Inutile

By Gregory John Ferris

C'est simple comme bonjour

For Henry Percheron, a retired homicide investigator, it was perhaps appropriate that his own death was violent. Known variously as Perch and Ronnie, Percheron joined the ranks of the dead for whom he had so diligently worked in life. The detective's death held for others a lesson than he himself had not learned in while alive. He left behind both the lesson and the chore of solving his own murder case to another Louisville police detective, Castorina Ertras, his former protégée. Whether this was by either design or simple misfortune is another unanswered question in this Louisville mystery.

It has been five years since the mysterious events transpired at Cave Hill cemetery during the Kentucky Derby. At the time of this writing, neither professional law enforcement nor amateur sleuths have been able to resolve inconsistencies in the volumes of witness testimony, let alone bring the case to closure. The victim, Henry Percheron and lead suspect, Mosgrove Templeton, are both dead. Templeton benefited from the support of those who in normal circumstances, would have been his most ardent pursuers. The person most capable of solving this puzzling case was instead the reason for its existence. The computer system that was designed and trained in large part by Percheron's past investigations provided no useful insight into what was Percheron's final problem.

Instead of computer power, it may require the irrationality of one human to understand and explain the passions of another.

I've been informed by legal experts that I cannot be sued on behalf of the dead. I doubt that the dead themselves can haunt me, at least during daylight hours. As far as the living, many of those connected with the events of Cave Hill have either left their positions of power, Louisville itself, or both.

I offer this as my contribution to the growing number of articles and publications that attempt to answer most, if not all the questions around the movements of the late Henry Percheron during the weekend festivities of the Kentucky Derby. As in any unexplained death, who, how, why, et cetera, are the most relevant questions. I will do my best to answer all of them, but will undoubtedly find myself offering to the reader a distinctly unpopular opinion.

I interviewed many people in the course of my research, from the celebrated to the unknown, those who knew the truth and told lies and liars who unknowingly divulged truth. I questioned police officials, both active and retired, neighbors, ex-girlfriends, and those who claimed to be ex-girlfriends. In brief I spoke with any and all. I told each of them, slow down take a breath, relax, I have time to listen to you.

Jessica Villier, immensely popular in the entertainment world, knew Henry Percheron since childhood. Ms. Villier spoke with him a few days before his death, and was the one who discovered his body only hours after his death. Fate made of her a suspect, attractive in the many senses of that adjective, and yet each moment of her time was as accounted for as each frame in one her numerous films.

She was the most documented of women in Louisville, Kentucky that weekend, being both beautiful and having strong, local ties. If this had been a movie, she would have been guilty, her guilt unprovable. I cannot say more, as the living can avail themselves of libel courts. I will instead offer my conclusion as to what really happened in the epilogue, after presenting as comprehensively as possible, the chain of events and coincidences that have played such havoc with the resolution of this mystery.

The world of sports over celebrates pitiful achievements. The games themselves are a series of meaningless consolation prizes, remarkable for their insignificance. Some have likened murder and the solving of murders to if not a sport, a game, nevertheless. Jessica Villier has recently finished a film on the Cave Hill events, playing the most personal of roles.

I am interested to see which conclusions are presented in this upcoming Villier film, *In May*. The director is known for his iconoclastic tendencies. Will the answers be made clear or will the film's ending leave the audience with a tantalizing mystery still unanswered?

Will the movie show the love in this sad story? It was not the love of American movies, neither was it the love of Irish art. It was the love found somewhere in between, somewhere in reality.

Detective Castorina Ertras left Louisville within 18 months of the murder. The most common question on social media is who plays her in *In May*. Castorina had known Jessica slightly many years ago, when Castornia had been her babysitter. That had only been discovered during filming, according to my sources. How would that relationship be portrayed in the film is the topic of gossip as well. The film will have its say, but I will have mine here, in print.

In another confluence of events, the three-year-old son of Inutile, More Than Useless, is expected to run in the upcoming Derby.

As to you, my readers, I suggest that you too, slow down take a breath, relax, and take time to listen to me.

CHAPTER ONE

It was his first time dead, and by the look on Henry Percheron's face he was both surprised and disappointed at what death held for him. The lead detective, Castorina Ertras, recalled that strange expression from the first case that she had worked on with Perch. She had been newly assigned to his team, and he'd made the same funny face to prevent her becoming sick at the sight of what was to become commonplace to her. Despite the horror of seeing Perch dead, a slight smile curved her lips at the memory of their early days together in the field.

Percheron was an old Louisville name, not an old, rich Louisville name. One four letter word made for a world of difference.

Her former mentor had died in a place reserved for the dead, his body lying face up in between the intermingled graves of sinners and saints. "Which was he?" detective Ertras wondered. Like most humans, he was undoubtedly a mixture of both.

She knew the victim, retired senior detective Henry Percheron, well enough to think that he had been more saint than sinner. Still, she wasn't looking forward to discovering the sorts of truths that everyone kept hidden, even him, Henry Percheron, Perch to his friends and colleagues in LMPD.

This investigation was going to be a final examination given by her former mentor. Ertras couldn't help imaging that Perch had chosen her explicitly to solve his murder. It was a clear case of murder. It was difficult to shoot yourself twice in the back and have the result termed suicide. He'd fallen where he had been shot, in a remote area of the large Louisville cemetery at Cave Hill. No blood trail, no signs of a struggle, and when she saw his hands zip-tied behind his back, there was no doubt in her mind who had done this. You made this too easy, she nearly said aloud to Perch, as if to tease him with the simplicity of his own murder.

He'd treated each case, if not quite as a game, then as a puzzle to be solved. He saw homicide as an endless series of scavenger hunts, each of which unfortunately had to end, usually with his winning, if murder can be said to have winners. While Perch was courteous to the victims' relatives, it was clear to his colleagues, that he enjoyed the, there was no other word more appropriate, the game. Maybe he needed to render murder less brutal in his own mind, in order to succeed. Who was Detective

Ertras to critique his technique? Her role, then, as now, was to catch, not to judge.

Detective Castorina Ertras took a few minutes to reflect on the surroundings before she refocused her attention on the scene. Would Perch be interred here? In Cave Hill for certain, but not in this exact spot. Generations of Percherons were buried somewhere in the cemetery. She wasn't familiar with the cemetery herself, as she had no relatives, living or dead, within 3000 miles. She was a new American living in what used to be called New France. She glanced around, her blond pigtail following the swivel of her head. Her blue eyes and fair hair constantly amazed locals who expected something different of a native-born Spaniard.

This exact spot, was that significant? The zip-ties wrapped around Perch's wrists spoke of planning, possibly of multiple perpetrators. Was the site of the murder relevant? She looked again at the chipped tombstone against which her friend's body rested. John Dietz it read, born 1840, died 1903. It was just another name to Ertras, someone long forgotten, as Perch would be in a few years. That was life, and death. Would John Dietz enjoy a celebrity type revival, given the circumstances? Who was this long since dead man of the 19th century? Was there a link between the two men, other than their both being now forever part of the past? Louisville was small enough and friendly enough that families settled here for generations, centuries now. Or was there a link between the long-deceased Dietz and Jessica Villier, the vivacious Louisville native who had become a successful actress. Villier had returned for the Derby and had discovered the murder scene a few hours ago, when she'd stopped by to visit family graves before resuming her life elsewhere. Did she know Perch? Was Dietz a common ancestor? Or was it all just random?

It was the noise of a new case, noise that she hoped would resolve itself into a recognizable tune. Ertras' list of leads to investigate was growing by the second, and she scribbled another note in her old-timer notebook, no batteries needed. She noticed the small headstones for children, where the cold marker was heavier than the forever cold child.

Ertras let her mind disengage again for a few minutes to let the surrounding scene paint itself anew. This Sunday after Derby was like so many, a clear, warming day. She heard aircraft overhead. "Angels over angels" she mused. Perch's own grave, where would it be? In his family section certainly, but unlike many Louisvillians, Henry Percheron had no family in town to mourn him. His branch ended with him. Ertras would attend his service as would scores of other officers. Maybe four score and seven of us, she speculated, her eyes catching sight of the union and confederate tombstones in the distance.

More unknown dead, from a war fought between what had been to herself and her immigrant family, two foreign countries. The revolutionary soldier helped put the US together, the Union troops lay together in rows having died in their attempt to keep it together, and now it seems that the country was as divided as ever, and only needed to finalize the divorce that would end a multi centuries long experiment .The country was tearing itself apart, and the few who tried to mend the widening tears were mocked. It was ironic that so many flee war and arrive in America, not realizing that war awaits them there. All she knew of that conflict, glancing again at the Civil War section, was a few words uttered by one of its last victims at the site of another, more famous cemetery. She had learned that one speech and had even found a version in Spanish for her parents. They had thought it to be lyrics to a song, similar to the mistake they have made in thinking that Lewis and Clark was a contemporary musical duo. But that was all history, as was her dead mentor, friend, and colleague.

Ertras' mind was full of morbid and painful thoughts, in contrast to a day that spoke of beauty and promise. Perch had no surviving family, just a long-term girlfriend. "No, that isn't correct, Perch had a brother. They were estranged, it was too late to fix that now," she thought sadly. The brother lived somewhere out west, a destination comfortably vague. Maybe the distant brother would rejoice at the news of his sibling's death. He'd have to be found and notified regardless. Ertras jotted a note, a few words that condensed a family's quarrel down to a barely legible smear of blue ink. At the same time, given the numbers of fans and former residents in town for Derby, the brother might

3

just as well be in the city. If so, then the brother was a suspect, just like the actress who had discovered the corpse.

The smell of peonies filled the May air. For the two detectives on the case, Ertras and her assistant Jackson, the odor aroused in each a distinctive memory. Her Jackson, Ertras smiled at the description, as if Jackson were her version of what she herself had been to Perch. Not quite the same, she corrected herself, and inhaled again.

For Jackson, the smell of peonies was the final scent of death, the closing of a life where there was nothing more to be done. This death scene was unusual for the young, male investigator. There was no blood, rain the evening before had seen to that. It was quiet, the grounds green and manicured, no empty cans, bottles, or needles lay within sight. Nor were there any locals with cellphones, recording and commenting on the scene like amateur reporters. The body was decently dressed in business casual, there were no signs of a struggle, no residual debris of violence. The only witnesses at this point were beyond being able to testify. Famous victims. Famous villains. The positive impacts people have seemed to reduce the size of their headstone. It was more reminiscent of a funeral visitation, than of a murder, and the nauseating odor of the peonies discouraged him, as it led him to consider already that there was nothing more to be done. The flower was a bad omen that this case was over before it had even begun, that it would not be solved.

Ertras inhaled again the air wonderfully perfumed with peonies. The scent was one of the pleasures of her own, private fifth season, spring/summer, a few weeks that was neither one nor the other, but also somehow both. It was a season that proclaimed everything was possible. The flower helped to calm for her what was a disturbing scene, one more disturbing because of its serenity. Unlike Jackson, Ertras knew the victim very well. It was as if this was years ago, and she was attending a forensics investigatory program. The scene before would have been an examination, with her old mentor playing the part of the victim. It was all too real, and the reality that this was going to be a test of all that she had learned over the past 15 years, brought the sense of nausea back. She breathed again the sweet air. May was the best time to visit cemeteries. The new life makes the loss of life, especially young life, more bearable. The new distracts the old, like a newborn kitten. Today she could not afford distractions.

Uniformed police officers searched diligently despite their own distractions when they saw well-known names on the tombstones, those of famous men and women as well as their own family names. For most of them this was the longest time that they'd passed in a graveyard

Death has shifted to the east as it had for the bulk of Louisville's history. The burial ground in the Portland area filled years ago. Just adjacent to Cave Hill, in Cherokee Park, the rolling terrain served as another sort of graveyard. There, small white balls fell into slightly larger, reused graves, from which they were quickly exhumed in order to complete their nine or eighteen lives for the day. In most cemeteries, death now was isolated, walled off, the sole subject deemed taboo. Cave Hill presented itself as a place of life and death, not life or death.

Ertras and her team searched the surrounding area for a radius of fifty yards for anything that was unusual. Other than finding another body every other step, there had been nothing odd. Just headstones of varying age and vanity, flowers fresh and dried. It would be impossible to determine who had brought bouquets recently, a public appeal would be required, and undoubtedly ineffective. One officer found a few damp, torn open, empty sugar packets from Starbucks. "Were they a clue, or just carelessness," Ertras wondered, noticing that a few of her searchers were holding coffee cups with the same, ubiquitous logo. She had the packets bagged. The only other real clue, which she held in a separate evidence bag was a betting ticket from yesterday's Derby. These were the sole items found on Perch's body. There had been no phone, no jewelry, no wallet, money, keys, absolutely nothing. Nothing except for his medical insurance card, and this one ticket, a winning ticket she had noticed immediately, $2 placed on Inutile to win. He would no longer need either of them.

Jackson provided little else of value. "Guards at the front entrance report hearing what could have been two shots just before the derby. Could have been firecrackers. Or a car backfiring."

"Cars don't do that any longer. Did they hear any shots during the race?"

"No. They were all inside, watching it on television."

"I see."

"One neighbor reported seeing a drone, but they are becoming as common as birds around here. It is a good place for hobbyists to practice. See, there a few flying even now. Hell, they might even be ours or the TV stations. The neighbor wanted to know if we could stop the flights, as her husband wanted to shoot them if they flew over his house. I told her to contact the FAA in Middletown. I saw the husband for a second, I suspect he'll go with the twelve gauge solution".

Jackson's attempt at humor was met with the silence appropriate to the surroundings. "From what I understand there was no aircraft during derby itself, it only lasts what, thirty minutes or so altogether, except for approved ones. I'll check with the FAA tomorrow", he said, this time with no hint of humor.

"We can put out a request to the public for any footage of the cemetery from yesterday."

"If there is any, it is either already on YouTube or being put up for bid."

"Yeah" Ertras sighed. "Ok, thanks Jackson."

After her team had completed the survey of the area, Ertras asked Cave Hill staff if they, being much more familiar with the grounds, would repeat a search. That was effective, not in finding anything, as her team was very good, but it would help Ertras later when she questioned them, some of them repeatedly. It made them feel involved.

As expected, the staff found nothing. The grass held no footprints, no cigarette butts. Visitors seem to fear the consequences of inhaling tobacco fumes so flagrantly in the presence of Death itself. There was nothing unusual except the broken lock on the door of 19th century mausoleum. The family tomb dated from the Civil War. Rich in the time of war, but just as dead.

The Civil War was everywhere if you looked for it. Some fools said that we were on the verge of another, they just wanted the easy way out, assured that their side would win because their

6

cause was just. "The same old, tired stupidity," Ertras sighed again.

Today's locals were the descendants of slaves and slave traders, of those who sold bullets and those who absorbed them. Or like, her, Ertras, a recent immigrant who had no interest in her adopted country's past, only its future.

The warning, "Don't go past 6th street after 6 pm had, in 15 years, extended to don't pass 9th after 9." That was progress of a sort. In 25 years, it would extend to the Ohio river, 20 blocks or so beyond. It didn't take a realtor to see that the property west of downtown was going to shoot up in value like one of those rockets that she watched climb into the sky before exploding in a blaze of color and sound. "Where would she be then? Would she still remember Perch?"

Ertras noticed that the names of those who spoke glowingly of and profited from war overshadowed those of its combatants and victims. Maybe there was equality and justice in the afterlife, but she thought not. Comparing the magnificent effigy of the media barons to the crumbling, nondescript tombstones of the dead soldiers made a mockery of fairness. "Life sucks, and so does death, apparently," she concluded.

Ertras slowly turned around, making a complete rotation as she surveyed the upright marble tablets and towering monoliths that surrounded the crime scene. Many dated from a time when such memorials were popular. There was fashion even in death. Each of the names carved on the stones were possible clues that might explain the motive for this murder.

There was already a prime suspect, one whose name would come to the mind of many people when news of this killing spread: Mosgrove Templeton. But Ertras needed to be thorough, "she was not the judge" she told herself again. Take for example, the broken lock. That might be crucial. Hopes were dashed in learning that the lock had been found broken weeks ago, and while the lock still closed it did not lock.

One of the groundskeepers had investigated at the time but had found only a few empty beer cans. He had cleared those away and swept the cobwebs. "Had the residents enjoyed the distraction provided by the lock breaking interlopers," Ertras wondered nonsensically. Instead she had asked the groundskeeper, "Is that normal?"

"Is what normal, broken locks?"

"Yes, broken locks. But tell me, this intrigues me, the cleanup that you performed, why?" His answers surprised her.

"It was open. We don't keep keys for these mausoleums unless the family requests it. We can break in if we need to, but I don't remember us ever doing that."

"But the cleanup, why?"

"We are caregivers."

"But they are all dead, what care do they require?"

The perplexed man responded, "They are still here ma'am", and Ertras felt a chill race up and then back down her spine. "It's because they are dead. They can't clean for themselves. And their families are either not present, not willing, or not able."

It dawned on Ertras that this middle aged cemetery employee was one in a decades long chain of the sort of strangers to whom people assigned their babies, their adolescents, their college bound children, their aged parents, and eventually their dear departed. Strangers who cared.

"You did replace the lock?"

"No. We usually send a letter to the next of kin, but I am not certain if that was done. You could check with the front office. Given the age of this mausoleum, I doubt that any letter was sent. Who would we send to the key to? I may be wrong. The front office will know for certain."

Ertras would learn later that such letter had been sent with no response.

"That horse, it used to be a unicorn", the caretaker said, pointing to a rampant horse atop a large tomb nearby. The original unicorn was broken a century ago and replaced or repaired several times." A private jet passed overhead. "Vandals are a persistent tribe", he continued in a voice tinged with sorrow. "The family eventually decided to add a unicorn as a bas relief." He delivered this information in staccato bursts, perhaps doubting Ertras' comprehension skills.

"Who was he?" she asked idly.

"A comedian. Two words to describe a life. Dead now, of course. As is his fame."

Jackson hurried over, attracted by their animated conversation.

"I wonder if the same person is buried more than once?" Jackson asked as he reached them.

"What?" Ertras and the caretaker exclaimed in unison.

"The same person, reincarnated, he or she would need two graves, right? Or I am just being weird? I don't like cemeteries."

The caretaker frowned at this sacrilege, but Ertras understood Jackson's sentiment. "It's not weird. First time dead. That is what I called it years ago. I asked Percheron once if he'd seen corpses who had died before, a repeat offender so to speak. He worked so many cases, that after a while they began to resemble one another."

"Zombies?" Jackson questioned.

The caretaker interrupted, not sure if the detectives were mocking him, and not anxious to have his suspicion confirmed. "I need to talk with my staff for a moment. I'll be right back, detective", he said, phrasing the words as a request, and then strolled away when Ertras nodded yes.

"And I don't know, his look was noncommittal", she continued her Perch story, turning back to face Jackson. "Once, he told me, he'd had a victim whose final expression could only be described as one of boredom. So, maybe, maybe, who knows? Not me. Next door in Eastern cemetery it is just the reverse, many bodies in the same grave."

Both detectives were aware of the years' long scandal where those accustomed to life's indignities were forced to endure another one in death. Rent is never cheap, especially when you are no longer alive to earn it. But Eastern Cemetery was not today's case.

Percheron's killer had shown the courtesy to avoid the derby festivities, but just barely. City officials would strive to keep bad news from the front page, but that would be impossible, as the local newspapers were forced to compete with Facebook and its thousands of unpaid but vigilant reporters. Ertras' most pressing concern was Lou247, a continuous streaming program whose goal was to describe and record life in Louisville, a variety show that showcased local news, delivering truth wrapped in enough entertainment to make it not only palatable but enjoyable. For the

LOU247 reporters, their education in journalism had taught them that if you don't know the facts, report whatever the hell you want. If bad publicity was better than no publicity, then the same axiom held for news.

The best that the police could hope for was a brief delay. A short, vague statement implying that it was death, possibly by natural causes, would push the shocking news of the murder of a homicide detective to Monday. Most if not all the visiting celebrities would have flown away by then. The annual post Derby migration had begun immediately, minutes after the famous race's winner had crossed the finish line. Ertras too was in a race. Overhead, private jets climbed, the wealthy and famous departing Muhammad Ali airport for the next venue on their magnificent tour of life. From their perspective, the remaining fog filled hollows of the graveyard formed a milky white image resembling an X-ray of bronchial passages.

Did any of the passengers possess knowledge helpful to this investigation? Unlikely, and if some of them did, which ones? She could not stop hundreds of private flights. Nor could she prevent the thousands of lesser mortals from quitting Louisville by commercial flight, by private car or by RV. Each one was a potential suspect or witness. No, the best she could do was to obtain a list of well-known attendees and retain it for future reference. If she hit a dead end, she'd contact some of the B level faces. It wouldn't help the case, but it would provide her with additional time. Time could be an alibi for a detective as readily as for a criminal. The press would give even subprime actors front page coverage. Ertras wouldn't even need to leak the news of the interview, the attention starved celebrity would readily handle that. Ertras put that thought aside, plan B for B celebrities. She laughed at her pun, humor was not one of her strengths, neither in English nor in Spanish.

She was certain that the local media was anxious for bad news after the preceding two weeks of Derby. It was the media version of Lent. The media was barely able to contain their impulses for 20 or so days in mid-Spring. Violence, hate, and divisiveness were all subjects to be avoided during the holy season. It was agreed to grudgingly, the press resembling a family relation that should be banned from reunions, but who was tolerated because everyone enjoyed his tales of misfortune and moldering skeletons. Ironically, the dead editor Prentie's tomb was near enough to the murder to warrant a mention in the local paper the following day.

Some of the local papers benefited from a sophisticated understanding of honesty. Too much criticism of the locals was the quickest path to bankruptcy. Blaming the locals, that was the niche of the alternative press and their irreligious fanatics who hated everybody not them. Their true market was the young drinker with neither children nor a real job. They were always angry and smug, and 100 percent anti-police.

Jackson interrupted Ertras' daydreaming.

"I bet that Percheron didn't like cemeteries either. They probably reminded him of work."

"And now it will for us," Ertras said without emotion. She continued, rebutting Jackson's speculation. "If they did remind him of work, he would have liked it." Jackson raised his eyebrows at this insight. He was under the impression that only he had odd thoughts.

"They say that detective Percheron solved all but one his murder cases. Is that true, Cas?"

"It is," confirmed Ertras. "That is what they say."

"According to what the staff here says, this case might be more difficult than we expect. There might be too many spirits hovering nearby, muddying the water," Jackson commented, wiping mud from his right shoe onto the grass to emphasize his point. "I'm just joking, Cas. Folks are sensitive about spirits here, aren't they? Who the hell would kill a former cop so publicly?"

"Spirits," Ertras repeated. "He tried that once, on the case that he never solved."

"Really?"

"Yes, really. Add that to your list of things to research, it may be important. Yes, really," she repeated, seeing the surprise on her assistant's face.

"Ok, Cas. This place is depressing all the same, and what the hell is that stink," he uttered, as the caretaker rejoined them. "Peonies'," he responded to Jackson.

"I thought so," Jackson said sharply.

"They're wonderful," Ertras interjected.

"You see this as a place of disappointment, I imagine," the caretaker speculated, not expecting confirmation. "Most people do, it has been that way for decades now. But visitors used to see cemeteries as places of hope. Hard to believe, isn't it. But that is the truth."

A moment later he asked the detectives, "You knew him well, then?" Not accustomed to receiving responses, he answered his own query. "That should help you find out who killed him." Ertras hoped that he was right. After a few more questions, the interview ended, and the caretaker left them.

As he looked at fading roses on some of the surrounding tombs, Jackson's mind flashed back to yesterday. Twenty-four hours ago, he had driven to the Middletown Kroger's to see the Derby rose garland that was on display. Ahead of him, a young girl was making her way across the parking lot to the grocery. As she walked, the precise left to right and back again switch of her jeans covered rear reminded him of a fine Swiss metronome.

Jackson enjoyed viewing the garland in private. Later it would be ceremoniously loaded in a Kroger van and accompanied by several Sheriff's vehicles, where it would be delivered to Churchill Downs. A few hours after that, while Percheron lay dead here in Cave Hill, the red and green blanket would be lain across the withers of the new champion.

With another look around at this unusual crime scene, Ertras sighed and said to her colleague, "Ok Jackson, let's begin at the beginning. I'll talk with Melissa, his girlfriend. You, find Templeton."

The Sunday after Derby, few in need of one would be able to reach their attorney. The talented lawyers were all recovering from the many parties held throughout the metro area, while the unskilled ones pretended to be unreachable in order to appear important. It was one of the few times where pride overwhelmed greed in the legal profession. Hopefully, Templeton would be without counsel. "Under normal circumstances, I would have loved a case like this one, on a beautiful springsummer day such as this," Ertras reflected. But not today, as she slid her right hand up the loose-fitting sleeve of her raspberry colored silk jacket and dug her nails into her left forearm. One pain to take away another. The day exhaled optimism, it was what she liked about this period in Kentucky, a private season that she thought of as springsummer, neither one nor the other, but a hybrid of both. This was going to be a painful season. There would be the unpleasant truths to which she would be exposed. As unpleasant to her as the scent of peonies was to her assistant.

CHAPTER TWO

It was Thunder over Louisville, the opening day of Kentucky Derby festivities, two weeks before the death of Detective Percheron. Few were thinking of Henry Percheron as either a living person or as a dead nothing. Mosgrove Templeton was among those few. And he was busy. Wind blew past his ears, softly at first, and then more and more insistently, as if she had something important to impart. He liked the sound of her voice, he always had. She was dependable, a visitor who could cross the prison walls and be with him whenever she wanted. He listened attentively to her, despite her incomprehensible, whispered poetry. He listened anyway, hoping desperately to understand for once. Let it be today, Templeton prayed, but his plea was in fact little more than a futile command. The wind left him as suddenly as she had arrived, and he was reduced to listening to his own respiration.

He wondered if he was insane. It didn't matter. He had the joy of kook, happiness without cause. And yet, he was happy to be invisibly insane. It was better unshared.

"There is a reason that we can't hear each other breathe, or feel each other's pain," he told himself, but only wished that she had told him what that reason was. Few take advantage of selecting their own exit and after so much vacillation on his final choice, he had passed and left it to fate. He too would soon be a dead nothing. But Ronnie, aka Henry Percheron, would die first.

"There are no do overs for today even if you believe in reincarnation for tomorrow," he said silently. And he believed in nothing, or nearly nothing.

Templeton let his hatred build. They had sentenced him to life but had reneged when he had fallen ill. They bragged that it was a humanitarian gesture and that, given his condition, he would pose no danger to the community. He would prove them wrong. Their decision would be fatal for more than just him. They were not going to break the law without consequence. He hadn't been able to escape what they called justice, neither would they. Compassion has a cost and he would present them the bill.

He glanced at a photo of a royal wedding in the newspaper that lay beside him on the car seat. She was a divorcee, wasn't she? How far the royals had fallen. They couldn't escape scandal and humiliation. It wasn't right. He'd been raised in a world where divorce was not an option. Beatings or a reciprocal push down the stairs served the same purpose and could be forgiven by the same power that forbade divorce. No divorce. It was simple. They had divorced him. It was another contract broken by the government They just did not want to pay his medical bills. They would pay. Of that he was sure.

Templeton parked outside the tennis courts at Joe Creason park. It was funny, the owner of the local newspaper gets a small plot and a big stone at Cave Hill cemetery while his reporter gets an entire park named in his honor. That was the sort of justice that he himself merited.

As he descended the combination road and walking path, Templeton was thankful for the wonders of the modern pharmaceutical business. The battery-operated oxygen compressor was magic, akin to transforming lead into gold, as it reduced his labored breathing to something approaching normal. The bridge over Beargrass Creek was closed for repairs. It was a pleasure to see that parks were still being funded. Better yet was the sight of discarded hypodermic needles. Maybe some of the disappointed police cadets who'd been turned away from the academy due to city budget cuts would be here learning to use a shovel instead of a taser. It made him laugh until he began to cough uncontrollably, the phlegm mounting in his throat, a reminder by the cancer, that it would have the last laugh, not him.

He turned left at the bridge, following the trail that extended through the northern side of the park and into and through the nature preserve. The trail paralleled for a short distance the creek and Newburg road, which lay beyond the flowing water. In his mind, he magically transformed the drone of the traffic to the roar of a rushing creek, a flow of water that was in fact more placid than powerful. He'd learned to master pretense in prison, there he'd created his own mental castle into which he could withdraw at a moment's notice, his own lord, secure and in control. The wind was there to reassure him. On the outside, abandoned by the serenity of daily prison life, it was more difficult to pretend. Pretense was proving more and more exhausting but more and more important in his remaining months.

"Big four bridge. It was foolish to have gone there. It was too visible, and the only escape route involved his drowning. This would surely be better. Did he have the strength to overpower his former friend," a torrent of thoughts rushed through the ex-convict's brain.

The doctors promised him a few months, illegal narcotics could lengthen or shorten that estimate, it was his wager to make. Alone, even high, his plan required physical strength.

The ground was damp, the weeks before Derby were often this way. If they placed bets on weather conditions for this time of year, wet would win. He moved slowly, the trail more of a groomed cow path. Branches and the occasional tree trunk proved that trail maintenance was not a daily chore for the park crew. "Prisoners would do a better job," he judged.

The nature reserve was a combination of reds and greens that offset the brown, muddy earth. The greens were of varying tints, as if each plant had its own idea of which hue was genuine green. Soon however as if by consensus or peer pressure, the leaves would adopt the same uniform color. "Vert, verdatre, verdant. Green," He remembered that from High School French class. He hated green except for in Nature. It was the color of life but had been stolen for use by the world's militaries and prisons. Death coopting the dress of Life.

His mind was wandering again. His presence here was not intended to be only a simple walk in the park. Fair is fun and fun is fair. He heard in the distance the distinctive sound of a baseball smacking the leather. It emitted a contented sigh of finality. "Remember how we would change the rules, Ronnie? I'm doing that now."

Red. Oh yes, there was plenty of that. Cardinals and robins abounded, trees were splotched in red paint, marking the red maple trail. Red again. The paint reminded him of blood on a sturdy branch, left beside Ronnie's body. No, that would be murder. That would not be justice. It had to be suicide. Red. He spotted the flash of crimson nearby, traversing from right to left. A woodpecker, a pique. Fragments of French came back to him. He and Ronnie had known each other for ever, but high school French was where they had first competed as young men. Like most competitions it was for the attention of girls, French was simply the arena. There had been one girl, a brown girl. She was attractive in any color but being the only brown girl made her the obvious goal. It would have been the same if she'd been green and not brown.

The path under his shoes was brown, and while there were a few sections with an incline, none were steep enough to stage an accidental fall. Even if one were, he was neither strong enough nor agile enough to risk grappling with Percheron. Any of the fallen branches or even a rock would serve as a lethal piece of nature. He could just murder the old fashion way and leave the body in the undergrowth to be eaten by coyotes, but they did not venture this far into the city. It was ironic, the zoo was less than a mile away, but no predators of any size lived nearby. He could leave the body to disappear slowly as an unburied corpse, but he didn't want the mystery of Percheron's disappearance to survive his own death. He wanted to taste revenge again, he'd forgotten what it tasted like, but these scouting trips were increasing his craving for it.

A deer started away among the trees and it startled him. He was rarely startled in prison. Many inmates saw prison as a refuge. So had he, for too long. But that was then.

He couldn't get to the governor, whoever he was, but Percheron was local, once even a friend. But a contract was a contract. For Templeton, six months more would have constituted a life sentence; he was that ill. Templeton had become an expert at pretense over the years, was that insanity? Probably not, if he could pose himself the question. Or did the cancer in his lungs have a relative in his brain? It didn't matter now.

Between the oxy and the oxygen, he had enough energy to push on. If he needed a further boost, hatred was freely available. Hell, it made for a great hangover free cocktail.

"Sanity is overrated. Passion can push itself across the finish line with ease, compared to sanity." He was tired of climbing the steep grade. "Who would ever do this for fun?" Templeton trudged on.

The periodic pop of tennis balls hurtling from tightly strung rackets blended with the squeak of rubber soles on the asphalt courts to form a song of approaching summer. Soon, the splash of happy children in the nearby pool would add to the orchestra.

Unless the public pools had been cut from the city budget, as shot spotter had been. Not that the two costs had anything to do with one another. That was the point, distribute the pain equally.

The cuts were approved during what some saw as the best of times. The crowd at a new bar made to look like a gas station remade into a bar was evidence that the economy was well. The Mercedes Benz dealership had expanded into a new location, opening for business while still under construction. Local traffic was continuing to congest and although new Kias outnumbered German vehicles, each typically contained only a single occupant at rush hour.

"Yes, Derby would be perfect. The governor would be in town. This could not be any better.

Fresh cut flowers are so effective at bringing attention to the presence of death."

A few miles away, standing on the Belvedere plaza above one of the interstates that cut through the city, retired detective Percheron was speaking with a former colleague, Eli Heinsdorf, also retired.

"It's out of hand, if you ask me. Technology is no longer a tool to extend our innate abilities but as a cold replacement for them."

"You're exaggerating, Perch."

"I'm not. At the rate police work is adopting the future, versus the glacial "progress" of the criminals, soon they will be classified as an endangered species, worthy of government protection. They'll be hunted to extinction by computerized precision."

"Like grey wolves? I think that now you are underestimating the 21st villain."

"I don't know much about internet crime, I've specialized in the humdrum beat of violence, retail crime is as smelly as retail sales. Unions won't help us, me and the rest of the current ranks will be or have been pensioned off or offered a buyout."

"Ok, Sherlock."

"Don't call me that, please. Perch is just fine."

"You were the best, Perch. You probably still are."

"I'm good with the dead, I only fail with those still living. Technology has made me obsolete; I could no longer compete. I'm glad. It opens new doors. I've puttered around for a year now."

"You need to find something. Otherwise dementia sets it. Don't be a wus. You handled murderers with ease, retirement should be a breeze. If not, and you lose your mind you won't remember anyway. Seriously, you are still adjusting to retirement, give it-"

"Time? Sure, if you say so. Why not? I'm going to have a beer, I see a break in the line at the Miller truck. It's Miller time." As they stood drinking their beers, the conversation resumed.

"And now what?"

"I don't know. Maybe fish, or travel."

"Everyone says that they will fish or travel. Knowing you, it won't happen."

"Knowing me, you'd be wrong. I made sure that my passport is up to date."

"That doesn't mean anything."

"Does this?" Percheron illuminated the screen on his phone and a few seconds later, held the screen up for the other man to read, a smirk visible on his face. Perch looked younger now than he had in the past few years preceding his retirement last May.

"Paris? You are really going to Paris? You always did like to prank people. All this talk of frittering away time and having to fish. Paris. Alone? What about your girlfriend?"

"Melissa left."

"Good for her. She wasted her time with you. A relationship with you was never going to progress to what she wanted."

"She said the same thing. Did she text you a transcript of our last conversation? Or do you follow her on Twitter?"

"Neither. I understand women."

"Sure you do. She was correct of course. The three of us now agree, the relationship was not going anywhere other than where it was. I was content with it. She wasn't." Perch sipped his beer, while the other man stared at the small screen.

"She bought me a drone for Christmas, last year."

"That was nice."

"Nice is a four-letter word."

"Have you played with it?"

"Have I played with it? What am I, ten years old?" Percheron said, then paused. "Sure, that is what I'm supposed to get ready for. Play, another four-letter word."

"So is work."

"I took it out a few times, we've become good friends, one drone to another."

"Maybe you will meet some queen bee in Paris. Wait, this is a one-way ticket."

"I can spend 5 months in Europe without a visa. That is long enough."

"Long enough to get your fill of Europe?"

"No, there isn't enough time for that, not at my age. But five months is long enough to see if there is the right woman for me over there, the right life. Right enough for long enough. My short-term plan is to not make any long-term plans. What is the French word, staige? I'll take the future in months long increments. Who knows, maybe I will be able to appreciate living in the moment. It's like training for a sprint when I've only ever run marathons."

"I don't know you at all, do I? You resemble Perch but you're not him. I visited a butterfly farm once in Aruba. You remind me of that, one creature that changes over time, the same but different. Your ex-girlfriend will be not be happy when she hears what you've done. She'd have enjoyed Paris. Hell, I may need to leave Louisville for a few weeks as well if she discovers that I knew about this and didn't tell her. When do you leave?". He stared at the phone again. "I really can't believe that you are doing this. Honestly, I didn't think you were this smart when it comes to life."

"Intelligence is for idiots," he said in a voice devoid of irony. "I don't leave until after Derby."

"It's so out of character. Are the French police recruiting an old, one dimensional American street detective who speaks marginal French? Big city retired cops should move to the provinces."

"Paris is not the provinces. It's the exact opposite."

"I'm talking about police here Perch, in the States. That would satisfy many of us, a job is just a job. A job. That is all it is to at least half of the guys. But not for you. It is not simply a job. It is you."

"Look at the screen again. It was me."

"OK. It was you."

Ertras approached the two men, she had spotted them by accident among the 600,000 or more attendees. Perch was not a tall man and melted easily into crowds. They embraced for a moment; it was still awkward for them both.

"You look happy, Perch." The other retired cop saw this as the moment to leave them and strolled off search of his children and grandchildren. His own cell phone would make this so easy despite the crowd size. Percheron had retired the Monday after Thunder, a year ago, coordinating his last day so that he could claim the largest annual fireworks display in the country as being held in his honor. "And now Paris," Heinsdorf thought, threading through the crowd."

"You look happy" Ertras repeated.

"I am, Castor. I can enjoy events like this as a participant and not as a guard dog. Not like TSA agents working at Vegas or Orlando. Are you working?" he asked, knowing the response.

"Always. I'm worried about Templeton." Ertras scanned the crowd.

Perch was unconcerned, keeping his eyes on Ertras. "He will need to manage his own health, not mine."

Cas and Perch discussed his upcoming plan to travel, but he did not share with his former mentee the details, particularly not that he was leaving Louisville indefinitely.

"What could you possibly do in Paris that a thousand others haven't already done, many of them well: paint, sculpt, cook? That makes no sense."

"It will be new for me. And it isn't a competition with anyone."

"You never needed to compete, it came easily."

"It's becoming even easier."

What is?

"Nothing," Perch responded simply, using that one word like a lane change indicator in the conversation. "Who knows, I might even consult."

"With the French police?"

"I'm kidding," Perch responded, but Ertras wasn't sure that he was.

"Although it might be intriguing, and murderers are murderers around the globe." He hated saying goodbye.

"It was great seeing you again, Castor."

She smiled when he referred to her as Castor, he was the only person to call her that, and was sad when their conversation ended. As they parted, her former boss gave Ertras the same weird grin/grimace that she had seen during their first case together more than a decade ago, and would see again in fifteen days, at Cave Hill cemetery.

Percheron was smart but could feel himself slipping. Retired athletes no longer need to compete, but he did, despite what he had just said to Castor. There was nothing else for him. Despite their brief careers, sports champions were forced to accept periodic defeats, even at their peak prowess. They were accustomed to losses. He now understood the fear felt by gifted athletes when their powers began to weaken. Losses now and again prepared them for the irreversible loss that the future was bringing to them.

For him, it had been too abrupt. He had lost only once, and now years that seemed like seconds later, he was not even in the game. The stages of death, how many of them were there, six, or seven? It didn't matter, the result had been the same; retirement. He hadn't met any retirees who regretted that step, and he was encountering more and more of them recently. Some were bitter, because they'd been retired by their employer. But none admitted that they hated their new state. They had all found "things to do". They never phrased it as something new to be, just something to do. Like watercolors in kindergarten, or prison. It was playing Sudoku while waiting to board a plane; that was awful enough. This retirement was and would be much worse, and the flight would be to parts unknown, a one-way ticket to oblivion. Useless, now and forever more.

He had nothing else to do, let alone to be. He would come to resemble one of the numerous criminals that he'd sent away for long sentences. Maybe he could run for judge. No, that was a stupid thought. There was no puzzle in judgement. It was following a recipe, not creating one. One of his putaways had sent him a birthday card last June. Percheron's birthday was in November and it took him a minute to understand the sentiment of the sender. The convict's birthday was in June. Inside the card the felon had written that for his birthday he'd wished that Kentucky still had the death penalty, so that we would not be forced to spend another year alive and in confinement. He had remembered that con, he was smart too, an embezzler who had murdered his partner and the partner's wife to cover his thefts. Oh yes, he was smart, that one, but not as smart as Percheron. Maybe he was as smart as Percheron now. He was younger than Percheron, and yes, Percheron was slipping. And now there was Templeton to add to his worries.

CHAPTER THREE

The pair of gunshots affected the inhabitants of the city in ways unforeseen. The dense 32 caliber bullets were like two small stones tossed into the center of a farm pond. The ripples of two separate circles spread in all directions, the ridges of one cancelling some of those of the other circle, but magnifying others. The resulting collisions were unpredictable, as were the results. Life forms on the surface shifted, some fled, some froze in place, waiting for the wave to pass by. Below the surface, who knew what, if anything, had changed. "Very little," Ertras guessed.

Detective Ertras managed to speak to Doctor Kaplan early on Monday at Baptist East Hospital. It was two days since the murder. Perch's girlfriend, Melissa Higgins had told Ertras the previous day that Perch had a colonoscopy scheduled for Oaks Day, the Friday before Derby. She had planned on taking him to the hospital herself, but since Perch and she were, in her words, 'taking a break from each other for a while', Perch had made other arrangements for transportation.

Ertras listened as the doctor closed every door that she tried to open. Every inquiry and search for a path to follow was stymied by the doctor telling the truth. If he would only lie to her, it would be more useful.

"I'm sorry detective but yes he was here. It was a normal procedure. I'd suggest that you review our security video, but the video is only retained for a few hours. We must balance HIPPA concerns and liability insurance. Attorneys are the only species of shark that bites by opening their mouth.

Mr. Percheron said he was going to walk to his car after the procedure. He was fine when he left. We make sure of that, again attorneys. Normal precautions were advised, including that someone drive him home. But we can't prevent patients from driving. He knew the process from previous tests."

"He did that often? Schedule these exams?"

"No, let me check, just to be sure," the doctor responded, checking his iPad. "Yes, that is right. No not often. He did such a good job that it made my examination that much easier. He told me that he fasted 12 hours more than suggested."

Ertras smiled, the doctor returned the smile, but did not know why. "He did like to plan and follow rules. Would you call that behavior obsessive?"

"Maybe. But it worked. I saw him half as often as most patients. Soon, these examinations will be performed remotely by machine. And I won't see anyone."

"Where does technology end?" Ertras asked rhetorically.

"Of course, I don't really see their best side."

"So, his exam was normal? The results I mean?"

"Yes, perfectly normal. He was as clean as a whistle. Clean as a whistle, they all want to hear it phrased the same way."

"Let me ask you, did you check his health beforehand?"

"Before the colonoscopy? Of course, but not in depth. BP, weight, oxygen level, pulse. All by the book. The pathologist will tell you more, but Mr. Percheron appeared healthy enough by all our standard, mandatory measures".

The doctor paused, then asked, "How did he die? I'm not following where this is going. Should I? I suppose you can tell that I'm not keen on attorneys, but in this case"

"No, there is no need to call your legal office, Doctor Kaplan. I didn't mean to imply anything about you or your staff, doctor. Detective Percheron was shot twice. We know that he came here for the colonoscopy but after that no one can recall having seen him. That is almost 30 hours from the time that he left here and the time that he was found shot to death."

"He mentioned stopping for a milkshake. That was the last time that I saw him. It's a shame." The detective and the medical man shared a silent moment, each alone in their own thoughts.

Several minutes later, Ertras was questioning the doctor's nurse.

"Have you heard of a man named Mosgrove Templeton?"

"Oh sure. Who hasn't? He is a long time criminal, a celebrity criminal."

Ertras winced. "That's one way to describe evil. Not the phrase that I would have selected but there it is," she thought.

"Did you see him around the hospital on the morning of Detective Percheron's procedure? That would be last Friday. Assuming you know what he looks like, that it."

"Oh sure. I know what he looks like. No, I didn't see him here."

Ertras turned to leave.

"I think it was the day before, or maybe the day before that, Wednesday. Wednesday or Thursday, it was one day or the other."

The detective asked very clearly, "Are you saying that Mosgrove Templeton was in this hospital on the Wednesday or Thursday before Oaks Day?"

"Yes."

"How can you be so sure?"

The nurse was not used to being questioned in such a manner, even doctors had learned to respect her.

"If you don't believe me, you can ask my ex sisters-in-law Joyce Small over in oncology. He is one of her patients, both here in the hospital and privately. I've said enough."

With that, it was she who turned and walked away, leaving a puzzled Ertras in her wake.

The doctor and his nurse having departed to attend living patients, Ertras reflected on the conversation.

"So Perch had driven himself. Where is the car?"

A quick check of the hospital parking lot showing no trace of his car, Ertras called the station to issue an alert for Percheron's vehicle, based on whatever they could find in state registration. It was possible that the car was in the garage at Perch's house, but that search would happen later today or tomorrow.

"If the car wasn't there, where was it?" The detective had forgotten that Melissa and Perch had broken up, "taking a break" was the phrased the girlfriend had used. Perch had mentioned at Thunder that he and Melissa were on the outs, but Cas had little interest in the romances of other people. In this case the breakup sounded more like a complete rupture.

CHAPTER FOUR

It was a blur. Already his dream, so vivid when he and awoken was gone, expelled from his mind like his most recent exhaled breath. There was no possibility of retrieving either.

"Maybe he had killed Ronnie. It was all a muddle. Between the drugs and the booze, he had no tolerance for either any longer, he sometimes felt delusional. Was that it? Was he following his mother into dementia?" His mind and heart were both racing.

His name was Mosgrove Templeton, a name above his station, an appellation that reminded a person of a sophisticated confidence man. His childhood and true friends called him Grove, his criminal associates referred to him as Moss or Moz, while law enforcement knew him simply as Templeton. At this point in his life, he seldom heard "Grove" directed to him.

When the police had shown up at his door earlier, he had refused them entry. They had no warrant. Templeton had demanded to speak with an attorney. A few phone calls between Jackson, Ertras and the city attorney resulted in a public defender arriving at the home that Templeton was renting. The only statement he would provide, delivered via his attorney was that he would not consent to any interview in a police station.

If they wanted to speak with him, two and only two detectives could come to his house. They would not be permitted to bring any electronic recording devices, nor could they bring any weapons into the house. Oh, and they would be searched upon arrival.

Neither detective had ever heard of such demands being made by a prime suspect, but this was a new world for police nationwide. There was reality and there was YouTube, it was difficult to conclude that they weren't becoming one and the same.

They agreed to the demands, but the city attorney had the final word. She consented as well. "Too readily," Ertras thought. It wasn't her who would be under the bus if something went wrong.

And then, as soon as the city attorney publicly announced her agreement to these conditions, Templeton said that he would instead come to them, tomorrow. He wanted no police in his sanctuary was how he phrased it. And now it was tomorrow.

Templeton sat in the small interview room on the Monday after the Kentucky Derby. He was pleased with himself and smiled as he reflected on yesterday's accomplishment.

He had refused to open the door to the police when they had arrived at his house the previous day. He had told the numerous officers outside of the door that he would come to the central police station the next following day, once he had consulted with his own attorney. Both sides recorded the conversation through the front door of his small home, and curious neighbors recorded the police from their own front windows.

When she introduced herself, Templeton laughed, and then asked in a mocking voice, "What the hell sort of name is that?"

"It's Spanish," she replied with a trained smile. She had heard this comment before, it was part of the small talk that proceeded most encounters with suspects. It was always tedious.

"Castorina Ertras," Templeton repeated her name awkwardly. "Maybe you could teach me to say it correctly, I'd love to roll your R's," he said with a grin."

"And you are Mosgrove Templeton."

"My friends call me Grove."

"I see," she said, "Mister Templeton."

"Maybe we could become friends while we practice rolling those R's of yours. I bet that I could really do well with them."

The sparring would end soon, he was attempting to gain dominance, he was destined to fail. This was her game, her rules.

Her thoughts accompanied by a mental sigh, she committed herself to remaining polite and professional, an odd combination given the circumstances. Otherwise Templeton would become petulant and would tell her nothing.

Men, especially criminals, were so moody. Their lack of self-control was the origin of most of their problems, but they never learned. They were too hormonal for their own good.

The more he said, the more likely that he would disclose an inconsistency, a thread that she could pull.

So far, he had said nothing of consequence, she had taken no notes.

It was a technique that Perch had taught her, but it was not uniquely his.

Suspects and witnesses unfailingly played to her notebook. Her writing in it was proof of their importance. When her fingers stopped moving across the page, they were often visibly deflated. Ironically those who spoke at a pace slow enough for Ertras to take accurate notes were often lying, while those whose words gushed from their mouth too rapidly to transcribe were truthful.

"Truth is rare, it requires only a few syllables," was how Perch put it, "it doesn't need thought."

"I'm afraid that wouldn't be appropriate Mr. Templeton for us to be friends. This is an official investigation." Ertras delivered the line in her best bureaucratic voice.

Jackson appeared distracted, but he was simply bored with the opening sequence. It was watching opening credits while awaiting the main event.

"Ronnie was my friend," Templeton said in rebuttal.

All these names and nicknames that jostled about during the investigation, they were costumes that the fortunate, herself included, were able to wear. Sometimes the costumes were also disguises. We have the luxury of being different characters like father or mother. In this case the ones with nicknames were all childless. "What would it be like to only be one person?" she pondered briefly. "Had Perch been only one person?"

She reflected that the girlfriend had one name, Melissa, no nicknames for that one. Melissa had been jealous of her, Castor. Perch had been the sole person to call her Castor. It had been a sign of semi-formality that the girlfriend had misconstrued as intimacy. Everyone else spoke to her as Cas or Cassie. When she and Perch had taken to embracing one another when they'd seen each other after his retirement, the girlfriend had one again bristled.

"You spoke of killing detective Percheron," Jackson said, beginning what he expected to be a short interview followed by a confession.

"I did. I also spoke of winning the lottery. That didn't come to pass either."

"They are not the same thing."

"Listen, the governor was aware of what I said at the time. He didn't take it seriously, why are you? He commuted my sentence despite any prison talk."

"He should have taken it seriously. If he had, Percheron would still be alive."

"So you say. But you have it all backwards if you think that I murdered Ronnie. We worked everything out when we spoke. We left on good terms when we last met."

"So, you lured him to this alleged meeting?"

"It was he who set up the meeting. Was he luring me?"

"And when was this meeting?"

"It was before his suicide."

"Don't play games, Templeton," Jackson exclaimed, ensuring that he did not shout. "There is no way it was a suicide."

"And where was this meeting, Mr. Templeton?" Ertras asked.

"It doesn't matter. Let's just say it takes two to tango, either at Blair's Ballroom or anywhere else in Louisville. It's clear that you two are convinced of my guilt. I'm not going to freak out simply because you two have already panicked. Panic is a choice not a disease that you catch."

"Trying to lure him. You admit it?"

"Yeah, but instead he set up a meeting on his own. Shouldn't you be wearing one of those body cams? You cops are monitored more than endangered animals today. The young thugs keep us up to date as they arrive. They can track you as much as you track them. People think that we teach them when it is actually the reverse."

"You teach each other how to get caught and screw up your lives. By the way "thugs" is a considered an insult on the outside. Things have changed quite a bit"

"Thug was never a compliment. These young criminals, strange how the terms gangster and thugs were back from the 1920s or was it the 30s, are once again in vogue. You're not inclusive, you're very prejudiced against people who want nothing more than to kill others and take their property. They come to prison uneducated and leave even less smart." He paused for breath.

"You have to give the criminal a break occasionally. Otherwise they will pack up and leave town, and then where would LMPD be?"

"Society would be better off.""

"Society is just a four-syllable word. You are going to be out of work soon. Look at who you arrest. These miserable excuses for villains that pass for 'society's' best criminals today. We have really dumbed down our crooks. I blame the schools."

Jackson said, "Everyone blames the schools for everything. Get in line."

"What did you and Percheron discuss at this alleged meeting?"

"Life."

"A strange topic for a dying man."

"Not really. He told me "there was no longer an outside, just degrees of imprisonment, whether it was jail or the graveyard." At least it has trees, and birds. I told him that I had seen an albino cardinal the other day, a female. An outsider to the other birds. He asked me if I found that to be an omen. He no longer knew me".

"Oh?"

"I no longer look for hidden meanings, grand insights. She was just a bird. A colorful creature bleached of her vibrant color. Vibrant due to her lack of color. In a world of red, beige is startling."

"You two seem to be quite the philosophers", Jackson quipped, but Templeton ignored the jibe.

"I don't want to go back to prison. Ronnie believed that I did. That killing him was worth dying in prison. He was wrong, for once. I needed to cut out the bad parts in order to get the good part flourish. I still have a good part."

"I've heard this same "I've changed" claim from better actors than you. You can save it for the tabloids. You should sign up for Facebook, you can tell your BS story yourself to the world."

Templeton was effective at ignoring taunts, they fell at his feet like exhausted arrows.

"He said that I was as mad as my mother. Perhaps I'll take her madness over his sanity. Or mine. That is the question, isn't it? It's not to be. But am I insane now? Or is this all seen through the rage of dementia? I no longer understand this world, I feel like Rip Van Winkle, or one of those countless Cave Hill dead returned to life. Would Hell be as frightening, as the world has become?"

Ertras was going weary of this mental meandering. "Who helped you?"

"I called UBER dead. You know that I work alone."

"I know little about you, beyond the fact that you're an old, dying con. A waste of oxygen for a while longer."

"Yeah, I'll be joining your dead colleague. But I won."

"Won what?"

"I get to attend his funeral. He won't be attending mine. I said, I work alone. Who would I call for help?"

"Your old gang."

"They are beyond old, they're all dead. Are you gullible enough to think that I was able to raise some of them from their graves to help me put someone else in one? They should relegalize duels, they kept people honest, or polite. My old gang, as you refer to them, they're dead, and, by the way, they couldn't afford to be buried in Cave Hill."

"Some could. Crime pays."

"Don't spread lies, detective. Crime is a waste, I know that."

"Is that your alibi, that you are reformed?"

"Don't be a bigger idiot than what you've shown me so far."

"And your girlfriend?"

"Who?"

"Joyce Small."

Jackson said nothing.

"What about her?"

"She could have assisted you."

"She is not my girlfriend. She is my nurse. The state pays her, can you believe that? The governor refused to treat me in prison, then must pay double on the outside. Is that justice?" he asked rhetorically." There was a pause while they all reflected on what had been said so far.

"The country is so screwed up. I'll be glad to leave it. So was Ronnie. That explains his suicide."

"Shot in the back twice, with your gun?"

"Who said it was my gun?"

"We will find it. Good luck finding an attorney who will present suicide as your defense, let alone a jury who won't laugh him, and you, out of court."

"I won't be alive for court. The three of us in this room can agree on that outcome."

"You may have wanted to stage his murder as his suicide, but something went wrong. We'll find the gun, we will clean up the timeline."

"Cleanup as in get witnesses to remember what you want to have happened? As you said, good luck with that. We are both short on luck."

"We don't behave that way, if we ever did. This case is being run by the book."

"Sure, I have a copy of that book on the shelf at home. Grimm's fairy tales. I stole it from prison."

"How long have you known your girlfriend?"

"She's not my girlfriend."

"I mean your nurse."

"She's not my girlfriend. I'm honest enough to know that I have nothing to offer her. Maybe now I do, given your insane theory about me being involved in Ronnie's death. I'm, oh what is the word? Hot. Yeah, I'm hot now, I've been on the news and on Facebook. Yeah, I am aware of Facebook and these other public confessionals. I can probably get laid now more than when"

"That when you were a man?"

"Joyce is my nurse, maybe even a pallbearer in waiting. I'll encourage her to buy herself something new for the funerals. She can wear the same outfit to his and mine. Or not. That would be gauche, right detective? She will need two funeral outfits, plus others for her television appearances. If I did have help, it wouldn't be a woman. I don't trust them, and I doubly don't trust women with tattoos."

"And men with tattoos? The prisons are full of them, carnivals with concrete walls instead of canvas tents."

"I don't trust them either, with or without tattoos."

"So you trust no one."

"Do you? Mistrust is an occupational illness. For both of us."

"Who are your credible suspects?" Ertras asked as a way to find some opening in Templeton's defense.

"Outside of me?"

"Is this a confession?"

"I'm not credible as a suspect, not to the three people in this city who still think logically. If I generate eyeballs and clicks, those who sell clicks and eyeballs will paint me as a suspect. Truth lies in whatever is profitable."

"Profit is truth", Ertras repeated. "I'll make a note of that."

"If you need to make a note of that, then you obviously don't understand the world that you live in, and I've overestimated you. Anyone listening to this interview later will think that is you who had been locked away from the world for the past eighteen years. Not me."

"Let's return to the topic that brought us here, the murder. Why now? And why there? What possible motive could there be other than revenge? You are right at the top of that list. Establishing credibility with other gangs? Random is not likely."

"He dumped his girlfriend", Templeton added.

"Maybe", Jackson interjected.

"He did. He told me himself."

"He told you that he dumped her? That doesn't sound like something that he would do."

"Did you even know Ronnie, detective?" Templeton asked caustically, emphasizing the word detective. "Ask her yourself, I can't do everything for you two. They broke up. Those were Ronnie's words."

"That I believe", Ertras said, nodding her head slowly. "I met her a few times, she's a real estate agent."

"I know," replied Templeton. "Half of the women in this town are nurses or real estate agents. How sick is that", he continued, laughing at his little joke.

"She had access to his house, his medicine, any medicine or drugs that would render him pliable, she knew his routine and his schedule for that day. She would have been picking him up if they hadn't split from each other. Maybe she came by and met him at the door of the hospital. They have cameras. Check on that," Templeton said authoritatively.

"There is no video, it wraps every few hours." Ertras shared this information with the suspect, not knowing why. Jackson turned away from Templeton to hide his surprise. Perhaps Cas was disclosing these details as some sort of gambit. He would not have done it himself. Templeton noticed the male detective's movement and smiled at Jackson's discomfort. "Thanks for the display of trust, Detective," he said politely to Ertras. He then sat back and smiled his broadest smile. He had failed to establish dominance with the detectives, but he had held his own. He could still land a solid punch.

"You probably don't know this," he had said as he regarded the detectives, "but the leaves of an oak differ from those of a maple. There are reasons for that. They sing in the wind. Each has its own song."

"I did not know that," Detective Ertras responded.

"Years ago, when I was innocent," Templeton said and then paused, "more or less," he continued after noticing the facial expression on Ertras' assistant, "they all would want me to be guilty. The judge, the police, they all wanted a simple solution. They thought me guilty, so I became guilty."

"I see", Ertras said dryly.

"Today, when I might be guilty, the evidence that you've presented might convince even me. But I just can't remember. Now, finally, they all think me innocent, they need me to be innocent. Your assistant would be terrible at poker, Lieutenant. One glance confirms that I am right, what is your name by the way?"

"Jackson."

"I hate referring to people as if they only had existence as being someone else's possession. Jackson is your family name?"

"Yeah."

"Mr. Jackson here understands the politics of the situation."

"The murder, you mean?"

"Murder is such an unpleasant word. We can use it here, behind closed doors. But I can't guarantee"

"You aren't in a position to guarantee anything."

"You must be very good at your job to have made your rank despite your lack of political sense. Jackson you'd best pay attention to where your captain is flying the plane. It could end badly for you. Disastrous."

Jackson remained silent. So far, each phrase that passed from Templeton's lips had their unspoken twin in his mind. The male detective found himself nodding in agreement. Absent the governor's commutation, this case would have been a gold mine for Ertras and him. Instead it was a tar pit that he would be lucky to escape.

Templeton continued his explanation.

"The governor thinks me innocent; he has no choice. I'm pretty sure that I am innocent. Ha! Do I see a glimmer of hope in your eyes Jackson? I might be able to save your career. Or should I just crash this jet into the nearest mountain, taking all of us at once. I could just plead guilty. the governor's smile wouldn't be as wide as it was Saturday at Churchill. We could all join Ronnie at Cave Hill, the ultimate destination for those who have become useless."

"What the hell does that mean?" Jackson asked, puzzled.

"I may not be able to win this race, but"

"There is no race Templeton," Ertras interjected angrily.

"You like to have the last word."

Templeton said nothing, refusing to make the detective's point.

"Do you drive?" Jackson asked calmly.

"I'm a dying man, who just got out of jail. I haven't had time to get a license. I don't have a passport either. If I did drive, my car wouldn't have all the modern technology, it's just a way to spy on us."

"Us?"

"Us, all of us. You included. Normal people like us."

Ertras smiled but said nothing.

"I don't like technology and neither did Ronnie. Did you search his house?"

"We went through it" Ertras lied. The search was a task still to be done. "Why?"

"Did anything strike you as odd?"

"Such as what? And how would you know?"

"From what I saw through the windows. That isn't a crime, or not much of one. I saw no high-end entertainment, no big screen, nothing like that."

"Templeton has no reason to lie about something so trivial" Ertras told herself. "So?"

"Nothing. I lost my train of thought. Oh, wait, no it's gone."

"And when you speak"

"Now I remember. Technology is sucking all the fun out of life. I used to feel locked up in prison, because, well, I was locked up."

Ertras smiled again despite herself at this unexpected awkwardness on the part of Templeton.

"Out here, in the so-called free world, all these kids, and middle aged men even, they lock themselves away with their smartphones, hell, they do it in public, like they are consulting some oracle on the screen. They are voyeurs. I should know, I met more than a few in prison. They put themselves in isolation like the worst of the worst."

He paused, gathering his thoughts.

"Today's criminals, I'm not talking about those they call thugs. At least the thugs are upfront about it, you may not like or respect their uniform, but you must admit that they wear one.

No, the others, they are sneaky, they commit their crimes from afar, like a missile launched from the desert sky. What they used to call strong arm guys are obsolete."

"You just told us that thugs are a regular military organization," Ertras asked. "Which is it?"

"Both. They both exist but the real money is being made by the nerds. They are the white-collar criminals, although they work from home or Starbucks, and I doubt they wear collared shirts. These guys are the strong minds, and not the strong arms. Smart guys and not wise guys."

"They are all men?" asked Ertras, feigning hurt.

"I was going to say, and some smart women. I suppose" added Templeton.

"I suppose," echoed Ertras. "Keep him talking" she ordered herself. She hoped that he would ramble into a confession. Across the room, Jackson gave her a glance of approval.

"Technology has yanked all personality from crime, now it is all bits and bytes, maybe a flash of light or an annoying sound effect, if you are lucky."

"The thrill is gone," Ertras summarized.

"That is the truth, inspector" confirmed Templeton. Ertras had difficulty following the career she had with the aged con. Between his references to her as officer, up to captain, demoted to sergeant and then elevated to the nonexistent rank of inspector, Ertras wavered between believing that Templeton was slipping mentally and theorizing that he was deliberately annoying her.

"Perch had other interests", Ertras offered.

"You're telling me that Ronnie had hobbies?"

"Yes."

"Hobbies are for Brits and soon to be dead Americans."

"So, you must have picked up a few yourself, recently. Considering" Jackson said with a stab.

"Touché."

"We were kids. Back then we could be kids. It was ok to be kids. We would have bristled at being called children, if we'd known the meaning of bristle. Children were the kid version of kids, and we were kids, full grown kids. We wore military uniforms. Not our own of course, but those of our fathers and now that I think of it, of their friends. It's hard to think of them as having friends, but, oh I don't know, we were them, our parents I mean, and we were ourselves, we were us, themselves, both at the same time. We carried guns."

"You did? Guns?"

"Toys. Guns. Back then there was no difference between them."

"And Percheron?" Jackson asked.

"And Ronnie what?"

"Was he your friend or your enemy?" Jackson detailed the question.

Templeton paused. Stalled more accurately described his silence.

"Friend or enemy? Is that your question?" Ertras' silence was both affirming and demanding. "It was a different world back then. It was better."

"So, you want to go back there?" pursued the policewoman.

"Who wouldn't, Sarge? But that is fantasy. It's not possible. Life runs in one direction, and as much as I'd like to run it in reverse, I can't. And neither can you. Frames don't work any longer Ertras" the lack of a title emphasized his disrespect. "You and LMPD won't frame me for this killing. It's a trap, one of yours or Ronnie's, but it doesn't matter, you're his woman."

"I am not his woman."

"No, you aren't, he no longer has anything. But you were." He was going to say more but decided not to. After a moment he spoke again.

"Ronnie understood. The governor wants me innocent, who am I to argue?"

Templeton stood and turned to leave.

"If you think I'm guilty then send your evidence to my attorney."

"You know that it doesn't work that way".

"It should." He paused, looking directly into her yes.

"Am I free to go, detective Castorina Ertras?" Templeton asked in a formal voice.

Ertras nodded and saw her prime suspect stroll calmly out of the interview room.

Cas turned to Jackson, "What we think was his first victim was found floating in the Ohio river."

"Drowned?"

"No. Death was from a gunshot. Then she had been dumped in the water. Templeton was strongly suspected but never charged."

"He got lucky."

"She didn't."

"He is right about the politics of this."

"I know. And now he needs medical treatment and thanks to the fact that many people don't like the governor's party he has become a cause célèbre among the fools on social media. They clap and bark like trained seals."

"But the governor released a dying man to enjoy his last months in freedom."

"Actions don't matter. He is the wrong color, the wrong gender, he belongs to the wrong party. Shoot first, life is a video game. It's so easy to judge people today, it's impossible to forgive."

"I'd have thought that he looked progressive in front of the young voters."

"That is an oxymoron. And it had the perfect tone of vengeance for the boomers."

"How's that?" questioned Jackson

"Release Templeton and let him die in the gutter, un-mourned and uncared for. The commutation was a death sentence for a convict previously sentenced to life.

The reaction now that Templeton is the prime suspect in Perch's death is completely the reverse of what the governor likely anticipated.

The boomers are upset that the governor released a weak but nevertheless dangerous wolf into the city where he killed a local hero in such a public in your face way."

"Among the lambs of the internet, it's seen as sweet justice."

"Murder is not justice."

"No, of course not, Cas, but it's a different world. People want to be associated with celebrities so badly, that they will settle for scum like Templeton." Jackson was silent and then asked, "Templeton is really that ill?"

"He must have been checked and rechecked. Otherwise, he'd still be locked up, and you and I would not be here today, struggling in this, what did Templeton call this"

"A tar pit," Jackson provided

"Yes, a tar pit. Another name for a cemetery."

"La Brea, that is Spanish," he said proudly.

"Templeton can't afford the care, and he will probably be dead before trial meaning that he will be innocent before the law."

"As the governor wants."

"You agree with Templeton on that conclusion?"

Jackson nodded slowly.

"Yep," he uttered. "Even with medical treatment, he will not last until the end of any legal proceedings. The amount of donations pledged on his behalf for health assistance is insufficient to prolong his life. It's less of a GoFundMe for him than it is a go FU by him to us. He wants to stretch this embarrassment out for as long as he can for the governor, the city, for us. What about the first murder? The one that Templeton was never charged with?"

"The autopsy suggested that she'd been shot with a small caliber handgun, maybe a .32. She was a thin girl, and the bullet exited. If she was shot on or near the river, the bullet is somewhere on the bottom of the river. If the gun used to shoot Perch was also used 30 years ago to shoot the first victim, Sherry Pregel, there is absolutely no ability to prove it."

CHAPTER FIVE

Two days after Thunder over Louisville, Melissa and Templeton met as her house.

"Ronnie and I are through, Grove."

"I'm not surprised, Melissa. He has ruined both of our lives."

"No, we did that to ourselves."

"He has ruined our futures. Both of us had plans, yours included him and mine excluded him. He's screwed both of us."

"No, I don't" Melissa paused, not knowing what she wanted to say.

"You disagree, Melissa?"

"No," she said simply after a long pause. "But we are all adults, Grove. We don't go home and cry because we've been disappointed and didn't get our own way."

"I agree completely."

"You do?"

"Sure, we are adults, we can behave as adults."

"I'm glad to hear you say that. I was worried"

"Let me finish. We don't have to take no for an answer." Templeton looked as if a new thought had just struck him, and he said nonchalantly, "I saw him with a youngish blonde woman at Thunder. Is she the reason he dumped you?"

"He didn't dump me, he"

"He eased you out, is that it? People have become loathe to face reality during my absence."

"So have you, Grove. You were in prison for murder, not on some university sabbatical. Your absence, ha!"

"This blonde woman, she looked like his type."

"A younger version of me? Is that what you mean?"

"You do resemble each other. They seemed quite close."

"What were you doing at Thunder? Were you stalking him?"

"Don't be silly. Everybody was there."

"She is Cassie Ertras, his ex-mentee and partner."

"They embraced each other and even kissed each other on the cheek."

"Hell Grove, this is not high school. That's just Ronnie doing his French thing."

"Her name sounds Spanish, they do the French thing as well? Oh, which French thing are you talking about?"

"You know, the kiss on the cheeks."

"During my sabbatical, the term French kiss must have taken on a new meaning. Oh well, you know more than I do."

Neither spoke for a minute, as each sipped from their overpriced paper cups.

"I've never seen police partners embrace like that before."

"It only began after Ronnie retired. They are no longer partners," Melissa said, recognizing immediately the double meaning of the word partner.

Templeton said nothing but waited patiently. He had learned patience, he hated it as much as the prison food, but it had been necessary to accept both.

"What else did they do?"

"I don't know, I wasn't surveilling them," he said, truthfully, and then followed immediately with a lie, like medicine in candy. "They strolled off through the crowd, hand in hand."

"They didn't'!" she exclaimed.

"Maybe you are right, he could have been leading her through the crowd. It was very crowded; it was never that big years ago. I noticed that Thunder is more popular than ever."

He saw with satisfaction that his lie had taken root. Her own suspicion and festering anger would fertilize it

Over the next few days he found out Ronnie's schedule, the colonoscopy set for Oaks Day. He wondered if Ronnie still visited Cave Hill from time to time, perhaps something could be arranged

Two days after she had first informed Melissa about Perch's death, the woman sitting across from Detective Ertras was at ease. The shock had worn off and Melissa had time to apply makeup for this interview.

She was nearly the same height as Perch, they would have been a perfect match as dance partners. Melissa kept her hair long, it was probably effective in her job as a real estate agent, Ertras thought.

"It hurt more than normal, not that I have been dumped often, or recently. Ronnie was a decent guy, which is why it hurt."

"You had history together," Jackson suggested.

"Is that what you call it, Detective?"

"How would you describe it, Melissa?"

"We had more than history, Detective. What is you name again?" Melissa asked

"Never mind," she went on before he could respond to her.

"Don't tell me. I don't care what it is. Knowing it isn't important to me." She turned to Ertras, then seeing that she was correct in having expected no sympathy from the other female in the small room, she rotated back to the now insulted unknown male, whose mouth remained partially open.

"We had a lifetime together," Melissa answered, restarting the interview from zero.

"A lifetime together and another one apart," Ertras launched, hoping to elicit an involuntary response from the middle aged widow and ex-girlfriend.

"So what?" parried Melissa. "We are friends, we were always friends. Years ago, when he wanted more, I didn't. And then later, when I was ready"

Jackson reopened his mouth to speak, then closed it again, saying nothing. Melissa had paused, offering the detective a chance to speak. She felt contrite for being rude. As the silence extended itself, Melissa simply supplied the obvious ending, "Ronnie wasn't ready."

Jackson asked, "how many years did you and Ronnie date?"

"Recently, you mean?"

"After the death of your husband," Ertras clarified.

"Or did you," began Jackson

"No!" Melissa said emphatically. "I was faithful to my husband. Don't even go there," she commanded, but the three of them were aware that the police would go wherever they needed to go.

"It was a good marriage that quickly went bad," Melissa was explaining. "He was married two days a week, it was a part time role, not a career. It went bad."

"Like a sensitive Bordeaux," Ertras thought for no reason.

"Then suddenly, one day it got much better."

"What happened?" queried Jackson

"My husband died," Melissa replied unemotionally. She paused, then laughed.

"His leaving me was the happiest day of my life." She laughed again, longer this time. Ertras wondered, was the laughter sincere or was Melissa only trying to relieve the stress of their questions. "Probably both," Ertras decided.

Jackson restarted in with his bad cop voice, "Tell us about the big dump scene with Ronnie."

"He was such a great guy," Melissa began, lost for a moment in the world where Henry Percheron, her childhood and lifelong friend, still lived. She was no longer smiling, the laughter now vanished, like Ronnie.

Ertras again asked herself the same question that she had posed so often already in this inquiry. "Was this an act, which emotions and words were real and not deflections?" Jessica Villier was not the only accomplished actor in this play that Ertras was trying desperately to direct well. A play to which no two people had the same script, not even her and Jackson.

She felt a wave of vertigo and grabbed the back of one of the white plastic chairs for support. Little about this case had the sense of being real. She was used to dealing with liars and their untruths, but this was somehow different. She could not describe it, even to herself.

Melissa was speaking. Ertras was glad that this session was being recorded as she wasn't sure if she'd had missed something critical.

"As I said, I wanted Ronnie to remember that moment, and frankly I was hoping, praying, that he would change his mind."

Her explanation contained too much honesty to be true, Jackson judged. "You were mad?"

"Absolutely. I was angry, and sad, and lost and hopeless, I was all of that and I feared that very soon I was going to be nothing."

"You did very well on your husband's life insurance policy and the settlement from the mine." The accusation was presented as a statement of fact.

Jackson went on, "He was an OSHA inspector, checking on coal mines and was presumed killed in an underground explosion and collapse."

Ertras' horrified glance at her subordinate mirrored that of Melissa. His behavior was cruel as well as stupid, even for a man.

Melissa turned to Ertras and explained.

The money she had was a given, her husband was long dead. The money was assured, it too belonged like her late husband to the past.

"Ronnie's decision had concerned my future, our future. His choice had been to relegate me to his past. Like my husband was for me. I felt dead. Like my husband." Ertras understood her at least

Melissa spoke again. "You know how Derby is like Christmas, detective?"

Jackson and Ertras both nodded, the two holidays resemble each other in Louisville.

"Spiked eggnog or julep," Jackson said to himself.

"Well, I was expecting a marriage proposal, not a dismissal."

Melissa wanted a happier memory; she changed the subject.

"Different info on opposite sides of the headstone is his final joke, one that will last for decades."

"What do you mean by that?"

"Perch and I talked about burials once, back when I think both of us saw a future together. He said that the tombstones were bragging in stone. He suggested that it would be fair to let detractors carve whatever they wanted to say on the reverse, as long as it was in poor taste."

"You mean good taste."

"No, he meant poor taste. It's even more appropriate today. Remain silent if you have nothing good to say is heresy in the

49

social media age. I'm rambling, I know. I'm just" she paused and then let that thought drop.

"So, his headstone will have its back constructed from blackboard material."

"Slate?" suggested Jackson.

"Yes, that's right. Slate." Melissa paused, then let go forever of that happy memory.

Without their prompting, Melissa returned to the weeks between Thunder and Derby and her relationship with Perch.

"Ronnie barely had time for me when he was working. Once he retired, I expected that he'd fill the free time with me. Instead, he tried all and everything to provide whatever was missing.

"Other women?", asked Jackson.

"Are you kind when you aren't working?" Melissa asked in return, then continued immediately. She wanted no answers from this man.

"Not as far as I know. And I made a point to know as much as possible."

"Are you certain?"

"I wish that it had only been a woman. I could have competed easily with her, whoever she would have been. You understand that, don't you Cassie? But with dead bodies dropping all over town, he was always on the go. Afterwards it was fixing cars, birding, French lessons at the Alliance Française, various Meetup groups, radio planes, a stint as a private investigator. If it could serve him as a diversion he'd give it a try But none of these gave him the around the clock excitement of his job. It was his life, it was life."

"Was he investigating anything recently."

"No, he abandoned that post career as well. But then, I haven't seen him in a few weeks."

"Oh? Why was that? I thought that you were still friends."

"We broke up." She laughed.

"It's not funny, but when I say it aloud, it sounds like we were back in high school."

"You dated that long ago?"

"Yes, with a marriage for me in between. We lost contact and then got back together a few years later, after my husband died."

"Hmmm. Do you know Mosgrove Templeton?"

"Grove? Sure, since elementary school. He was bad even then. Smart, clever, but bad. It's an unappreciated gift.

"Do you know his girlfriend?"

"I didn't know he has one. She must be crazy."

"Do you know a Joyce Small."

"Yes, we are friends."

"Were you aware of Percheron's upcoming colonoscopy?"

"Yes. Why?"

"Did you"

"Wait, you asked me about Joyce Small. Joyce is Grove's nurse. Are you saying that Joyce is Grove's girlfriend?" Melissa laughed, looked at Ertras and Jackson, and laughed again.

"We are not sure if there is more to Templeton and Small than just patient and nurse," Jackson stated, his voice without emotion.

"Just because you say that in such a formal manner, detective, doesn't make it any less stupid" Melissa said, grateful for a chance at payback on the male in the room.

"You may be right," Jackson said quickly.

"Did you swing by to pick him up afterwards? Maybe met him at his car."

"What?"

"Did you pick Percheron up at the hospital after his colonoscopy?"

"No. I called the night before and offered. He took my call rather than letting it roll to voicemail."

"He didn't block you after the big breakup?"

"It was a breakup like any other. He isn't, wasn't like that"

"Like what?"

"I was important to him." Melissa paused. "Some guys would behave that way. Not Ronnie".

"You were important. He hadn't got around to blocking you yet. He had new important things, maybe a new, important other woman?"

The question had been thrown by Jackson, but Melissa addressed her answer to Ertras.

"That won't get a rise from me, Cas. I spent too many years with Perch to respond to bait."

"Too many years? How many is too many?"

"You should have come to this interrogation better prepared, Cas. I did."

"I see. Preparations often involve hiding something."

"Whatever. I'm here to help you solve this awful killing. If you don't want my help, I'll offer it to the chief directly. She'll see me."

"That is your prerogative, but we are not finished here."

"You act as if we are. I expected better. You asked me if Perch and I were together for too many years. It was more than five and less than six. That is not as many as I was hoping for. But, it's over now. I have memories of a sweet past. And I envision a future not so sweet. Finding the killers will be, oh what is the silly word that people use, closure. As if closure is healing."

"Maybe it is a start," Ertras said gently, switching to sympathy.

"Maybe."

"Why do you say killers, and not killer?" probed Ertras.

"It's obvious. It could not be done by one person," Melissa said adamantly.

"Was that accurate?" Ertras wondered. "One person who could get very close to Perch, who knew his mannerisms, one person could do that."

Melissa was reading her mind.

"Oh, you think that I could have done this horrible thing by myself?" Waiting for no reply, Melissa went on, "You could have done this yourself; you were just as close. Maybe even closer, recently. I think that he trusted your more."

"Why, because I had no ulterior motive? I wasn't husband shopping."

"You probably were, just not with him. Or maybe even with him. Who knows?"

"I need to ask you again about your breakup," Ertras commented, putting sympathy away for the moment.

"It was over something trivial, no, that isn't right, see I am trying to help Cas," the delayed response to the discarded sympathy finally successful. "Not trivial exactly".

"Do you think that it was contrived?" Ertras asked, testing to see if Melissa would project her own deceit onto Perch.

"Percheron lived in a contrived world."

"What does that mean?" interjected Jackson.

"You know, Cas, maybe this unnamed detective should be conducting this interrogation, he and the chief, not you. You are too close," she finished saying. The remark could not have been truer. Ertras knew it as well as anyone.

"Everything with Perch was contrived. He was a great guy, but he wasn't perfect. He won't be canonized, Cas."

The repeated use of her first name was rapidly annoying Ertras. It was just a technique; she would ignore it. This woman liked to play games. Perhaps that explained her long-term success with Perch. Melissa was still speaking.

"Perch was tightly wound. He was poor at relaxation. He so wanted adventure in his daily life, but the unexpected seemed to escape him.

"Until a few days ago," Jackson said involuntarily.

"Or he escaped it?" asked Ertras.

Melissa hesitated, and thought for a moment, before nodding in agreement.

"I think that you're right about him escaping."

"Until Derby," Jackson added unnecessarily.

"Why did you two never marry?"

"It would be trite but true to say that he was already married."

"To the job?" Jackson provided.

"No, to the game. Your police department gave him a place to play his game, and money on top of it. He'd have done it for nothing. He reminded me of an athlete, or maybe even Sherlock Holmes, a prodigy in his field, but outside of his crime puzzles, he was boring."

"And bored?" wondered Ertras.

"He was a bit autistic I think, disguised as boring."

"So, no violin for him?"

"Violin? No, why? Oh, that is a Sherlock Holmes reference. You are just as bad."

"The girlfriend was doing very well in judging her," Ertras realized, annoyed.

"Let's get back to the breakup."

"He was going on and on about his latest infatuation, model planes or drones. It was a hobby, that's a poor choice of words, he was looking for something, anything to replace police work, the crime games that I mentioned earlier."

Jackson and Ertras both nodded encouragingly

"He didn't complain, but he may have been drowning in the vacuum left by his retirement. Can someone drown in a vacuum? Perch will know the answer to that question," Melissa said, using the wrong tense.

"Without police work he was nothing."

"And how did you feel about it?"

"About police work? It was a job, like any other. Retirement is a reward, not a penalty."

"How did you feel about Perch's "drowning"?"

"Terrible. I knew that there was little that either of could do about it, the crime game I mean."

A thought came to Jackson about Melissa concocting a crime game for Percheron that went wrong. He glanced at Ertras who indicated that she had the same idea.

"But he could do private investigation work, you hear about that sort of thing often. But that wouldn't be with me. I expected that retirement would be our fun time, that we would have our shared hobbies. Like Tango, which we did a few times at Blair's Ballroom. Tango was a team activity. I liked it, it was"

"It was what?" demanded Jackson, his voice too loud, breaking the moment.

"It was intimate, but in a public way. It said, look everyone, Perch and Melissa are together."

"I see," said Ertras, filling the vacuum that was on the verge of drowning her.

"And then there was birdwatching, we were together, often hidden, whispering. It was erotic. The hushed voices."

"Don't blush, Cas," Melissa commanded. "Ronnie was a man you know, and I am a woman."

Jackson attempted to correct the course of the interview, saying in a neutral voice, "And then Perch started flying toy planes."

"Drones, I think. The same damned one that I had given him for Christmas. It was his new thing to do. Notice that I said his, not ours. It wasn't like painting, or dancing, or anything that we had done as a couple. But I knew that it would go the way of his other solitary pursuits, in time."

"He was slipping away?"

"Yes, I was afraid that he was slipping away, leaving us behind for" she paused.

"For what Melissa?" Ertras prompted gently.

"For a new girlfriend?" Jackson asked.

"Maybe," Melissa answered. "But even that would not have lasted. The birdwatching, the toy planes, I think that he saw them not as I did, as something that we could do together. It was like a stakeout, solitary."

Melissa stood and stretched, walked around the small room and sat down again.

"We took French classes, tango lessons, even the birdwatching, we secreted ourselves away. All of those were romantic, shared, like I said. I felt that they were bringing us closer together, that something would lead to something."

"Like dance contests?"

"No, not like that. Dance contests would have been just like the model aircraft, mechanical, like a job." She paused, attempting to summarize her emotions as much for herself as for them.

"I was wrong."

"How so?" Jackson asked, perplexed at Melissa's conclusion.

"It led nowhere. The more time we spent together, the more Perch began to miss his solitary life. He told me that our dual activities were not achieving his goal. He was stepping away."

"What was his goal?"

"I'm not sure that he knew the goal himself. I don't know. He then informed me that it was over. It being us. It being the past five years. It was so abrupt. I understood then what my nieces and nephews felt like when they were texted out of some relationship. It's like receiving a telegram in one of those old black and white movies."

"And now what?"

"How do I feel, is that your question?"

Ertras nodded yes.

"Or how did I feel then, and how did I react?"

"Were you angry?"

"Of course I was angry. Was I angry enough to kill him? Of course not. I hated him for making me start over, I know that it is too late to start over. I will never finish the race," she sighed, and Ertras speculated that neither would she.

Ertras persevered with her questions.

"What did you do?"

"I went back to work, such as it is." She added in response to their questioning looks, "It took my mind off what had just occurred."

"And between the Thursday before Oaks," not being able to bring herself to use the childish sounding Thurby, "until Sunday morning?"

"Nothing really. The market is slow those days, and I didn't want to see anyone. I stayed home and drank more wine than normal. I took a few walks in Lake Forest, hoping to see Ronnie on Friday or Saturday after the colonoscopy.

"Some folks might consider that stalking", Jackson commented.

"Do most criminals confess just in order to have you shut up? You are a yappy little dog."

"Are you a criminal, Melissa?" Jackson's retort came very quickly.

Ertras knew that these interviews could be cruel for all participants. She was good at her job because she could be cold. Her empathy had no endurance. Men had told her that she was a thirty second lover before leaving her for women with more emotional stamina.

"Melissa, the way you describe Percheron his life was one step away from acquiring a dog."

Cas and Ertras glanced at each other in hearing Jackson's comment.

"Why didn't he? Acquire a dog, that is."

"Perch with a dog? I don't see it. Do you Cas?"

"Hell, I don't know. Perch with a dog? Two weeks ago, I would have said no, but today? Maybe."

"He could have been allergic to dogs. You know as well as I do that folks here are allergic to everything."

Ertras returned to the breakup. She had what she needed from Melissa, at least for now. "Was she asking these questions unnecessarily, for her own enjoyment? Did she want to bring this woman pain?"

"Where did Perch tell you that it was over?"

"At Gander's."

Cas had decided to stop this line of questioning, but Melissa continued unprompted, perhaps needing to relive the moment in order to forget it.

"There is no classy way to breakup except by offering to be breaker instead of the breakee.

I wasn't having it. It was going to be his role. He would play the bad cop this one time."

Melissa laughed mirthlessly.

"You wanted to see him squirm," Ertras said. It was not a question.

"I wouldn't say that," Melissa protested weakly.

"It was his turn that day."

"His turn to die?" It was not a reasonable question, Ertras thought as soon as the words were spoken. But neither was murder in most instances.

Melissa ignored the question.

"In the past two years, Ronnie had abandoned so many pursuits. I was just one of many. The only one with emotions" Melissa's voice was resigned to her loss.

"Perch preferred the beauty of illusion to the reality of the thing, whatever that thing was. It was what made him so effective, his imagination. It also made a discontented man." On that the two women agreed.

Jackson tried another tack.

"You claim that Perch dropped pastimes so readily in retirement."

"Yes."

"But he had stuck with murder for decades. It has no beauty."

"Not to you or me it doesn't. Or maybe it does to you, and to you too, Cas. You are both in the murder business. They say that there is no accounting for taste."

"Or that beauty is in the eye of the beholder," added Jackson hopefully."

Melissa veered to another idea.

"He retired at a good time. It was the right time for him."

"Is it the right time for me?" wondered Ertras. "This case feels like it has been going on for years, and it was only hours. Was it progressing?" She had no clue amongst all the clues.

Melissa was still speaking.

"I got the feeling that he feared becoming stuck in the past, not that he didn't love it there."

Ertras nodded slowly as Melissa continued.

"He was afraid of being seen as obsolete. It was silly."

"Why?" prompted Jackson

Melissa wanted to ignore this man and his questions. The answer was obvious.

"The world was leaving Perch behind." She sipped from the can of Coke in front of her. The liquid was flat and tepid.

"He had trouble enough, disappointments is a better word," she explained while thinking of her own, the detectives contemplating theirs.

"The 20th century had been bad enough but the 21st was far worse. In his eyes. I think. I don't really know what I'm saying. I miss him and now," here voice trailed off. There was nothing else she wanted to say. She too felt flat and tepid. She was empty.

"Things are getting better," countered Jackson, dissatisfied with this sudden evaporation of what had been a promising interview.

Melissa sat immobile for over a minute before she acquiesced to responding to this latest question. She was tired of their questions and more tired of her answers. She understood how feeble her replies were.

"Technology was making Perch obsolete. He was a chess grandmaster whose whole existence was replaced by a free online game. He became nothing."

"He retired."

"I wonder now if he wasn't retired before retirement."

"What do you mean Melissa?" Ertras asked. She had been watching the witness closely and was suspicious that this psychological talk was intended to distract her from asking hard, specific questions. Technology didn't kill Perch; someone used a gun and hand-ties to murder him.

Ertras went on, "He retired. He was a bit disoriented and sad. That is the fate of every retiree that I've ever met."

"You mentioned earlier that you know Mosgrove Templeton.

"Yes".

"Did you handle the sale of his late mother's house in Middletown?"

"Yes".

"Why?"

"Why? That is, or rather was, my profession. I'm mostly retired now. I handled that section of town, among others. Plus, Grove trusted me. I knew his mother. We both did. Ronnie and I."

"I see. And your commission?"

"I took the minimum, he was a friend."

"It sounds like he still is. Thirty years and a murder or so later? You have low requirements for friendship."

"And you have low standards in other areas, from what I've been told."

"By your accomplice?"

I don't have an accomplice, you saw to that during Thunder. You and Ronnie were quite the couple."

Jackson's head swiveled from one woman to another, it reminded him of the professional tennis match he'd seen in Cincinnati years ago, when he was as yet unfamiliar with the rules of the game. He felt the same confusion, and he took in the verbal exchanges without understanding their true meanings.

"No, I had nothing do with whatever happened between you and Perch."

That phrase made everything clear to Jackson. This was a simple case of one man killing another, and politics and romance were on their way to turning this into a scandal. He needed to bury this, before it buried him and his career.

These two women before him saw themselves as rivals of a man who was still alive in their minds. Neither would admit it, either to him or to each other. It reminded him of that reality show that his sister so enjoyed, where women compete and humiliate themselves in an attempt to win a prize that is not worth having and where second place earns one the chance to transition from humiliated to humiliator on a subsequent season of the program.

Melissa's mind was dealing with her own reality.

"This can't be happening, these detectives consider me a suspect," she thought. It dawned on Melissa that she should stop talking, or to think before answering. She did a quick review of the past three weeks, but it was too much to classify intelligently while she sat in this room. She needed time to think, her story was not as simple as she had first thought. "Maybe Grove could help. No, that was the worst solution, no, not the worst. They were in this together, whether she liked it or not. She would need to speak to Grove soon. But how?"

"Booze, broads, and bucks. The big three", Jackson said during lunch at Brasserie Provence, a French restaurant that they'd stopped at before driving to the exclusive enclave of Anchorage to interview an additional witness and then on to Lake Forest to conduct a search of the Percheron residence.

"Templeton doesn't fit into any of those categories. As far as we know. Does he?" questioned Jackson. This murder is not rational."

"Forty percent of the country is on drugs, and you expect rationality?" Ertras had stated the statistic with the level of seriousness found only in women. Jackson reflected for a moment before offering his own perspective on the state of society.

"People abuse neither drugs nor faith, there is no safe dose. Drugs and faith are the abusers, not the victims. Oh well, not our problems."

"No, he doesn't fit," Ertras said, returning the discussion to something that was their problem. "His motive is more biblical."

I haven't read the Bible. Can you fill me in?

"There's no point to it," Ertras replied, distracted by the arrival of their soup.

"Oh, that makes me feel much better," Jackson quipped, his attempt at a clever riposte escaping the notice of his boss, who continued with her own thoughts.

"Revenge. This murder is all about revenge. At least that's what I think at the moment."

"Revenge or vengeance?" Jackson asked, perplexed by this sudden detour into religion and ancient beliefs. Discussing taboos had become the final taboo in his opinion.

The fact that the crime scene was the land of the dead, filled with competing advertisements for the afterlife, made this case uncomfortable for him. It was like investigating a murder that had occurred at the morgue, it was against the rules of the game. "A game," he was reflecting, when the words of Ertras ferried him back to the current version of reality.

"Revenge. Whose revenge? Templeton, the ex-girlfriend, one of a dozen other embittered convicts."

"He didn't lack for enemies."

"And former friends."

Instead of disagreeing, Jackson offered, "So we are back to Templeton? With or without an accomplice?"

"Probably. I wish that I had taken vacation."

"Overtime is there for the taking at Derby. No one takes vacation. Including murderers."

"If I had," Ertras continued, ignoring Jackson's logic, "this investigation would have fallen to someone else."

"And you would have canceled whatever lame trip you were on and returned to Louisville, demanding to lead this case. You need to do this, for Perch, using the familiar name for someone he had only met once or twice. And you need to solve this for yourself and the entire force."

"I know."

"I appreciate the pressure that you are under, Cas."

"Pressure that we are both under," Ertras told herself, not relishing the responsibility she had for both of their careers.

"The way it looks at the moment, the best that we may be offer to the public is a killer himself already half dead."

"A scape goat," Ertras added. The waiter had brought their main course, and she waited to speak until after he had left.

"It might come down to either the head of Mosgrove Templeton or that of Castorina Ertras. Welcome to the front row of the toreador, "bullfight", she interpreted without prompting.

Don't worry, you're safe. I will keep you far enough away from the splashing blood.

"And female drama", Jackson thought.

"A scapegoat or one or two sacrificial lambs," mused Jackson. "I am definitely never going back to any church," he promised himself.

Ertras took the long way to Anchorage. Whether it was to delay an unpleasant task, or to reflect further on Melissa's words was not clear to Jackson. Rain and lightning accompanied them. Driving down Ward avenue, an intense yellow light erupted and then just as quickly vanished from sight about a quarter of a mile ahead. In few minutes, driving slowly along the narrow, puddled road, through gusts of wind and rain, they arrived at the scene of electrical lines dangling like dark Christmas tinsel from one of the poles that paralleled the route. Jackson called it in to dispatch, and the two sat there, waiting for a utility truck from Louisville Gas and Electric.

Ertras said little during the delay, letting the sounds of rain and windshield wipers combine to form a soothing melody. She would look for fishing tackle in the victim's home, either later today or tomorrow. It was a simple task, routine. She forced herself to depersonalize Perch, she would need to do it sometime, now was as good a moment as any. The investigation was too personal not to treat is dispassionately.

Jackson too, was quiet, grateful for the silence. He checked a few messages on his smartphone, then leaned the seat back and closed his eyes.

"Let me see your hand", Ertras said suddenly.

"What?"

"Your right hand. Let me see it."

Dutifully, Jackson extended his right hand to Cas. She inspected it and then said mysteriously, "As I expected."

"What?" Jackson asked.

"It's all due to that smartphone that you can't put down. Look at your fingertips."

Jackson regarded them, as for the first time, and noticed their smoothness. "Hmmm."

"That device is sucking you in more and more every day. First your fingerprints disappear and then, poof, all of a sudden you will be gone, like Alice in Wonderland, through the smartphone glass."

"What are you talking about?"

"I've seen it before. You better moderate your usage, or you'll just disappear one day."

Jackson regarded Cas' face, then his fingertips again, and then back to the now smiling face of his colleague.

Laughter was added to the music of rain and wipers, and too soon the arrival of the efficient utility workers put an end to their respite.

CHAPTER SEVEN

Jessica Villier had left Cave Hill cemetery on the Sunday after the Kentucky Derby before the police were through questioning her. It was also rumored that she had in fact left before their arrival. Her departure was either due to a terrible shock according to her publicist, or it had been done with regret as it was a marvelous opportunity for additional exposure. Villier' detractors chose to believe in regret.

Those people who actually knew the actress were confident that it was genuine grief on the part of a young woman who had lost a long-time neighbor to a violent death. Ertras had no opinion.

Ms. Villier was staying in one of the exclusive areas of Louisville, so exclusive that while surrounded by the city of Louisville, it was its own town, a secular Vatican. The actress was the guest of someone whom Ertras would never have occasion to meet. The home itself was on a five acre estate in Anchorage with its own bridge over a stream, two guest houses, elegant 1909 construction which brought its own maintenance challenges, and numerous large trees with branches stretching in all directions seemingly searching for help. Water was still dripping from the leaves and the air felt refreshed.

The two investigators walked slowly up to the front door of the mansion. Jackson felt himself in a foreign country.

In general, people follow the rules that they accept and ignore the rest. They did so in the west end and behaved the same way Cherokee Triangle, or in the enclave of Anchorage. It was not a matter of affluence. Wealth and poverty both brought contempt for law. They shared a conviction that the law was for, if not the small people, then the others, the fools. They weren't shy about it either; your disagreement placed you among the fools.

As the two detectives waited for the celebrity, Jackson remarked, "You notice how in some small towns where there are four churches at each intersection, all different. It's like the book of Ruth, "Your god is not my god, and your people are not my people, and sure as hell, your law is not my law."

"Yeah, just like that. Or something like that. But I thought that you were a confirmed pagan."

Any Jacksonian response was cut off by the arrival of Jessica Villier.

Perch's death had affected not only Ertras, but also this beautiful woman before her, expert in
displaying or concealing emotion. Villier was Perch's one-time cute little girl next door. Now she was his potential killer. Jessica could likely control her expression as well as she did her weight. This actress might be the best trained liar that Ertras would ever question. The word liar was harsh, but accurate. "Were her own skills of interrogation sufficient," Ertras wondered.

"Thank you for meeting with us, Ms. Villers."

"Please, just call me Jessica. My attorney was not supportive of me meeting with you."

"I understand that. It is sound legal advice. I myself can say nothing to convince you to not follow your attorney's counsel. But what would Perch advise you, if he were here, Jessica?" Ertras cajoled.

"Ask your questions," replied Jessica, as she prepared herself for this cold reading of a very personal script.

"Did you kill or have killed Detective Percheron because of some personal animosity?" Jackson pounced. Ertras stared at her assistant, nonplussed. It was such an implausible theory that would have made her laugh in other circumstances, but not today. Did he have a ploy in mind? "No," she decided, Jackson had just carried himself away in the moment. The hypothesis was so silly, not the silliness that could stand in for truth, like an accomplished understudy, but the level of silliness that was ridiculousness undisguised.

"Jessica, just tell us what happened on Sunday," Ertras said as way of apology.

"When I saw him lying there, I thought that it was an elaborate hoax, a joke that he had organized with my crew. I was so happy to see him stretched out on the damp ground, it sounds horrible now, but at the time it was too real to be real. It was too well set."

"You thought that it was fake?" Ertras asked, taken aback. "Why would he have done that, Jessica?"

"He wasn't too enthusiastic about this project, I think he was doing it more to make me and my parents happy, than for any other reason. And so, when I saw what I thought was a gag in the cemetery, I laughed and said aloud 'Oh, Perch'. I really thought that he had had a change of heart, he was excited to do this. I was just so happy." Jessica paused and then finished. And then I wasn't. This is all so horrible."

Was Jessica referring to the murder or the now cancelled project. Surely it would be cancelled. Ertras phrased her comment carefully.

"Yes, his death is upsetting to all of us. He was a mentor of mine, so this is doubly painful. Will you continue with the project?"

"Which? The film project?"

"Yes. Is there another project?"

"There are always other proposals and plans in process. I don't know if the one with Perch will move forward or not. It really could go either way. If it was purely my decision I would" she paused again, "I'm sorry I don't know what I would do. I feel that I owe him something but I worry that whatever I could do without him would be so much less without his involvement. It could become an insult rather than a tribute to him. I'm rambling, but"

"Rambling clears the head" Jackson said unexpectedly.

"Yes, yes it does. I like the sound of that. If I decide to move forward that might even be a good film title, 'Rambling Clear'."

"Let me start at the beginning", the actress requested.

Thursday morning, Thurby in Louisville parlance, Jessica had stopped by with a small entourage to say hello to Percheron who was in prep for a colonoscopy.

"Of course, I didn't know that at the time. How could I?"

"Did he mention anything about leaving Louisville?"

"I was going to ask, there was a for sale sign in his yard, but it just slipped my mind. I wanted to talk more about the film, and we did, but it was really awkward. I sensed that he was still hesitant, not anxious to talk, but we did for a bit. It was clear that we couldn't have a meaningful conversation through a bathroom door."

Villier gave Percheron a rain check for brunch with her and her parents for Sunday after Derby, before she returned to California.

"I was confident that we would have time later. But we didn't."

"And your entourage, where were they during your conversation?"

"Nearby."

"In the same room?"

"Yes. Or down the hall. Mostly down the hall."

"They weren't bored?"

"They are here for me, not the other way round. I have a role to play around the clock. Sometimes it involves me being the bad cop."

"Which is what exactly?"

"You must know better than I, detective. That was one thing I wanted to discuss with Perch."

"Oh, being a bad cop?"

"I wanted to see him as he was, not as the kindly cop next door that I remembered. If he really was the man of my memories, fine, but to be honest, I was looking for a dark side."

"Because of something that you suspected about him?" Jackson asked in a quiet voice.

"No, not at all. I just needed to make his character more complex. If he couldn't provide a dash of the sinister from his own spice cabinet, so to speak, I was positive that he had more than enough experience with authentically bad cops that I could add some of it to his screen character."

"So the movie was not going to show a perfect cop?"

"No."

"It figures."

"Are there any?"

"I think that you just told me that you used to live next door to one for years."

"Perch wasn't star struck around me, even when I became one. It was more the reverse. He was like the lone ranger, but that movie has already been done," she said seriously.

"He was willing to accept my ideas. I even suggested that I play him, instead of the villain in the movie, the idea came to me suddenly, but it sounded perfect. What do you think?"

Ertras shrugged. Other people's work was of no interest to her, neither their work nor them.

"Perch said fine, that women in the workplace was the biggest change in his career, even more significant than advances in technology."

"Did you discuss anything else?"

"About the movie, sure."

"That isn't what," Ertras began but Jessica continued her line. Ertras wondered if any of this was rehearsed. Was one of the entourage an attorney?

"I indicated to him that I really needed to hear about some juicy murders, as he had worked so many of them. This all sounds like"

"Like what?"

"I don't know. Perch told me that the murders were rarely juicy, as I put it, but often bloody. He was willing to help as long as he received"

"All of the credit?" suggested Jackson.

Jessica turned to glance at Jackson, then returned her gaze to Ertras. "None of the credit. He wanted absolutely no credit at all."

"That was Perch," were Ertras' only words.

"And now he is dead. I feel terrible, as if I am somehow responsible." After a short pause, while each person in the room reflected on their own short lives, Ertras asked unemotionally, "Are you?" her calm delivery unable to disguise the brutality of the short inquiry.

"This is the reality of your work, I see that, detective. The bad cop."

"We are all of us very far east of Hollywood, Ms. Villier. I'll repeat the question, were you?"

"No. I don't understand any of this. It is out of control. Everything in my life is scripted. It has been for years. My public appearances, my personal appearance, my work. I say my, which usually means mine, but I am not sure that I have a mine these days, or whether I play a character in a long running production titled *Jessica Villier*. There was a song by Dido, called Life for Rent. Have you heard it?"

Ertras nodded in response. "Keep her talking, it was probably 90 percent untrue or irrelevant, but this witness was used to being heard."

"No, I am not responsible, I can't see how. But"

"But what?" queried Jackson.

"I'm involved. Involved but not responsible. I am now a character in his production, and here I was thinking that he would be a character in my production. That word again, my. It's not mine".

"It would appear so," Jackson said, hoping like Ertras that Jessica would continue and finally provide salient information.

"This is not scripted, not some publicist's stunt, something that you, the police, have cooked up for the film? Perch is truly dead?"

"Yes. You mentioned a film several times now. Is there a specific topic in mind?"

"Some of us."

"Us?"

"Me, my agent, a few unknown but talented writers have been discussing a film about one of or some of his cases. Maybe his first, the one he didn't solve."

"These writers are friend of yours?"

"Writers don't have friends, only ingredients. I'm still within my use by date."

As they walked back to their car, Jackson mentioned that Jessica had appeared in a motion picture about the Derby early in her career.

"Maybe I should see if there is a family link between Secretariat and Inutile," Jackson offered hopefully."

"Sure, why not," Ertras responded without thinking, before countermanding her order. "That won't lead anywhere, I doubt that a horse kidnapped and shot someone during Derby week and no one noticed."

"I also verified that Percheron's brother was nowhere near Louisville. This was confirmed through cell phone records, and although I know how you feel about relying on electronic witnesses, I also had local police in Colorado swing by his residence."

"Good."

"The brother appeared genuinely surprised but not saddened. He did not ask about any inheritance, and when the officers mentioned the possibility of one, the surviving sibling had requested without hesitation, that it be donated to a Kentucky charity, possibly a police charity."

"Did the police in Colorado consider that a bribe? Did you consider that a bribe?"

"No, why would I? Do you?"

Jackson continued, " I called myself and got the same story direct from the sibling. I even asked about personal effects and mementos, pictures and items like that."

"What was the brother's response?"

"He told me that there was nothing personal between them of value, let alone to discuss."

"I see," Ertras said, despite not seeing at all. "OK, so much for family. Let's look elsewhere."

Driving past the mowed fields on either side of the Lake Forest main entry, Jackson noticed a man playing Frisbee with his German Shepherd while nearby a teen flew a small radio controlled plane. As they entered the subdivision, the car shuddered as is passed over a section of cobblestone. Ertras smiled contentedly. She remembered this from before, she imagined that both the vehicle and herself cleansing themselves of real and figurative mud from the outside world.

Lake Forest was a neighborhood of trees. "Does Templeton listen to those as well, or are those citified trees too discreet to tell the convict stories?"

Jackson's mind was elsewhere. A girl, maybe she was a young woman, even the uniformed female police officers in town often resembled adolescents in Halloween costume, Jackson had noted, was riding her bike perfectly, easily cruising around and joggers and dog walkers as if she was an actress in a choreographed film scene. Who knew, maybe she was. She sat erect on the robin egg blue two wheeler, it was what they used to term a girl's bike.

Jackson was reviewing scenes in his mind, running the action back like a fanatic film projectionist. He thought back to the swinging hips that he'd seen Derby morning. They were both women, he decided. They both had the poise of women leading

71

the white life in the east end. Kentucky sure had some women, these two recently, and that Jessica Villier today. He was startled from his mental ramblings by the sound of the driver side door closing.

Jackson hurried to catch up to his partner, who was descending the shallow stairs that led to the lake.

"Perch liked to walk around this lake and discuss cases with me. I imagine he did it alone as well. Let's try it ourselves."

"Cases like this one?"

"None of the others were like this one."

They ambled around the lake, a pretentious word for a three fingered shallow pond, an aerated collection pool for goose droppings.

"Things are different today from yesterday," Ertras said matter of factly.

"You mean that yesterday Perch was alive." Neither was being literal, it had been days since Percheron's last breath. Ertras nodded once, she was sparing with both her words and her actions.

"And tomorrow will be more different yet," the assistance remarked, filling the silence. It was enough to start Ertras speaking.

"The geese are back, but I don't see any goslings. They are well hidden."

"Or not yet born," suggested her companion.

"Or not yet born," Ertras agreed. "The swimming pools are still covered, they'll open on Memorial weekend," she stated. "Spring is speeding into summer. A month from now this will be the same place, but somehow different."

They walked a minute in silence, and then Ertras went on.

"I was here once in June with Perch, the ground was absolutely covered in green birdcrap. Geese can be filthy creatures. From up in the air, the whole world must appear to them as an open air toilet," causing her fellow stroller to cast a quick look skywards, before deciding that he could only be an unresisting victim to whatever birds decided. He would just hope for the best.

They walked on a bit more carefully, easily avoiding the droppings that they could see on the asphalt path, thinking about the crap of this murder case.

"The case will be solved by June," the assistance said confidently, phrasing his question as a fact.

Ertras kept her opinion to herself, responding, "No children."

"Percheron was childless, yes, I know."

"I mean here. There are no children here now, this place is a set, where adults are performing their calm, boring theater, slow, thoughtful walks. Like we are doing now. In June, the new troop arrives on this stage, it's not a play, but real play. It will ring with the sounds of life and new laughter."

"I don't follow."

"You don't need to, it isn't related to the murder. This little park is on the verge of life, it's alive, unlike"

"Cave Hill."

"Yes. And me. Pay no attention, Jackson, I'm just a bit melancholy."

Her assistance simply nodded. They were both melancholy.

"Cave Hill used to be like this, a shared space. One intended for both the living and dead, where the living could come to visit with the memory of their loved ones, but also take strolls, play games, even picnic."

"That sounds a bit creepy, Cas."

Ertras laughed.

"I guess that it does. But it was perfectly normal one hundred and fifty years ago. Or more," she added wistfully. They'd reached the lake's drain, where the water was recycled to the fountain in the center of the lake's surface. "A jet d'eau" she thought, remembering the huge spray of cold, fresh water that she'd seen on Lac Lemain in Geneva.

"That is what I keep thinking".

"About life and death?"

"No, not that. Yes, but no, not directly. Something tells me that this crime has something to do with the past."

"Unrequited love, revenge?"

"Something like that."

"Those are always somewhere in the win, place, and show results. Homicide 101."

"The scene of the crime may have been selected not because of what it is today, but what it meant to the killer, or killers from another day, one long ago. The crime seems organized, well planned."

"And your belief is that there is a distant connection, maybe one as far back as the dates on the nearby tombstones?"

"Yes, something to that effect. The site was special for some reason. Either it was the location for some previous personal event, perhaps an earlier crime, or one of the graves holds a special meaning for the killer. All we know for sure is that Perch didn't pick it himself."

"You could be over thinking this, Cas. What if it was just selected because it was convenient?"

"Templeton qualifies for the murderer list on multiple counts."

"Such as?"

"For one, he visited Cave Hill many times, he lived nearby as a kid."

"Doesn't that make every local over 55 a suspect?"

"Only the living ones," Ertras joked weakly. "And those who still reside in Louisville."

"That eliminates 5 people, I'd wager. How else does Templeton make the suspect top of the online voting?"

"This is not a coming of age story, but one of coming to old age."

Sounds carried across the lake from varying distances, each arriving with its own sense of urgency. Church bells, train horn, the klaxon of an ambulance, and much smaller and closer the irritated buzz of a stressed insect, the alluring call of a cardinal. All had their own overarching priorities. The needs of other voices would just have to wait.

"Jackson was oblivious to these competing cries for dominance. Or was he focused, while she was distracted by the unimportant?" Ertras asked herself. "That was happening more and more frequently. No, it wasn't she corrected herself; she was just stressed from this case. And the other times, was that stress as well?"

"What are you thinking," Jackson asked. Silence was unbearable, while for her the tranquility was soothing.

The ring of Ertras' cell phone satisfied Jackson's craving for sound. It was the pathologist. After a few 'yeses' and 'I sees', she disconnected. She turned to her colleague.

"I walked around here many times with Perch. When the goslings are grown, the sidewalks are just covered in crap. Even more than now. Geese defecate every 12 minutes on average."

Jackson said nothing. He waited.

"Perch hadn't shaved or eaten. It was impossible to determine how long the zip-ties had been around his wrists, they weren't painfully tight. Our pathologist has determined that he had nothing to eat at all after he left the hospital."

"I see," Jackson said, wondering if his *I see* was the same as Ertras'.

"Not even a last milkshake."

"What?"

"This comes down to cold revenge, enjoyed over thirty six hours or so. No food, no water, he was treated like a snail, some of which had been found on his clothing Sunday morning."

"That was a bizarre comparison, Percheron to a snail. More of a sacrificial lamb," Jackson reasoned

"Why was Perch so clean?" Ertras asked aloud. There was no answer.

They heard the sound of geese honking overhead, nearby, but it took a few seconds to spot them, the sound seeming to come from multiple directions at once.

The police pair were seated on a green metal bench that faced the closed neighborhood swimming pools. It was a peaceful setting, the bench placed where the two fingers of the lake met. The lake was shaped like a large peace sign, Ertras found it relaxing, despite her reason for being here that afternoon in May.

Above, the flock pivoted as one, they too thought the lake an attractive destination.

The flight descended, one goose continuing to honk, providing last minute instructions.

There was one minor splash, no mishaps as the air wing metamorphosed into a fleet and paddled silently away from the detective audience.

"Was Percheron interested in birds?"

"Not particularly."

"What was he particularly interested in, if not birds?"

"Nothing really, other than murder."

"Not you?"

"What?"

"I have to ask. Others will be asking you these same questions. Or worse ones."

"I know. Everything and everyone is so related in this case."

"Louisville is a small town."

"It is smaller today than a week ago." She paused, thinking of another way of answering the question other than with the truth.

"No," was all she said, because no was the entirety of the truth. "He enjoyed the company of his girlfriend, Melissa."

"But that ended, shortly before his death. And you don't see any connection?"

"Of course I see a connection. That is the problem. To be honest it is one problem among many. Everything is connected in this case."

"Most people are killed by someone close to them."

"Life can be messy. And death even messier."

"Is that a lesson from Percheron?"

Ertras nodded.

"So, you and Percheron, there was nothing between you too? Other than work?"

"No."

"And the worked ended when he retired."

"I hadn't seen him in months before Thunder."

"Was that a planned meeting?" Jackson pressed, and Ertras acquiesced to the pressure. These were all valid questions, ones that she would have posed if their roles had been reversed.

"Cas, we earn the same salary whether we solve a particular crime or not. And if I screw some up, there are always others. It's like multiple suspended sentences or at worst, probation. We have the same rules as the criminals, players on both teams get warnings beforehand. Plus on our side, we can't be easily cut from the team. But, we do our best. Most of the time."

"So, what are you saying?" prompted Ertras after a moment. "That we purposely make an effort to not solve certain crimes?"

"You can delay this investigation."

"No, I can't. This one is"

"Personal? Political? Important?"

"It's personal."

"Too personal, in my opinion".

Jackson stood and approached the shoreline as the geese paddled past. They stopped and turned back as the detective retrieved some French bread from his jacket pocket and began to toss portions on the water. His right foot suddenly slipped on the wet grass and last year's leaves, and he found himself ankle deep in the surprisingly cold water. The thankful but wary birds greedily gobbled the rapidly sinking bread and were polite enough not to laugh at their benefactor. The laughter came not from the front, but from behind. Jackson turned and stepped back unto dry land and moved quickly to rejoin his boss. Between laughter, Ertras managed to comment, "You walk just like a duck". Her laughter was genuine. She could not recall the last time before today that she had laughed with someone, and not at them. Although to be fair, this situation was somewhere in between, Jackson had brought in on himself, and would have laughed just as hard had their roles been reversed. Her colleague joined her, he too needed some humor today, and if it had to be at his expense, he would pick up the check.

A collage of other funny moments flashed through her mind, a selection of souvenirs overrepresented by the man whose murder she was now tasked with solving. Perch would have enjoyed the irony of the situation. This stroll around Lake Pointe had been intended to be both nostalgic and a means to spur thoughts and theories, it could have been a joyous occasion, as much as a murder investigation could contain a joyful component.

She recalled the suicide that she had worked years ago. Following the collision of a human and a train, rarely was there evidence enough to rule the death anything but murder by self, unless the murderer was completely unskilled.

Always back to death, Perch had taught her too well. Or maybe she had been too motivated a student, as obsessive as her mentor had been.

"Jackson had slipped on leaves," Ertras thought back to one of those other strolls around Lake Pointe. It had required three laps before Perch had settled on a course of action in the case. She forgot now which case it had been, but she remembered that it was in the autumn, not springsummer as it was today. Perch had remarked on the newly fallen leaves, how they ran along the path, chased by the wind. Despite their best efforts, they would be swept up in a rafle, she had looked up the French word later, and then they would be either bagged and buried, or burned. Fleeing to a neighboring yard would avail them of nothing. It was a dark image painted by her mentor.

Perhaps this most recent stroll with Jackson had succeeded. Her head was clear, at the low cost of two wet feet. She could keep this on the rails. Whatever this was, it included her, she understood that very well. This case was easy in the abstract, impossible in the land of realism.

She imagined that the leaves on the surrounding trees absorbed not only sunlight but also human emotions, love, hate, despair, and that when they had enough, the leaves fell on their own accord, burying the feelings below ground, to be recycled for future generations of leaves and humans.

Percheron's house was neat as befitted a home for sale. "A home for sale, a life for rent," Cas sang silently as they searched the residence.

Several witness claimed that Perch had tried multiple hobbies, like a surfer trying on various suits and sportswear, knowing that nothing would be to his liking. Ertras reflected on his life, while she stood in his house, holding in her right hand a poem that represented one of those futile attempts at change. Whether the blank pages before and after the short two stanzas were an indication of an unfinished work, with more to follow, or were intended to frame a completed masterpiece was unclear. It wasn't very good poetry, or maybe she wasn't very good at appreciating poetry.

The paper contained several scratch outs and line redirects. It was a calloused piece that was both a first draft and a completed work, she finally decided. She read it again.

In the web resides
Not a girlish spider
Instead smolders in silk
A churlish dragon

Feared not by peasants
But believed by all
For their flames of self
Marry well those of Dragon

"It stinks," Ertras concluded. Perch was no poet.

It was sad to conclude that such an important person in her life had been limited. She understood now that Perch had excelled at solving murders but little else. She hadn't understood anything about him before, and now he was dead. "And yourself," she wondered, catching a glimpse of her reflection in the foyer's mirror. "Castor, are you good at anything except solving murders," she whispered, chancing that Jackson would overhear. Her reflection said nothing, embarrassed at being seen in public, in daylight, clothed. Truth was best delivered in the dark, naked.

"Home for sale, Life for rent," Cas hummed. Jessica Villier's reference to *Life for Rent*, sprang into her thoughts. The actress said it represented her life, but it could just as easily be said of her own, or Perch's.

She was an immigrant, but both she and Perch had spent almost the entirety of their lives in Louisville. And yet, now after his death, he appeared to her to have just been passing time. It was like his car had broken down and he had to wait 30 years for it to be repaired. And now that it was fixed, and he was ready to continue his delayed adventure, he was hit by a bus and killed on his way out of town. His house now for sale, his life no longer for rent. He had decided to buy a life elsewhere, Ertras reasoned. "Too late, too damned late, Perch," she sighed softly enough that her pity snuck by, unheard by Jackson.

"And what about herself? Was she repeating the same mistakes of her deceased friend and mentor?" She decided then, that perhaps this was Perch's last, unintentional lesson. "She would leave the police when this investigation was completed. here? Spain? A foreign country, where her parents lived? No, she would decide later, it was just a detail, the important question had been answered."

A print of *Chasse-maree a l'ancre* was mounted above the fireplace. It was the sort of painting best appreciated from a distance, like life. The nearer it was, the more obscure it seemed. It was a painting that no longer sang to her. "Death can be messy, life even messier."

Below the now disliked artwork was a small frame photo standing upright on the mantle. The photo was in a green version of sepia, the water, the clothes of the fly fisherman, the moss covered sides of the ancient stone bridge. It was peace encased in glass and brass.

Ertras pocketed the framed photo. Although Perch had been coy in whether it was him or not in the photo, she had her doubts, as the man's image exuded a contentment that she had never seen in Perch himself. Still, she liked to think that she was wrong, just this once.

Nothing else of obvious interest was found during their search. The ticket to Paris that one witness had mentioned was found, along with a small, nearly packed valise on a nightstand. "Who would unpack it now?" she wondered.

Two books were beside the valise, a small French/English dictionary with the English half torn out. Perch was the opposite of a pack rat, he collected nothing. It dawned on Ertras that Perch's lack if desire for possessions extended to his having few friends or close acquaintances. In his personal world he only had a small suitcase as well, and had to be very selective about its contents.

The other book that Perch had deemed worthy of taking was a thin tomb on pronunciation.

"He would know what to say and how to say it. That was enough. That was Perch."

"Perch taking up fishing. Fly fishing? What did it matter? It was just a photograph. It was a minor mystery, not deserving of the time and thought she was assigning to it. Almost everyone she knew dabbled in activities that were quickly dropped. Did robots fish? Where did that come from," Ertras thought. She had seen a few fishing shows, and while Ertras didn't begrudge anyone their own channel, she found fishing programs particularly puzzling. Who watches other people fish? It struck her as being in the same category as sports or pornography. Would there soon be robots fishing, with other robots engaged to watch them?

An old Cartier wristwatch lay on the office desk, still running for now. Perch had bought it secondhand at Merkley-Kendrich. He'd needed a watch, and it was stylish without being ostentatious. He considered it a temporary possession, one that he could resell once it was no longer needed. That day had come and gone, time had outpaced his timepiece, and the watch sat unused but faithful awaiting, his return. The desk on which the Cartier rested was equally obsolete and almost seemed bored from lack of activity.

Jackson's voice was overly loud in the empty house.

"Templeton was evasive about driving. I bet that he does."

"So?"

"What kind of car does Templeton drive? Does he own one? We didn't have a search warrant to search any vehicle."

"Check with the Transportation cabinet. He probably drives an old, expensive car."

"A BMW?"

"I doubt it."

"Cadillac? Yeah, a 70s caddy."

"Cadillac. You and I are both too young to use the word Caddy. Why did you ask if Templeton owned a BMW?"

"If he did, we would be home free. Any owner of a BMW who is charged with murder is guaranteed to be convicted. Juries for some reason are tough on them."

"I would be too."

"Why?"

"Just because." Ertras smiled to relieve the building tension. "Damn, if Templeton had only bought foreign. I could be on a beach somewhere this week."

"Yeah, me too. Joyce and I were planning on a quick trip to LA," using local shorthand for the coast of lower Alabama. It's a shame that Templeton didn't splurge on a new beemer, instead of an ancient cad, an old ca di lac, Jackson enunciated.

"An old Cadillac," Ertras repeated, her voice distant.

Nearly 50 years... Jackson began to speculate. Maybe a convertible, where the top has been redone. I don't"

"Old Cadillac," Ertras repeated a bit louder. "Old," she said, distilling her burgeoning thought to it's one word essence.

"Ertras?" questioned Jackson, the tone of his voice and the use of her surname indicating worry.

"Old. That is a lead. I'm certain of it. It may be the lead." She chuckled, and added pithily, "Old may be the new lead".

Ertras broke into a laugh of such a strange, nearly insane fashion, that Jackson's concern mounted rapidly and he took an involuntary step rearward.

His action, in turn, precipitated a similar rise in Ertras' mental state and an immediate backward move on the part of Ertras, the two movements appearing like the opening sequence of an erotic Latin dance.

It was the eroticism of the unknown, the excitement of heightened sensitivity, the thrill that comes with either enlightenment or danger. In another setting, it would have ended in sex, but not here.

The bizarre moment passed for Ertras and Jackson, but its memory would remain permanently with each of them.

"Don't worry my friend" were Ertras next words.

"It is old and new. Let me explain. Everything about this case is old." She paused, then recounted a series of examples, marking each by rapidly extending fingers of her left hand like the blades of a fistful of switchblades.

"The victim, the suspect, the relationship, the gun, the cemetery, the Kentucky Derby, these are all, each and every one of them, from the past. There is nothing new."

"And so what?" Jackson asked, beginning to sound fatigued from this emotional roller coaster that Cas was driving.

"So, the motive, the triggering event of this murder lies in the past. Unless," she continued, while Jackson groaned inwardly. The ups and downs were giving him vertigo. He had never enjoyed amusement parks. They smelled of sweat, and spilled sweets, punctuated with the odor of diesel fuel.

"Unless what?" he forced himself to clutch tighter onto this verbal ride.

"Unless I am grasping at straws. This is unlike any case that I've worked. It is like an old time murder, like one that Perch would have worked, back when it was appropriate to say caddie instead of Cadillac. Hell, Jackson I don't know." Ertras turned to leave, "I'll be in the car."

Cas remembered the poem, it was in the other room. It was bad poetry and so she left it behind, taking with her only the best memories of Perch

Jackson stood alone in the now even quieter house. Cassie had left the house abruptly. "Had it been too much for her? He could carry on with the search alone. Should he? No, probably not," he sensed. "Initiative in this investigation was a double edged sword and his new crazy idea about Jessica, she was really gorgeous, was initiative enough." Jackson hesitated.

Until now, he had said nothing to anyone about he and Joyce Small, Templeton's temporary nurse and suspected girlfriend. Whatever was between Jackson and Joyce was in the past, or soon would be. He would say nothing.

As fas as finding anything significant in Percheron's home, especially evidence that incriminated Templeton, he didn't want to be the one to find it. He was more than happy to let a follow-up team, if there was one, uncover the dirt. Jackson told himself to keep his own hands clean and himself safe. Without another glance around the room, he walked quickly to and through the front doorway, closing the solid wood door behind him as quietly as his boss had done a minute before.

CHAPTER EIGHT

Only two homicides had occurred over Thunder weekend, and both had the decency to take place away from the festivities and after the last firework had extinguished itself in the Ohio river.

Because of this happenstance, the deaths did not register as Thunder fatalities, as the cutoff was 11:59 PM, Saturday.

One of the homicides had been a clear case of murder, the chaotic arrangement of brilliant 9mm shell casings around the body was silent testimony to death at the hand of another. Cartridges were cheap and so was life. It had all the hallmarks of a mundane 21st homicide, only the location in a cemetery would make it more than a fleeting story.

It was an old cemetery, one placed on flat land when flat land was abundant and the dead were few. Gradually, as the ratio inverted, the dead were interred in hillier areas, Cave Hill being the most well known.

The body had been discovered in Portland cemetery in the far west end of Louisville. The caller was anonymous, as so far were the perpetrator or perpetrators. The motive was also unknown, although the few who read the newspaper account anticipated anything other than drugs.

Of the second homicide there was no doubt as to either the motive or the killer. It was just another opioid overdose by the victim in one of the middle class neighborhoods. Two homicides tied to the drug epidemic the detective on the cases had decided, not directly related to either other, but certainly less than six degrees of separation apart.

One of the dead was black, the other white, but they were both now graying together in the morgue. Both had been young, they had shared that trait which was now forever gone.

One of the more imaginative scribblers of Lou247 speculated that the cemetery setting and the overdose was the leit motif of a newly discovered serial killer, one that planted evidence to make them appear unrelated. The proponent of this theory, that crimes were connected by being totally different, was mocked by his reporter colleagues, more out of jealousy that he'd thought of something novel than actual refutation of his hypothesis.

CHAPTER NINE

Eleven days before his murder, Percheron drove by the former home of Templeton's mother's house. He did not stop. Mrs. Templeton had been dead for over a year and his visits to check on her were no longer necessary. The house had been sold to new occupants.

He recalled those visits with a mixture of humor and sadness. Depending on her state of mind, she would either screech and curse him, or welcome him as her neighbor, in his guise as his late father.

It was a small house, just off Bragg Avenue, in an area which still had a country feel due to the existence of several large undeveloped multi acre lots.

She had been a pleasant, kind, and usually unassuming woman, a wonderful neighbor when he was a child. Unlike her son. The sins of the son don't accrue to his parents. Or maybe he had that the wrong way round.

"Who would she be this morning," Percheron would wonder each time? The same milk and cookies second mother of all the boys, or the bitter and angry mother who blamed his son, that is him, for Mosgrove's unjust imprisonments. Yes, he'd sent Templeton away a few times. He didn't want it to be personal, but it couldn't be anything but personal.

Her illness could make life incredibly beautiful or overwhelmingly painful, while any of her skeletons remained private and well hidden, even from herself. One day, she'd claimed to have been married twice, once to a young man and once to an old man. Her memory was damaged, it was in fact the same man at her first and only wedding and at her 50 wedding anniversary.

When she took him to be his father, she transited between decades on a schedule that was known to no one, not even her.

"Your boy could use some of these toys and clothes, Mosgrove is too old for them, and he is rarely home anyway. He's running around with his lowlife friends, he should just stay here in the neighborhood and play with the other boys his age, like your Ronnie," was a typical nonsensical statements that combined events from various eras and incorporated them into a claim that was at once both logical and worthy of a Rose Hill psychic.

Mrs. Templeton had told him on several occasions that she was 99 years old and could just fall dead as they were sitting there talking. Percheron had scolded her, saying that would be rude, as they knew each other so well, and that she was too polite to behave in such a manner. Of course, one day she did just that, she slumped in her chair, dead. Percheron had not been there. Mrs. Templeton had remained polite to the very end.

CHAPTER TEN

On his way to meet Perch's coffee buddy at Kroger's, in Middletown, Jackson noticed that Caterpillar loaders were busy on both sides of Shelbyville road. To the south, they were installing a sidewalk, finally after so many years. They were now finishing the section in front of Heady funeral home, whose current guests would not benefit from this recent civic improvement.

Across the four lane thoroughfare another yellow machine , this one a tracked model, stood by patiently, ready to tear down the former Applebee's restaurant. A large, crudely hand printed sign, proclaiming "Permit and Intent to Demolish", read like a final menu, offering a single course.

Death and taxes should be joined by change in the old axiom, he thought. Even old constants needed renovation it seemed. Applebee's became just Applebee's, familiar and therefore bypassed. Further along, developers had deforested the terrain, displacing deer, birds and other varieties of woodland creatures in order to construct there, among other frivolities, a sports store dedicated to all things outdoors, the outdoors excepted.

Jackson and Martin Aikens were at the Starbuck's inside the grocery store to discuss Martin's last conversation with Percheron, one that had occurred about a week before.

"Are you the lead on the case, Detective Jackson?" Aikens asked.

"No, that would be my boss, Detective Ertras. Would you rather speak with her, Mr. Aikens?"

"No, not really. But you're involved with the case? Important, I mean."

"Yes. You are not former law enforcement, are you?"

"No, I'm not."

"Do you have a record?"

"A record of what, our conversations? No."

"That isn't what I meant. Do you have a criminal record?"

"No, no record at all. I'm just a regular guy."

"Sorry to be so blunt, Mr. Aikens. Not everyone I speak with it a criminal, it just feels that way. So how long had you and Detective Percheron been meeting for coffee?"

"Oh for about eighteen months or so."

"After his retirement," Jackson figured.

"Perch and I had both recently retired, and this is a busy place, one see's everyone here."

Jackson was tempted to ask about the young woman with the tight jeans and incredible rear end, but decided against it.

"What did you talk about that day?"

"Oh the usual."

Jackson understood that this man wanted to talk, and that he would speak at his own rate. "This might be a waste of time", he said inwardly. "At least the coffee is good."

"We spoke of inconsequential topics, sports, politics, and religion, the latter two of which have become radioactive in the fast few years, don't you think?"

Jackson sipped his coffee, and took out his notebook. If he filled this one, he was in the right place to purchase another. He began to write.

"Take sports, Perch had begun

"It would be so much better if they eliminated instant replay and spy satellite level imagery."

"Why?"

"We just don't need to know everything about everything."

"We don't? Why?"

"You sound like an owl with an accent," Perch joked.

"Isn't knowing everything the goal?"

"What does your smartphone tell you?" Perch challenged, daring the other man to reach for his electronic weapon as if they were in a classic western movie.

After a moment, Perch said, good naturedly, "Let's just have a human conversation. You choose the topic today. It's ok to be wrong sometimes. Life is not a game show."

"I know. I hate these things", indicating the flat, rectangular device. It lay on the table between them, screen side down, loaded but on safe. It was still within easy reach should events necessitate action. "We've created iPhone dens that replicate opium dens of the past, each of us oblivious to others, lost in our own imaginary, dreamy, useless world."

And these phones are ubiquitous, they're found even in good neighborhoods. Even the police carry one on duty!"

"You think that this matters, that it must matter because it's important to you."

"If it's important to me, then yes it matters."

To you. Only to you. It doesn't mean anything to the rest of the city. Nor do you. One you are no longer a cop, and two, you're old. No, I'm wrong you're not old, not yet. But you're getting there. I bet that you've noticed it yourself. You no longer command respect, it's diminished to courtesy and then ignorance. You will be ignored, not even worth pity or contradiction.""

Detective Jackson, Aikens explained, "Age is like an involuntary diet, where despite how much you eat, you eventually waste away to nothing. One day you will disappear. If you are lucky, someone will notice before you begin to stink."

Jackson interrupted, amazed. "This was a typical conversation?"

"Yes. The ones with alcohol were a bit more animated."

"Where did those take place? Surely not here?" Jackson asked, looking around at their surroundings.

"No, not at Lucky's either," Aikens responded with a smile. "We had dinner once or twice at the Corner Café."

"In Lyndon?"

"Yes, that's the one. It's a place your parents would like. That isn't much of a recommendation. Perch considered it a Louisville treasure, a jewel that was organic, not manufactured. He kept it a secret, he considered it his local, only to be shared with a few."

"Shared with a few friends?" Jackson was thinking of Melissa and Templeton, although including Templeton among Percheron's friends was more than a stretch.

"A few friends? No, he didn't have that many. He was like his estranged brother, a collector. One collected things, Perch collected, memories, stories. Neither had much of their own to call a life. In almost every other facet of their lives, they were opposites."

"You met the brother?"

"No, but Perch mentioned him a few times. I am pretty good at filling in blanks."

"You seem to be pretty good at getting people to talk with you. From what I've seen and heard about him, Percheron was a very private person. Why did he open up to you?"

"I used to be an undertaker."

Jackson said nothing.

"You disappoint me, Detective. You are looking at me the same way that I imagine most people look at you when you disclose that you are a policeman."

Jackson smiled and admitted, "Guilty."

"Perch and I were both accustomed to working with the dead. I think that we had the habit of saying whatever we wanted to them. The dead would hear our opinions, our secrets such as they were. For each of us, the other was a surrogate for the dead that we no longer had. We missed them as much as their families missed them, more in many instances." Aikens paused.

"I see that I've shocked you. It's bizarre. But I thought that you might understand, as you are a homicide investigator. The fact that you don't seems to prove my point."

"Which is what, exactly? I'm a bit lost here Mr. Aikens."

"Perch had no one else to confide in after retirement except me. Not to be rude, but you just are not experienced enough to appreciate his loneliness."

"I see," Jackson replied, filling another page in his notebook.

"During these more open dinner conversations, did you notice if Perch drank a lot?"

"Not really. He would have one, maybe two glasses of wine. Or if it was warm, one or two beers."

"Was Perch suicidal?"

"I'm the furthest thing from a doctor imaginable. None of my clients ever got healthier."

"I'm asking for your opinion. That's all."

"No more than most men."

"Oh? Are most men suicidal?"

"Yes, certainly. I had an acquaintance years ago who told me that if he were less optimistic, he wouldn't kill himself. Not that day. He'd have jumped years ago."

"Did he?"

"No. He lived to be 87. You have heard of the fountain of youth?"

"Sure, it doesn't exist."

"Alcohol is the fountain of age. It exists. That is for sure. It's the male equivalent of makeup. It gives the illusion of charm, wit, good looks. It does wonders for self-esteem, but only temporarily. And now with all of these narcotics, it is American roulette. The odds are worse than the Russian version, but the final payout is the same. And when you add in poor diet, work stress, lack of exercise, all of these are attempts at suicide, deliberate or not, immediate or not in their effectiveness.

"And Perch?"

"As I said, no more than most men."

"Tell me more about your last conversation."

"He was worried about the police, what the future held for them, and for the country."

As Aikens continued his recital, Jackson turned his notepad to a blank page.

"Only criminals understand freedom. The constitution was written by men seen as criminals by the British, it has a certain *Lord of the Flies* feel. No taxes and guns for everyone, what is there not to like. Yet today, those are the types we imprison. In a perverse way, they are the few remaining patriots. Hell, the drug dealers are the only Americans on board with the metric system. Police are just on the forefront of multiculturalism. Without a shared history and culture the chance of a shared future is dimming. Maybe it's time to accept our differences and divide the country, put into law what exists in practice."

"You don't believe that."

"What I believe is no longer relevant, according to you."

"Someone famous once said that you are entitled to your own opinion but not your own facts."

"That was his opinion. My opinion says that I can have my own facts. Everyone has their own facts by now; they're like that cell phone on the table. Facts don't really exist in the practical world, anyway."

"You mean like how gravity is just an opinion."

"You can believe what you want if that produces the desired result."

"The end justifies the means?"

"Maybe, but the end justifies the facts, of that I am certain. Truth is whatever you want it to be. I've come to accept identity politics as long as I get mine. The televised talking heads will say anything for a buck. They truly understand their role. It's not their fault that the audience confuses the role with the actor. It may destroy the country as I've known it but that's ok, I still have my self-esteem, and my part of the American, oh sorry, I'll need to find another country won't I? But me, I've got that covered."

"Perch, you need a towel, you're dripping with sarcasm.

I'm not. It's not sarcasm, I can't do sarcasm. I've limited range as an actor. I've been told that often enough, just a few days ago, in fact. If you can't beat them, join them. One more pig at the trough won't empty the silo any sooner."

"Don't you find it contradictory? You've battled against chaos your entire career, bring order to Louisville. What changed?"

"The song *E pluris unum* is no longer on the charts. You can't find it on Spotify. It's been succeeded by something more appealing to a newer generation and less comprehensible to mine. We have outgrown the one god for all. That idea was never going to work permanently, anyway.

It's funny, I was called pig hundreds of times during my career. They were wrong at the time, I thought. But no, they were just premature."

"But you have so much more to contribute. Your name means a great deal to the families of so many victims."

"Do you remember Whitney Young?"

"Vaguely."

"The name of Whitney Young, book ends the city, but is now just a name. By the time your name is on a building, or heaven forbid, a park, you are only one generation from being forgotten. Less for cops.""

"You two certainly covered a lot of ground over coffee," Jackson commented when Aikens paused to sip his drink.

"I guess so."

The retired undertaker continued describing his last conversation with Percheron.

""So many destructive videos go viral that YouTube resembles a disease ridden swamp, unsafe for children and adult alike. It is a never ending carnival of freaks and horrors that is nonetheless as addictive and dehumanizing as my career was. It's a terrible thing for anyone to see. The internet is like an immense circus tent, there is room enough for every freak, cult, whatever on the planet. In its own way, the way that matters, between my ears, between your ears, the internet is even bigger than the planet. Technology beats everything, including other narcotics."

"Sure. The media, the arts, they've assigned themselves responsibilities that no one wants them to have. Are they the new police?"

"Perhaps. If they are, they are off the leash. They've become preachers instead of entertainers. They are just as annoying and pompous as their collared predecessors."

"Some preachers are entertainers."

"Rightly or wrongly, the average person has concluded that they don't need the weekly sermon. Right or wrong is a personal choice, polytheism is back in style. Personals gods are in the air, pervasive as the scent of tiger lilies here in Kroger's, appealing to some, repulsive to others. As to the police, we are a necessary"

"Evil?"

"I won't go that far, Martin. We are as necessary to modern life as indoor plumbing. It can still stink. But I'm no longer part of that we. The police are them now. And they have been assigned new roles that I never imagined. They're screwed. It's a no win. It's ironic that so many of them are veterans of the GWOT. I wonder if they think that their job hasn't really changed, that they are in a greener version of Afghanistan where most people speak passable English but are just as incomprehensible."

"And the rest of us, the civilians?"

"People love true crime, they never outgrow nursery rhymes, especially unsolved ones. Those can be sold and resold for decades, if not centuries. A few must die so that thousands can be entertained."

"A moment later, he added "I don't play the game of life very well, I was always better with the dead. So were you."

"Because we got the last word in with them. All games become boring. In out in out. It's breathing. You have to do it until you can't. That is life, Perch."

"This is the new me."

"I much prefer the older model."

"So do I, so does my ex-partner. But that model is no longer road worthy."

"Then find a new road, Perch."

"I have, Martin," he said with an unexpected grin, and then seemed to contradict himself.

"All of my ex-partners," Percheron said cryptically. "Even the new me prefers the old me."

"You've been so you to being right and getting your own way that you're angry, and frustrated, and completely at a loss when you're correct but you don't get your way."

"It's worse because of the reason."

"Which is?"

"Technology. It is now making choices for us and making decisions about us. We are no longer in charge.""

Aikens stopped speaking to give Jackson time to finish writing.

"Perch was very concerned about the future of the police. He was fearful that the police were the first and the last nail holding the country together. And that he could nothing to prevent its breakup and eventual disappearance through apathy and technology."

"He was giving up?"

"I'm not sure. I took it to mean that he wanted one final win. That is in fact what he told me."

"Did you find that arrogant?"

"Maybe. Arrogance and visionary can be two sides of the same coin. I asked him toward the end of our last conversation, it's funny what you remember, if he was still afraid of losing. "No," he replied, "I've come to accept that we've lost the season, maybe the police franchise itself. I'm just trying to win one last game." I thought he meant his move to France. Now, I am not so sure."

"You knew about France?"

"I heard about it somewhere."

"What is your theory?"

"I think that he wanted to finally get Templeton to either confess or to slip up."

"And the move to France? That was, what, a reward, a diversion, an escape in case things went wrong?"

"I don't know. It could be any of those."

"But?"

"Perch knew that Templeton was dying. The SOB is still dying. My belief is that the French trip was a deadline that he set for himself as motivation. And if he couldn't resolve the case by wheels up, the game would be truly over. It was," and the old undertaker laughed, "sudden death overtime."

CHAPTER ELEVEN

The two weeks of Derby activities was in full swing. On Tuesday morning, two days after the Portland cemetery murder, and more than a week before Derby, the mother of the victim was waiting to see to Detective Pure. She was seated in a small interview room when Jackson entered.

"Ms. Hayes?"

"Yes."

"I'm Detective Jackson. Detective Pure worked all night and is at home now. They should have told you that at the front desk.",

"Oh" was all that the mother responded. She was not used to talking with the police.

"If you like you can wait until he returns, or I can ask him to stop by your home. Or, if you prefer I can speak with you. I'm not working directly on this…on investigating who did this to your son, but Kyle, detective Pure, and I did discuss it. What would you like to do?"

"I want to speak with anyone who can help."

The woman went on to speak at length. Jackson listened. She spoke of how things used to be, how her great grandmother lived next to the boy who became Muhammed Ali, how there used to be doctors, and bakers, and all professions in what used to be a distinct Louisville community.

"It worked." In all the meanings of the word 'work', Jackson understood her to say.

"We were poorish, but," her voice trailed off, too tired to recount the complete list of what the former community no longer was.

"There was opportunity, and the young people chased it. Now they are chased by drugs and bullets. If he wasn't going to join the military to improve himself, I hoped that he would survive long enough to be imprisoned. Prison would have been almost as good, as good as enlisting I mean. Don't you think so, officer? He would still be alive, wouldn't he?"

Jackson only nodded sympathetically, he had no response. He had not been able to think of any before, when he had had this same one sided conversation with other grieving parents. It was like a bizarre improvised tragedy, one in which his character was forced to rehearse the same scene, hoping that the presence of a new actor each time would provide him with his own appropriate dialogue. It never did.

When this latest mourner had depleted her current load of anguish, Jackson nodded again. Having failed once more to find comforting words, he fell back on describing department policy and how they expected to bring her son's killer to justice.

"My son will still be dead."

Jackson said nothing, and after a moment, the mother spoke to fill the silence.

"I hope that you catch whoever murdered my son. If the killer is sent to prison, then at least his mother won't suffer the same way as me. Her son will be safe. That's the truth as I see it, prison is safer than all this," spreading her hands to indicate all that was not prison. Slowly, she stood and turned, leaving the small interview room.

It was early Tuesday morning after the killing of detective Percheron. Detective Pure tapped Jackson on the shoulder and asked him to sit in on an interview. "Just five minutes", he had promised, "it's about the Portland murder."

"Is there a tie in to my case, Cas' case?"

"No, not directly. But since you spoke to the mother, I thought you might want to hear from the grandfather," Pure explained, then continued, "of one of the killers."

Jackson raised his eyebrows.

"You don't have to say a word, just listen. That's all that I am going to do. He thinks that his grandson is innocent, since he was in jail when Perch was murdered. He'll find the truth soon enough. Just five minutes, Jackson."

"Sure," Jackson said, and they entered the interview room together.

The grandfather belonged to one of the several generations between slave and revolutionary, wiry, tough, resilient but flexible. A man of his time, Tom and Oreo were just words to him, they had little sting and bounced from him like hail during a hard rain.

For Jackson it was a repeat of the one sided conversation he had had with the victim's mother two weeks ago to the day. It was frustration at the changes he had seen, disappointment in the poor choices made by the young. He offered his theory, that his grandson's presence in their jail, should show the detectives that the grandson was innocent.

"Even the press says that these murders are connected, some serial killer attracted to the Derby," he had offered as proof.

"We have evidence that your grandson did this. I'm sorry."

"But the serial killer," the grandfather persisted.

"This will all come out at trial."

"The truth will out?"

"Yes, the truth will out."

"Are you certain?"

"Yes."

"I'm afraid that we never learn that truth until it is too late. We can't handle life, no human can. The greatest gift we have and we all waste it. No one does life well. Not any more." Exhausted, the elderly man stood and left the room.

Pure explained once he and Jackson were alone.

"We received a tip and we pulled in his grandson and his grandson's friend. They are guilty, there is no question about it. He didn't tell you the entire story, because he doesn't know it. Not yet."

"Oh?"

"My guess is that the grandson was too ashamed to tell his grandfather the truth. The grandson knew that the old man was coming to talk to me. To plead his case." Pure paused, letting his anger subside.

"Grandpa wasn't told about the evidence. They have the whole murder on video."

"We do? It was one of our sting operations? I hadn't heard that."

"No, it was not a sting. It was cell phone footage." He paused for effect. "Cell phone footage taken by the grandson and the friend. It was premeditated."

"Scripted?"

"Yeah. You could say that. They planned to kill the victim from the very beginning. They had no drugs, no money beforehand."

"Grandpa is in for another disappointment."

"Yes, he is," confirmed Pure. "It gets worse," he continued grimly. "The killers filmed it to build credibility. I wouldn't be surprised that they were going to mask their faces and post it online for money."

"When were they locked up?"

"Friday, early."

"So they can't be involved In Cave Hill."

"No. Not directly. But they might try to implicate someone else, some mystery man in order to increase their notoriety. Some unknown associate of theirs. If we had not arrested them on Friday, they might have confessed to Cave Hill," Pure said.

"That would have been perfect for the governor," Jackson said, stating the obvious.

"As far as Grandpa, he hoped that his grandson being in jail provided an alibi for them in the Cave Hill murder."

"If the two were connected. But they aren't. There is not possible way that the murder are related. It's disappointment all around."

CHAPTER TWELVE

Templeton was pouting a few days after Thunder. He had to settle for a simple murder, and he did not like simple. Big Four at Thunder would have been incredible, but impossible. His brief visit to the old railroad bridge had demonstrated that definitively. Cameras were everywhere, not just mounted on the rusty arches but in every walker's pocket. The phone addicts were as bad as the dopers, worse as they needed a fix every few minutes.

"They were as addicted as he had been to cigarettes," he smirked, reaching for his nonexistent Marlboros.

In prison he had reread *1984*, but had still been flabbergasted at the change in what was still somewhat recognizable as the country of his birth.

He was unprepared for what had come to pass for normal life. TV coverage and what was now called Homeland Security rendered his dream of Ronnie's death on Big Four moot. There was no realistic way to bring the murder to fruition. Homeland Security oh yes, they would be recording. He had read somewhere that the agency classified these big events as significant terror targets. "Simply to get free passes," Templeton speculated.

The Kentucky Derby would be 10 times more surveilled, no that would never work, nor would this bridge. The bridge to nowhere it had been nicknamed in the early 1960s. An eyesore it remained for decades, until the two cities on each side of the Ohio River had installed lights and constructed pedestrian ramps.

It was now the Louisville Highline, resembling the Coulée Verte in Paris in no imaginable fashion.

Still the Big Four was attractive as a potential crime scene, but his artistic nature was overruled by his practical side. Its openness was a handicap, and with his own lack of wind and stamina, Templeton recognized that he was just as handicapped. He remembered vaguely that Ronnie had a fear of drowning, his suicide by drowning would be immediately suspicious. No, on second thought, Big Four was a big bust.

He would need to find another place. He had thought of Portland cemetery, but it was too level, too open. It was still on his list of venues for this, his last crime, but he preferred something more upscale.

In the dark, gazing at the cherry cordwood turning to embers, his unfocused eyes detected the profiles and full on faces of human like creatures, maybe it was the vision of a wood spirit fleeing his burning home. It was silly, but calming to let his mind wander, to notice everything, to accept seeing what wasn't there to be seen. The fire would keep him warm on this cool, spring night, but her actions had left him cold. He'd forgotten that evil inhabited some women, his years in prison conditioning him to think that, like the wood spirit of a moment ago, that feminine evil was just an illusion.

The next morning, he attempted to revive the fire like an old friend, using whatever means lay at hand. Paper, damp from setting out overnight, and dessert encrusted disposable plates, both of these charred into nonexistence without taking flame, sad counterparts to the mass of humanity. Plastic tableware dissolved in an alien fashion, he wouldn't be buying that product again.

Smoke, the color of well-worn Levi's, drifted slowly to the northwest, seeming to saunter away from any association with his feeble efforts at recreating warm life. No smoke without fire, the present situation attempted to disprove that old saying.

CHAPTER THIRTEEN

The same three people were seated in the same interview room as before. Templeton's attorney was also present to make a silent fourth.

"Your first killing, no bullets recovered. Sherry Pregel was a thin girl, and the bullet passed completely through her."

"If you say so. The girl would have died anyway, her friend was killed in a car accident later same day. You might even say that it was quicker, less painful, and it gave her a fame that she would not have enjoyed otherwise."

"I doubt that the dead enjoy anything."

"That was a long time ago." Templeton spoke again.

"Ronnie asked me to meet him on Derby."

"Where did this supposed meeting take place? You neglected to tell us that during our first interview."

"I'm not that kind of man, detective. I don't rush things with women. I wanted to see you again. Now that you asked to see me again, I can tell you. Cave Hill. Where else would it have taken place? Aren't you paying attention?"

"No, not that meeting."

"There was only the one."

"The pre-meeting then. How and when did he and you decide on a meeting."

"At Check's. I was just getting settled at the bar, when he paused on the way out."

"Did you two meet often at Check's?"

"No. It was the first and only time. It was not a rendezvous. He paused on his way to the door and said, "Derby day, 4 pm, our place"."

"That's it?"

"I suggested Friday. He mentioned a colonoscopy. It was a brief conversation. I didn't time it. I told him that he didn't need a doctor to tell him that he was an ass. And then he was gone, out the door."

"Were there any witnesses?"

"I doubt it. If there were, they wouldn't recall it. There was nothing to witness, it was a five second exchange. I said nothing else to Ronnie, it was over like that, snapping the fingers of his left hand. Ertras noticed a slight tremble in it.

"Templeton won't be here much longer," she thought.

Templeton caught Ertras' glance and chuckled, "not much longer Detective."

"What did Perch mean by our place?"

"It took me a minute to remember. At first I thought he said R place, over near Blair's ballroom. I knew that Ronnie used to take Tango lessons at Blair's."

"How did you know that? You seem very well informed for someone in prison".

"My mother kept me up to date. More or less, much less towards the end. You know that. Ronnie used to look in on her while I was away. Old neighborhood ties still bind. Ronnie and the Tango. It takes a talented man to dance with thin women."

"Meaning what?"

"Meaning nothing."

"So you met at the R place bar"?

"It's a sports bar, with outdoor volleyball. But, no we didn't meet up there. I just told you that it was Cave Hill that he had meant. Do you have this level of difficulty with all of your witnesses? I would have thought that they would have put someone competent on the case."

He paused, "Aha, I see now. The powers that be want this to drag on and on and just fade away. And you are two part of the cover-up, or is it just one of you? Did you flip a coin to see which one sweeps while the other holds the dust pan? I expected better of someone that Ronnie trained. He did train you?"

"Yes, he did," Ertras answered. "And there is no cover-up, no pressure from above," she replied in her best firm voice. Her inner voice was not as confident.

"Not yet, you should say. You are running full tilt. Wait until you reach the end of your leash. Believe me, you're on a leash."

"So our place was Cave Hill?" Jackson prompted.

"Yeah. We used to hang out there as kids. We liked to explore the cave there. We would sneak into the cemetery, following some adults as they walked through the gate." Templeton laughed at the memory. "They were our blockers, our decoys."

"And what was the reason for the meeting?"

"I didn't know at the time. I figured that he wanted to make amends."

"And you? What was your purpose for attending?"

"I was never much on making amends, they cause me to break out."

"Amends for what?"

"For having put me in prison."

"You put yourself in prison. Try again."

"Or maybe to set me up for his murder."

"You aren't making sense."

"Maybe not, but I was willing to listen to Ronnie. It wasn't as if I were going to miss the Barnstable Brown party. Ronnie was selling his house and his car. He was leaving town. It was evident that he was not going to be in Louisville much longer. I wanted to see an old friend. He gave me a gun which my mother had given to him, or to his dad. I didn't quite follow that part. Anyway it was a gun that came from my house, or so he said."

Jackson sat up, attentive.

"I thought that this was some type of a trap. As soon as I opened the bag, and saw what was in it, I suspected a trap. Here I was, a convicted felon holding a gun that would have sent me back to prison.

"Isn't that what you wanted?"

"Yes."

"So it wasn't a trap?"

"I don't know. Like I said, that was what I thought, a trap. He always seem to anticipate my thoughts before I did myself."

"Is that why you were caught for the other murder. Your second murder, correct?"

Templeton ignored the crude attempt of a question.

"Ronnie should have taught you better. He was your teacher, from what I read online. Henry Percheron. Ronnie to me and the other kids. I was Grove and he was Ronnie."

"We know that."

"Back in the days before."

"Before what?"

"Before the after.

"You said that he anticipated your thoughts?"

"Yeah, I did. I also said that I wanted to go back to prison. But in the weeks since I was unceremoniously kicked out of prison, I'd changed my mind. At first, all I could think of was killing Ronnie or the governor, maybe both. The anger kept me going for a while."

"And the drugs."

"I don't have a long time to live, will you let me finish my story?"

"Is that what it is, a story?" Jackson mocked.

"Never mind. I don't really need to talk to you. I still have some rights left to me. If you have any question, just contact my attorney."

"Don't be so sensitive, Mr. Templeton," Ertras said, hating herself for being so polite to her friend's killer.

"I'm so used to hearing about jail house conversions, and you are the first ex-jail house convert I've met. You threw me off track. Please, continue, I won't interrupt again."

"You know, the recipe for hate is as easy as the one for simple syrup. And I prefer bitterness to sweet. So yes the drugs and the anger, they kept me going. Even up to the moment that we met at Cave Hill."

"How did you and Perch get to the cemetery?"

Templeton ignored the detective's betrayal of her recent promise to remain silent.

We met in a secluded section of the cemetery, one where we had played many times. I guess that you would call it one of the old sections. He said that he chose that spot because it was remote, and full of the old dead, from a time when neither of us had been born, and neither of us had problems.

"Not being born, you mean?" Ertras interjected.

Templeton only nodded, resigned to Ertras' need to make noises every minute, like some poorly designed cuckoo clock.

"That was when he passed me the manila envelope."

"Which envelope?" Ertras chirped on schedule.

"A moment ago you described it as a bag," Jackson added.

"It was sealed. I tore it open and found the revolver inside, a .32 according to Ronnie."

"You recognized it?"

"Probably. It looked familiar, I didn't doubt that it came from my parent's attic. I'm not really a gun guy, I've other things that interest me."

"You didn't recognize it as the one that you used to killed Sherry Pregel decades ago?"

"I see that I'm not the only one in this conversation who finds comfort in drugs. I think Ronnie thought the same thing, that I would see some old gun and confess to a crime for which I was never charged."

"You didn't say innocent."

"It's the same thing."

"Is it?"

"Close enough. Anyway, I didn't get all weepy and confess. Maybe he thought that I would shoot him with it. It is amazing how fast thoughts whip through the brain. Did he want me to shoot him, so that he could go out in blaze? Was it a setup, with police behind the large headstones and old trees? Was it my chance to kill him and make it look like a suicide?"

"That is exactly what you bragged about to your roommates."

"I live alone."

"The other convicts in prison. You said that you were going to murder Perch and stage it to look like a suicide."

"Did the scene resemble a suicide?"

"You should know."

"No, I don't. Did it?"

"No, not at all. You're a smart guy. An intelligent man, a dying man. Someone suggested that it was a murder staged to look like a suicide meant to look like a murder."

"My lungs hurts, my knees hurt, and your ramblings are making my brain hurt. Are we through here, or are you going to talk about some sea serpent in the lake at Cave Hill?"

"What about the envelope?"

"What envelope?"

"The one that contained the gun. Where is it?"

"I don't know. I left the gun there and I tossed the envelope."

"Where?"

"In the rubbish somewhere."

"Why?"

"You need to learn how to ask longer questions."

"Tell me why you tossed the envelope. Please."

"Because I saw at that moment that I was done with Ronnie. I had won the last match. In more ways than even he understood.

He was right, that going back to the past, to a time before either of was born had worked. He was the cure."

Templeton coughed, as if his body refused to believe his mouth.

"I was able to take that moment from the past back with me to the present, to the hour before Derby. I could start again, from that point onward, and I wanted nothing more to do with Ronnie. He was right, he had cured me, or maybe I had cured myself. I was still dying of one illness, but I was cured of another. And I had won. I had beaten him once again. I felt great."

"And the envelope?"

"It had his scent, his touch on it. It needed to be put in the trash. Plus, my prints were on it."

"You claim that your mother gave Perch the gun?" Jackson asked.

"She gave him boxes of things to take away. Melissa informed me. She said that Ronnie told her. I was out of town when all of this happened." He smiled at his euphemism.

"That was how Perch had discovered the weapon. The same one that had likely been used to kill the victim in the one murder he had not solved. Once in his possession he had no hope of using it to convict Templeton of anything. How had it been missed all those years ago? What to do with it?" the chain of events sprang into Ertras' mind, clear, logical, and unprovable.

"I see that the old busybody died."

"Who?"

"Buster Bodlyne. That was his real name. He is, or was a local historian. For him, history was a pastime, to me it is just past time. You won't be able to interview him now," Templeton joked and laughed until the cough cut him off.

"He knew a lot of useless history, but then that is redundant. So was he."

"Did you know him well?"

"No, I didn't know at all. I only knew of him. He immersed himself in the past to the point that he came to believe that he controlled it. It was reincarnation in reverse. He was crazy of course, living in the past. Most people live in the future, but it's a cold place. Contentment is not found in the future, it can survive only in the present. It's like a butterfly, tomorrow brings death.

Yep, Buster Bodlyne, he was like Ronnie. And now they are both gone."

"Years ago, when I was innocent, or nearly so, they all wanted me to be guilty, the judge, the police. They thought me guilty, so I became guilty. Now, when I might be guilty, when honestly I prefer that, you know, the evidence is pretty convincing... I just can't remember."

"You told us the exact same thing a few days ago."

"Did I? Truth bears repeating. The people that matter think me innocent. The governor is one of them."

"I think that you're guilty."

"You think everyone is a criminal. But you no longer matter, that is a shame. I'm sincere about this, we have the same goal in mind for once. Did you see his wide smile at Churchill?"

"Who, the governor?"

"Who else? He isn't smiling today. He released a killer, and someone just said thanks very much in a very deadly way on the biggest day in Kentucky. Do you think that the blanket of roses that they placed on Inutile could be reused on Ronnie's casket?"

"It reminded Jackson of those same roses on display at Kroger's, and the hypnotizing sway of the woman's hip on Derby morning. Was it really only a few days ago?"

"You are one sick SOB, Templeton."

"I know that. In more ways than one. So did the governor. He released me anyway. Now he is the one with the pain in his guts."

"So you admit killing Percheron?"

"I might. I might even if I didn't. But you do understand that I won't be convicted? It would hurt too many people who matter. I continue you to explain reality to you, but you are ignoring facts. I wanted to go back, but that was weeks ago. Prison life made me soft, people always assume that it hardens people. Only on the outside. I don't want to be weak again, I am going to stay here on the outside."

"You repaid Percheron's kindness with betrayal."

"What kindness? Decades in prison?"

"You were guilty. Your nearly innocent act is just a poor version of who, little old me. You were guilty then and you killed

Perch on Derby. I don't understand for the life of me why he approached the governor on your behalf."

"What are you talking about? He is responsible for putting me away."

"And for your release when he heard about your illness. He was a fool."

"Ronnie was many things, but not a fool."

"He tolerated fools to the point that he would act foolishly. Okay, it wasn't just your illness. Your mother dying could have been the final straw. Look, I don't care if you die here or in prison but someone is going to be convicted. You are the overwhelming favorite. In fact, you are the only horse on the track. You may die in the starting gate, but I will still award you the guilty prize. That, and a blanket of used roses on your casket, not on Perch's."

"Are you telling me that Ronnie is responsible for my commutation? I don't believe it.

"I don't believe in fairies either. Belief is overrated, on that we agree."

Jackson stepped into the conversation.

"That is the story that I heard. If push comes to shove the governor will release that info. As long as you are seen to be innocent, Percheron won't be tarnished."

"So, what? You think that I am guilty but you prefer to act otherwise? This is delicious."

"I don't know what I prefer, maybe the truth. Let's just say it is the power or circumstances," Jackson said, as if quoting from a future press release.

"La force des choses. Sartre's' better half," Templeton said jubilantly.

Templeton whispered in such a low voice that it was not clear that he'd intended the two others in the room to hear, "Ronnie should have told me that".

The assistant followed up immediately, "I heard rumors, Cas, it could be true. It wasn't a secret, a poorly kept one if that was the plan. It just was not publicized. It must have been

"Been what?" questioned Ertras.

"The governor would have demanded Perch's support. Maybe he just wasn't mentioned by name."

"And Perch would have declined comment to the papers."

"The papers may not even care, or simply took the governor's claim of police support to include the agreement of Percheron."

"Perch could be sly at times."

"All the time," Templeton corrected. "He instigated it. Is that what you are saying?"

"Yes, that's right. He was behind your release."

"Ronnie should have told me," Templeton repeated.

"When?"

"At Cave Hill."

"So you admit being there?"

"Sure. I already did. You should listen better. You have your witnesses. I don't dispute that. I have my witnesses as well. You dispute mine. The only problem, is that my witnesses are also your witnesses. You can't have it both ways, detectives. I arrived when they said I did, and I left, when they say that I did. It's all or none."

"Maybe Percheron did tell you that he had approached the governor about an early release for you," Jackson said, baiting Templeton. "Did he tell you that in an attempt to stop you from shooting him?"

"I didn't shoot him. You know, here I am, an ex con out for a few weeks, and I'm helping you to find witnesses, all honorable men."

"And some women," Ertras added. She wanted this witness to talk.

"I don't know about their honor. They strike be as being suspects as much as me, more, really. Talk to the governor. Will you believe me or him? I'd ask him myself, but I doubt that he'd accept my call."

"Plus, you no longer have a cell phone. How convenient."

"Will you believe him or me? There is no need to answer. I can see your answer in your eyes. We'll give you the same response. At this point in the scandal, the governor has no option to lie. There is too much documentation already in place, he can't use lies to spin this story. It's funny."

"What is?" prompted Jackson.

"Truth is the best policy here. It's refreshing to be on the side of law and order, especially with you two to protect me."

"You misunderstand the situation," Ertras stated.

"No, for once, I understand everything clearly."

"Drugs will do that for you."

"This is fun. Your theory is that I wanted to kill them both for freeing me from jail. When I thought that Ronnie wanted nothing more than to see me die in prison?"

Detective Jackson returned the serve. "You would have us believe in your ignorance. It is more likely that you that had already concluded that the governor was acting with Percheron's knowledge and consent, as far as you being released. Or Percheron told you on day one."

"Who is on drugs now?", Templeton asked Ertras. "Jackson here says that I committed the murder because Ronnie either helped to release me from prison, or because he didn't help. You just cannot avoid twisting evidence and logic to fit your bogus theories. They call that a fixation."

"You no longer have a cell phone. Why did you have one to begin with?"

"Why indeed? A cell phone is worse than an ankle bracelet. I left it at home most of the time, I don't like being tracked. Ronnie called me early Derby afternoon."

"Why?"

"To confirm our meeting. I should have kept that phone, it would have been a great alibi."

"How did he get your number?"

"I don't know, maybe he broke into my house, things like that have been known to happen."

"Anyone could have called you. And you claim to not know your own phone number?"

"I never called myself. If you want certain answers, you should ask your questions to yourself."

"Even if Templeton received a call, that wouldn't prove much, he could have called himself using another phone, or used Perch's if he had one," Jackson realized. He was at a loss. The phone call was meaningless. He could accept the convict's answer or not.

Templeton was experienced enough to remain silent. If he spoke, it would be seen as overselling his answer. Up until this moment, it had all just been an exercise, a game like those when he was a young boy, playing the robber, making up strategies and characters. It was all real now, the final game, the final out before returning home for dinner, a bath, and sleep.

"You bragged for months or years that you were going to murder Percheron. This was long before any hint of a commutation of your sentence. You just wanted revenge, and your old friend dead," Jackson said in a burst of anger.

"Have you been in prison?", asked Templeton. "Don't worry, the question is rhetorical. It was talk, just talk. There is little else offered behind the bars. It's like this conversation between the three of us, it wiles away the time."

"Time that you don't have," observed Ertras.

Templeton responded with a laugh, followed by, "I have more time remaining than your boyfriend Perch."

As Jackson was processing this mocking accusation, combining it with the comments of Percheron's ex-girlfriend Melissa, Ertras, half stood, before she remembered the presence of Templeton's court appointed attorney in the room. The lawyer was a cipher, this was likely the biggest case of his young career, hell, it might be his first. Templeton had brought him in, not for counsel, but solely as a way to charge the governor more money. Templeton was vengeful, that much was clear. This young attorney was sure to be replaced at trial by some media hungry non government employee. Ertras' cynical thought was followed by another, more anger inducing idea. Maybe a friend of a friend of a friend of the governor would step in and drag the proceedings out until Templeton's time was finally up. It would mean an unsolved mystery as to the actual killer, but that outcome was preferable to Templeton's conviction. Ertras realized at that moment that, barring a quick confession, followed by a speedy trial, Templeton was going to die an innocent man. She had to do her job quickly and correctly, two incompatible goals

"He was my friend long before yours, Inspector." Templeton's words brought her back to the interrogation, dreary in its cleanliness, a room, which reeked of nothing, certainly not fear or desperation. Or maybe it did and she was unable to smell her own desperation. She certainly felt it. Ever since they began recording interviews, the word interrogation had disappeared along with the cigarette butts and other detritus that used to decorate the floor. Even the walls had been painted in a neutral color to conform with psychological best practices.

"He was my friend long before yours Detective". Templeton repeated, as if Ertras had forgotten her line in a play.

"What is that supposed to mean Templeton?"

The attorney took his client's repetition to Ertras as a cue to him.

"He is Mr. Templeton, Detective Ertras."

The detectives and the suspect ignored him. They felt awkward for him for a second, his was supposed to be a nonspeaking role. They returned to their meeting.

Templeton was the first to speak.

"How long has Ronnie been dead? A few days? You are not going to solve this crime in record time. My bet is that you won't ever solve it".

"Would you bet your life?" posed Jackson.

"My life is not worth much these day, my young investigator."

"Why won't we solve this?" Ertras asked.

"Because you are too well trained. You will follow the evidence blindly, like two blind mice."

"And your advice is to not follow the evidence, particularly since it leads to you?" demanded Ertras. "No thanks."

Templeton turned to address his attorney.

"You should make a note of the detective's words. This is how act one of a police frame-up begins. I am watching empty the hourglass of my life. I can almost count every grain of sand. Death and I are both set in our ways, but he has the patience that I have always lacked.

"Shakespeare?"

"Templeton."

The convict went on.

"Here I am, persecuted by these agents of the law in my dying days. And the prosecutors are much worse, they like to burn people like me, regardless of the century. They worship some god they call justice but persecute me as a heretic because I don't. They play their game, I play mine. And you play yours. Unfortunately for us, they are more effective in convincing our fellow humans that their chosen sport is more attractive. They must have been raised spiteful little brats.

"Someone has to be in charge," Jackson claimed.

"That is why we change laws, to give everyone a chance to play. When you have as many people in prison as we do, the law is wrong. Your silence is agreement," ventured Templeton.

"I didn't know that prison doubled as a school of philosophy."

"You know a lot about a little," teased the former felon, "you need to discover the living world."

"I agree with that," Ertras told herself. "Perch offered me what I wanted but not what I needed. It came with a cost."

"He offered me a chance to redeem myself by confessing to an old murder. He never understood that we'd taken separate paths, they weren't going to rejoin further down the way."

"And you resented that?"

"Resented? No, I don't think so. I was fine with who I was, what I am. I wasn't about to confess to any murder."

"Because you're innocent?"

A tight smile flickered on his face.

"I don't confess, period. Except in your dreams Detective, only in your dreams. If you were as focused as your brag, you and I would not be having this conversation."

"Oh?"

"Hell yes, oh. You wouldn't be here, you're tired of the game. I see it clearly. You're a gambler who promises to leave after the next hand. For you the next hand is another murder. You and Ronnie, what a pair. Templeton noticed the quizzical look on Jackson's face. You didn't work with Ronnie, did you?"

Jackson shook his head, confirming the felon's guess.

"He and Castorina here," the use of her complete name by this man disconcerted Ertras, only Perch and her mother called her that, "they both depleted their lives chasing death. What could be of less importance than death? Well, Detective, this is the biggest hand that you'll play in the Louisville casino. I won't be alive to see if you escape your delusion after this round, or if you starting searching another instance of death to run after like a country dog."

He paused to drink water.

"I learned from childhood that it's all about me. I had the same instruction in school and in life as everyone else, but just because I came up with what some thought was the wrong answer, I was locked away in a decades long timeout."

"And with Perch?"

"Just the opposite, I suppose. On second thought, he might have suffered the same punishment. I never considered it that way before."

"We are getting way off the reason for this interview, Mr. Templeton," Jackson said glancing acidly at the attorney.

"In prison, we have everything, TV, books, foreign language studies, even a criminal justice system. Not everyone in prison is a heartless criminal. Just as not everyone on the outside is a paragon of virtue. On the inside we become you while on the outside you become us. You don't believe it because you can't see it. You are too close, you breathe it every day and miss the changes as they approach and take over.

I've seen your crimes, oh yes, I have. Surveillance is for and against everyone, you don't even have solitary confinement as a refuge. With the internet and the help of a few friends one can accomplish anything. Is it any wonder that the Chinese control theirs? It's only a matter of time until the government here sees the light and takes control."

"We'll let our own criminal justice handle your case. The judge and jury will decide."

"It requires years of law school indoctrination for judges to willing believe in such BS."

"Tell me again about the gun," Ertras requested. "Where was the envelope?"

"It was on one of the headstones."

"Which one?"

"I don't remember. If it's important"

Ertras shrugged in response.

"Ronnie pointed to it and said that it was for me."

"He didn't hand it to you?"

"No, and I thought that odd."

"Odd? How?"

"It was a strange way to present a gift."

"It wasn't a gift though, was it?"

"No, that's correct. I'd asked him, "A gift?"

"No," Ronnie said, "an inheritance."".

"So you took it?" Jackson inquired.

"Yes. The word inheritance intrigued me.

"So you took it," Ertras echoed her colleague, but hers was a statement, not a question.

Templeton remained silent for a moment, "thinking who knows what," Ertras herself thought.

"He wanted me to open it."

"And did you?"

"No. Not at first."

"Why not?" asked Jackson, perplexed by this breakdown in normal behavior. "Who doesn't open mysterious presents?"

"Because Perch wanted you to open the package", Ertras said, supplying a response for the middle aged felon. Templeton's silence was confirmation of the female detective's supposition.

"It was tacky," Templeton said, his voice cracking slightly, self-questioning.

"Tacky, in what way?" Jackson asked. "How do you mean, tacky? Was it in poor taste to offer a gift to a dying man", his question itself defining poor taste.

"No, just tacky. Sticky, wet, no, not wet, damp. I thought at the time that the envelope might contain a flask of bourbon that was leaking. I even smelled it, but it did not smell of bourbon." The detectives could see that Templeton was, in his mind's eye, back in Cave Hill, facing Percheron and holding a strange package.

"Or so he wants us to believe," Ertras warned herself.

Templeton himself had leapt back to that day in his thoughts, but then he went much further back, to when he and Ronnie were twelve or so, the best age he believed now. If heaven existed, everyone there would be that age. He remembered too, that all of his friend's fathers owned a flask, a remembrance of their own younger days. So long ago, five miles and fifty years away from where he stood now.

Templeton returned to the 21st century. Here he was no longer twelve, no longer young at all, no longer innocent. Now, five miles and fifty years away, he was dying, and innocence was a distant, faded memory.

"To be honest", Templeton commenced, and then abruptly stopped. "That's funny, even to me," and his persecutors couldn't restrain a smile at this shared moment of absurdity. "I thought that it was either a flask of bourbon, that was leaking", he continued, repeating himself, "or some type of a setup, drugs, a gun. It was heavy enough to have been a gun. He wanted me to open it, so I didn't. Not right away. Ronnie didn't play by the rules".

"Whose rules?" came the prompt from Jackson.

"Our rules, neighborhood rules".

"Neither did you," Ertras commented.

"You are absolutely correct," Templeton conceded. "I chose"

"Poorly", interjected Ertras, pouncing on the older man for no logical reason, and she regretted it.

"You would say that, Detective," Templeton responded with a sigh. "Your righteousness wearies me, regarding one and then the other of the two investigators with vacant eyes. "This was boring", he reflected, "These two were not very good at life. He wanted to move things along and these two inquisitors were plodders." Aloud he admitted, "Ok, I opened the envelope. Inside was a gun."

"It is illegal for you to possess a firearm," Jackson said in a voice too loud for the small room.

"So arrest me. But I don't have any gun that killed Ronnie."

"Go on", Ertras said in a voice so soft that the men were not immediately certain what she had said, and then, after the words had registered, neither was sure what their meaning was. Was Jackson supposed to arrest Templeton here and now?

"What did you do then?" asked Ertras, and both men visibly relaxed.

"It was an old revolver, it belonged to my father. Ronnie said that it did, but I wasn't sure. But Ronnie knew guns. Hell, for all I know it was a toy or a pot metal replica." Templeton continued.

"That isn't true," Ertras said in the same hushed tone.

"Sure it did", replied Templeton with a touch of anger in his voice.

"I'm sure that it did," Ertras agreed, once again confusing the men in the room. "But it was you who brought the weapon to the cemetery, not Perch. And while it may be been hidden in an envelope, it was you who pulled it from the envelope and used it to shoot retired detective Henry Percheron twice in the back".

Jackson smirked, now they were getting somewhere. The smirk expanded, stopped, and then collapsed as Templeton began to laugh and laugh, the crackling laugh of a dying man who still found ridiculousness funny.

The laughter stopped as suddenly as it had begun, as if it had been on a precise timer, and Templeton spoke.

"I suppose that I kept the gun in prison with me all this time. Detective Jackson here just told me that was illegal. That is more bad news for the governor. You know, come to think of it, I should really write him a thank you card. If it wasn't for him then I'd probably be dead by now, and none of these unpleasant events would have occurred. But then, we'd have never met. I'm not referring to you, Jackson.

Let me share a bit of prison wisdom with you," his unfocused eyes directed at Ertras. Her face was impassive.

"We each have our heaven waiting for us." Her silence permitted him to finish his statement. "I will not be there in yours, and you certainly will not be there in mine. You have five senses for a reason, you are focusing too much attention on just one of them to the exclusion of the others. The same with suspects. Unless I am under arrest, I'm leaving. You know the name and phone number of my attorney, and I know the way out."

For the second time in a few days, they watched as their prime suspect left them alone in the small interview room.

Ertras and Jackson drove separately to Check's to regroup. They found a table from where they could half watch the televised races, but isolated enough not to be overheard.

On the screen the young horses half strutted, half shuffled to the starting gates. All were well trained beasts, but they moved forward as if walking for them was an unaccustomed gait. Each jockey and thoroughbred was accompanied by a guide horse and pilot.

"Even the best of us need help in getting settled," Ertras reflected. "Except Perch. But he was a workhorse, not really a thoroughbred. In his vocation, being a workhorse was preferred, he had told her once. He was competent but not high strung he had claimed. It was a delusion," Ertras decided.

The 30 something man a few tables away was still deluded enough to be consumed by work, good for him. "He'll outgrow it," she thought.

It was the moment in every race, when all of the spectators and betters are equal, the equine favorite is not aware of his elevated status, and each of the twenty jockeys was confident in their mount and of their ability. The future was bright and fair to all.

"Let's assume that everyone is telling the truth," Ertras began.

"Ok. Including Templeton?"

"Yes, especially him."

"The convicted murder, the one who was the last known person to see Percheron alive, by his own admission? The same one who was selling his story to the press before Percheron's funeral? So we assume that he is a paragon of virtue, despite having told numerous witnesses that he wanted Percheron dead? The same man who destroyed his own cell phone that Perch supposedly contacted him on?"

"There is no evidence that Perch did contact him by phone. The call as Templeton described it would not have indicated the purpose of the call, nor proof of any arranged meeting."

"It was a weak alibi."

"It is not alibi at all. He had just woken up, probably still half drugged up or drunk, heard police at the door, destroyed whatever incriminating evidence there was in the rented house, phone included, and came up with his idiotic story."

"So you think that the phone might have contained calls or texts to his accomplice?"

"Possibly, or it might have been as he first said. He might have been carrying it when he murdered Perch at Cave Hill, and was afraid that we would track it and him to the cemetery."

"It would have confirmed our theory."

"Who today doesn't carry their phone everywhere? No one."

"Templeton isn't from today."

"I'm more concerned about where he was on Derby. He doesn't trust well, but he deceives extraordinarily well."

"He could have been a preacher. And yet you want us to believe him?"

"Just for the moment."

"Surely other vehicles came and went at the cemetery around the same time of day."

"There is no video of the entrance so that is only conjecture."

"It's a reasonable assumption."

"I can hear the phrase now, it assumes facts not in evidence. On second thought that would be the defense's position. They would love to have us raise first the idea of other suspects coming and going."

"We're stuck either way."

"I am afraid so. But we are not in court, we follow logic and the evidence."

"And if they conflict? Do we flip a coin?"

"Our coin has two heads, we follow the evidence."

"The guide at Cave Hill said that the artist John Audubon lived here. Did you know that he was an illegal French immigrant?"

"What is your point? That he was French or illegal?"

"So many German and French immigrants fled to America to avoid wars in their own countries."

"So?"

"Nothing. Nevermind. It was just an observation."

"Okay. Now, have you any observations about this case?"

"You mentioned earlier about this crime being tied to something in the past. You referred to the distant past. Percheron and Audubon were both French, in a way."

"Okay," Ertras repeated. "I understand now where you were heading. How long ago did Audubon live in Louisville?"

"He was here in the early 19th century."

"That would make it in the 1800s. Around the time of the Civil War?"

"No, earlier. Like 1805."

"1805!" Ertras exclaimed. "That is over two centuries ago. By distant past, I mean 50 to 60 years tops, something during Perch's lifetime. Although Perch might have been happier back in Audubon's day. For someone so logical, he had a romantic side."

"Oh?"

"Not in that way, Jackson."

"Oh?"

"Not with me."

"Oh."

"You sound like one of those birds that your long dead suspect, Audubon, drew so well."

"I didn't say that he was a suspect," Jackson responded defensively.

"Perch had a sensitive side, he was human."

"Oh?"

"Definitely an owl. That's what you are," Ertras said teasingly, winking.

"For someone who detested video games as monotonous, I never understood his fascination with the past. He wore blinders when it came to this subject, he saw the past as some idyllic pre technological life, but it struck me as just as inescapable and repetitive a world, only more smelly, as the computer realities that so annoyed him."

"Did he garden?"

"What?"

"Did Percheron like to garden?"

"No," Ertras responded without having to think. "No, not at all."

The assistant said nothing, enjoying his moment of having surprised his superior. He pictured himself at Lake Pointe with a fly rod in his hand, seeing a ripple and a watery disturbance before his fly was snatched by a bass.

"Jackson?" Ertras questioned.

"Yes?"

"Why the question about gardening?"

"I have friends who like to talk about their dreams, hell, who doesn't. They'd like to run a marathon or write a book, but they won't take the first step to achieve it. It's all or nothing. They want to win the lottery but won't take a second job, or economize to save money. They are content with the dream, it requires no effort."

"And so Perch was content with his little fantasy?"

"Yes."

"I'm not sure. I knew him better than you."

"I agree with both of your claims. You knew him better than me. And two, you're not sure."

"So it was just a crime of opportunity?"

"The evidence does not support that."

"It does not. Everything about this case reeks of a crime of cold passion."

"That is an oxymoron, Cas."

"I mean passion delayed."

"So that brings me back to the girlfriend, Melissa. Handcuffs, drugs, she had access to all of the evidence. Has anyone checked her house to see if he was there?"

"Of course, he was there, many times."

"What proof do we have that he was shot at Cave Hill? Sorry, I understand that this is personal."

"They are always personal to someone."

So, Melissa meets him at the hospital door and he gets in her car voluntarily. What about his car? It is still missing. Someone else had to drive that, Templeton? Or does Melissa meet him at the hospital's front door and they walk to his car, or she meets him at his car. Somehow his car and he both disappear. They need to take his keys, they need to overpower him or to trick him in order to accomplish that task. Do they drug him? Is the nurse Joyce involved?"

"There are too many nurses in this story already. One drugs him beforehand, and another one drugs him afterwards, all at the instigation of Melissa and or Templeton? These are guesses. You need to find out what the process is, did anyone remember seeing the keys, did he say anything about it?"

"If it was Melissa. she keeps him handcuffed and doesn't feed him for 36 hours. Why?"

"Maybe she doesn't want to deal with him needing to go to the bathroom, maybe she wanted their last meal together to be his last."

"Was he diabetic?"

"No, I already checked."

"You have had this theory for a while."

"Yes."

"What about other criminals holding him for information? Or maybe just to delay him until after"

"Until after what?"

"I have no idea."

"That could be possible. He wasn't tortured or injured in any way."

"Other than being shot in the back, twice."

"Before that. If they wanted information, either he provided it voluntarily, or they weren't that persistent."

"Twice, in the back. That is persistent enough for me."

"It was a .32, that is weak bullet."

"He is still dead."

"I know that. I simply commented that it was a 32. It was the first time I'd seen one of those in a murder. It's like something from the 1960s, 1970s. Organized crime."

"Don't even go there."

"But"

"But nothing."

"Templeton is from that era, he'd have owned a 32 back then."

"I know. Let's pretend that he isn't lying."

"If you say so."

"There is another possibility. Some random sadist. The prison has enough of those."

"So does my wife's side of the family."

"You're not married."

"That is the reason why."

Detective Jackson had been against marriage, marriage for him, since he had been a teenager and what he had seen in the interim had not changed his mind.

"The actress, did he have dirt on her that would kill her career? Oh, what am I saying, this is not the 1960s or 70s, as you said. Dirt is no longer dirty."

"Melissa, Joyce, these others, they are convenient suspects but they are not very plausible. The press would be more than willing to help us convict them and then turnaround in a few years to exonerate them and excoriate us."

"I need to leave, Cas. I'll ask a few questions again at the bar."

On his way out, Jackson posed the question to the new bartender who had just come on duty.

"Do you remember Henry Percheron? He went by Perch."

"Sure. It's terrible what happened. I didn't know that he had been a detective. He was quiet, polite. He'd have a beer once in a while, but he liked to mix them. I'd never seen anyone else do that."

"Like a shot and a beer?"

"No, like half Coors light and half West 6. He said it was a good combination of sweet and bitter. The customer is always right."

"You don't say."

"I do say that he was a good tipper. You learn to remember the good tippers."

"Do you remember anything else?"

"Such as what, detective?"

"Such as any enemies, any arguments, any plans that he may have discussed that would help us apprehend his killers", Jackson explained, using the plural, killers, in an attempt to expand the bartender's memory. Someone needed to think beyond just Templeton.

"I can tip well too".

"I'm sorry detective, but you must watch too many old movies. This isn't one them", extending his arms to indicate the bar, "and I am not some shady barkeep selling secrets and other information on the side. This is a suburban watering hole, a family place. If I knew anything, I would share it with you voluntarily, without expecting anything in return, especially not money. I didn't know him well", he was the first witness that seemed to fit into that category, Jackson thought, "but he seemed a decent guy, respected, decent."

"A pillar of the community?" Jackson asked, his voice lacking any hint of irony.

"Yep." The shortness and informality of the phrase covered it in truth.

"Well, if you," Jackson began, as he prepared to leave.

"I'll call if I hear or remember anything else," the bartender completed the detective's interrupted request, placing Jackson's business card carefully in his wallet. Jackson nodded, turned, and left the family place, empty handed but pleasantly cheered.

Cas had moved to a stool after Jackson's departure, where she studied the bar in more detail.

Numerous men and the occasional woman glanced at Ertras, with hope, or disdain, or with vacancy, she found the latter to be the most attractive, and the most frightening. And there was very little that frightened Ertras, for she believed in nothing, and expected nothing.

She pondered the rumor of a planned meeting between herself and the governor.

"It would serve no purpose," she reasoned. "He needs less coverage, not more, a meeting would only bring an unwanted spotlight. He prefers that any spotlight and its heat be focused solely on me."

Ertras let herself eavesdrop on neighboring conversations.

"His ex-life"

"His ex-wife?"

"It's the same thing, ex-life, ex-wife."

"Me, I'm a post lifer. I don't like it." The man paused, a pause that lasted longer than many conversations.

"Yeah, like that."

"Yep. It means no more complaining."

Two men were complaining about their exes and their lost families. It was normal, in the strange normalcy of men, that even their complaints were a form of competition. Who had lost the more, the claims mounted like wagers at a poker tables. Men should only marry in their forties or fifties seemed to be the general consensus, the shared flop, while the winner of the beer facilitated discussion would be the one who lost more than the others to their ex-wives.

"Both men were wearing short sleeved blue striped shirts, golfers. Probably four college degrees between them, and their combined common sense made then less clueless than the high school kid making fries in the kitchen," Ertras thought.

They introduced themselves to each other only at their end of the shared confessions, when they still possessed the cloak of anonymity. "Idiots," Ertras ruled against them.

"Bitter regret and the rare meeting with another victim of divorce were poor substitutes for murder," Ertras thought, reflecting on the compilation of suspects that she had arrested over the years who had said as much to her during their confessions. Some people simply enjoyed killing their fellow humans.

"This country is full of undug holes," one had said memorably during his attempt at explanation.

Murders mostly resulted from a lack of respect or money, which usually meant the latter, which can buy the former.

An elderly man in a worn, stretched out T shirt salted his meal of meatloaf, green beans and mashed potatoes so heavily it was as if he were attempting to thaw a frozen driveway. A moment later, when she overheard that he had just been discharged from Jewish hospital, Ertras speculated that he would soon return there. Had this man been a patient during Perche's brief stay?

"Forget it," she told herself, Perch was in the hospital for a matter of several hours, and not everyone knows everyone else, even in Louisville. The city had a million inhabitants, and coincidences happen.

Still, it nagged her, and she was only prevented from approaching this new, potential witness, by the man's words which broke through the pleasant bar hubbub. He and his female companion were arguing over some triviality, by the sound of it, the contretemps could have been part of their late afternoon ritual. . It was boomer silliness, where the choice between a lemon and lime slice in a club soda generated a philosophical debate.

It was time for her own ritual, her own home. Ertras had no more energy to read another chapter in another human's story book. If it were important, she could find them again, if both were still alive that is, she added, as the couple's voices rose, and Ertras made a hurried exit.

CHAPTER FOURTEEN

There were only ten days until Derby, he had to stop planning and move on to the action of this drama, he told himself. Mosgrove Templeton waited until Perch had started his car and driven away. Templeton exited his own vehicle, crossed Lyndon Lane, and entered the two story nondescript office building. "What was Ronnie doing here evenings?" he wondered.

He scanned the wall mounted occupant directory, one listing caught his eye. He went to the indicated office and opened the door, surprised that it was still unlocked. Inside, he was greeted with the sight of a middle aged woman and the word, "Bonsoir". Templeton responded "Bonsoir" in turn.

"I've come to the right place, I think. You offer French lessons, right?"

"Yes, we do", the woman responded in French accented English. "Welcome to the Alliance Française of Louisville. I'm Monique, one of the teachers." Monique turned to a framed photograph on the wall of an attractive, older woman.

"This is the school's founder, Evelyn Cohn. The Alliance has been in Louisville since 1904 and the school for over thirty years. Are you"

"Good" Templeton interrupted. "Sorry. But I met a fella recently, who said he was taking classes here, and I thought, why not try that myself."

"Are you new to the area?" Monique asked.

"I moved back recently. This man I met, his name was Percy or something like that."

Monique and the other two adults in the office, students, Templeton concluded, all stared blankly at him.

"Perch or Percheron?" he prompted.

"Oh" one of the students exclaimed, turning to Monique. "He must mean Henry, Henry Percheron."

"Ronnie going by Henry", Templeton thought, shocked to hear that Ronnie was using his given name in public, with strangers. Monique added to his amazement, when she added, "Oui, Henri is one of our students."

Disconcerted, Templeton carried on.

"Would it be possible to enroll in one of your classes? Tonight, I mean."

"We are nearly at the end of our term, but we do offer private lessons as well. Those can start at any time."

"If you are really anxious, perhaps you could finish out Henry's lessons, it's only for a few weeks, and while you might feel lost, I'm confident that it will be fun. Or at least different," one of the students said in a rush.

"Finish his lessons?" Templeton asked confusedly.

The second student explained it in a way that only added to Templeton's confusion.

"Henry liked these French classes so much that he is moving to France for a few months, maybe longer, I'm not sure. He is even selling his car. That reminds me, I need to ask him about that, my granddaughter needs a good used car."

CHAPTER FIFTEEN

Ertras felt that she way playing the character of a detective, this was only a role for her, she had no part in writing the script of this play. "If she was not the playwright then who was?"

The corpse of her friend, now or soon to be buried, was the sole component of this case that was neither a plausible prop, nor part of unlikely coincidences. "Was she going mad? Everyone is cursed in their own private way."

Her friend and former mentor was dead. He had worked the difficult cases. It was said that he had solved all but his first assignment, and that was put down to his inexperience and the killer's luck. Perhaps it was true, perhaps he had a perfect record, save one. Or maybe it was only legend. Everyone needs their legends, even law enforcement, maybe for them, herself included, more than ever. The press would do what they liked best, they would press and pry, and the legend would stand or fall. She hoped the former, but did not feel confident in her desire.

Perch's one loss. Maybe there had been more; she had never asked him about it directly. It had been a dull ache for the detective. That was how Perch had described it. Ertras concluded that it was this which made Perch so effective, he used that one loss as motivation for his dozens and dozens of wins. Perch had mentioned it once years ago, who in hearing Mr. Pregel, a first generation American, talk to his surviving daughter, had spoken as Perch had put it, "in heavily accented love that the young girl found embarrassing." Ertras had blushed, for it had been the same with her.

There was a song she remembered from years ago, *It ain't over 'til it's over*. For Perch it was certainly over, for her, she hoped that working this murder would not bring to her the same incurable ache. All she knew was that hope was neither a solution to this murder, nor a permanent salve for any future pain.

"Smoke without fire," she thought again, as the wind shifted and she inhaled involuntarily acrid smoke in her nostrils and felt it burn in her eyes. She stood and stepped back from her evening campfire, her eyes tearing.

She recalled the sound of crunching gravel from the cemetery. It was the sound of joyous arrivals and sad departures. The same sound but separate meanings.

"Had the guards at Cave Hill experienced the same confusion, not smoke and fire, but smoke and mirrors? The sounds that they had attributed to gunshots a few minutes before derby, could they have been what Jackson had first suggested, an imitation? Were they firecrackers set off by Templeton's accomplice to provide an alibi for the real murderer, the criminal known as Mos?"

She would need to run a test to see if shots could be heard in the guards' office when they were fired from the old 32 caliber revolver near the location of the Dietz headstone. It was simpler and less painful to use an actual site marker than the true murder scene. She was again reminded of the muffled but gunlike detonations of the burning cherry wood."

Ertras feared also that the murder would be forever linked with the Derby, and if the murder remain unsolved, so would she. America already had enough decades-long mysteries, shows about them appeared regularly on the uncountable television and internet channels. It would be a case that would involve Dwayne Stanton. Perhaps only he, aside from Perch himself, would be able to solve it to everyone's satisfaction. She herself would become a celebrity, better known if she failed than if success smiled upon her. Failure would finish her career with LMPD, and accomplish what her own parents had been unable to achieve: cause her to leave Kentucky. Her future was going to be either bigger and worse, for success would promote her out of the field, or smaller and worse. Failure would end her police career entirely, if not from incompetence, then from shame.

She was content, an unappreciated state in America, and enjoyed being a cog in a machine. She was a nondescript detective, she thanked her unknown predecessors who had made female police a yawnable offense. She received little publicity, and was thankful when they misspelled her name. "When the press spells your name correctly, you are about to be screwed," was Ertras' private axiom.

The smoke had raced around to find and embrace her. What was that phrase that she had heard once, it was from a Patricia Cornwell novel, "the flame snapped and waved as if it had something important to say."

"Was the smoke also sending her a signal?" The cherry wood suddenly took flame, and when, a few minutes later, the crackle of the snapping cherry erupted like poorly done special effects in an amateur theatre production, Ertras smiled, and then frowned. She was happy to have warm flame, but realized that she had missed whatever message the smoke had been trying to communicate to her. The fuel had become fire without smoke. It was no more helpful to her than smoke without fire. Ertras stepped back, turned, and headed back inside.

Home, bed, sleep, back in the hive where she was queen. The hive itself was silent, normal as it was empty, no workers, not even a drone. Her home was complete in its emptiness. The finished basement was a beautiful abyss, prepared for the next residents, for surely the house craved a family, with its attendant dirt, noise, and commotion. Maybe she should have invited the argumentative couple from Check's over to teach her house a lesson in getting what you wish for.

Ertras' residence was uncluttered. The house, she thought sadly, was as silent and as manicured as the cemetery where Perch's body had been found. Here, in this house, she was little more than the current occupant, temporarily above ground, only here for a test drive.

She was in her own mausoleum, Oblivion with four walls and a roof. It was ironic, after a day policing, she ended it by ensconcing herself in a gorgeous prison. She laughed aloud, but there was no one to ask her to explain the joke.

What if she were not policing? Cas had been toying with the idea for a while now. The shock and suddenness of Perch's death, the daze in which she had conducted the investigation, and then the unexpected inheritance and the equally disorienting reassignment away from the investigation had followed one upon the other at such a pace that she was left dizzy. The events combined to both force the issue upon her and to offer her a new direction. A week ago, there had been policing and nothing else. Today it could be no policing and everything else. From what her chief had not said, her career in Louisville, while not over, would never be the same. It wasn't her fault, it just was the ways things were, and would be. Was this the same choice that Perch had faced when he had retired? It was reaching the end of the paved road and facing the choice of continuing ahead on foot or turning around. Perch had not really had that choice, there was no possibility of turning back to the comfort of the pavement. Retirement had seen to that.

And now Perch's decision to continue on foot, in Paris, what a ramble that would have been, had been terminated before it began by two gunshots. Ertras walked to the built in bookshelves, filled mainly with DVDs. She saw none that spoke to her. She would sleep. Sleep would provide her with a plan. Ertras asked aloud, as there was no one present to inform on her, "An escape plan"?

She wanted desperately to switch it off, this job that was at once so addictive and yet so elegant, in a putrid, bloody, vomit covered sort of elegance. "What would her childhood friends say? What would they think of her now? Had any become her own Templeton? She had lost contact with most of them, which was difficult to do in Louisville. She would have to seek out the one that she saw from time to time, and ask him questions that only friends can, but which she never had asked. It would amazing to switch the job off, to dress and absorb the civility that plainclothes provided. It's not civility, she corrected herself, it's civilian. That could be funny, she'd file that one away. Maybe it was funny, who was she to determine humor? That was reserved to the living, and to Ertras, those consisted mainly of suspects or witnesses, who were sometimes both at once. Good and evil had a soft border, it shifted, like the Ohio River used to do before dams and flood control management. The river still ran wild once in a while, for old time's sake. That is what she needed, she told herself convincingly, I need a new path. Numerous bridges connected Louisville to Indiana and beyond. Why not just take one?"

It was time for decisiveness in her indecision. A simple no was sufficient to suppress doubt and open the door to tomorrow. With tomorrow settled, she slept.

He was in a bar where no one cares if they are seen there, because they know that they are not worth being seen. The beer was mildly bitter, he liked it. He swallowed his contentment in small quantities. Who was he kidding, it wasn't his choice; contentment was only offered in small dosages. It was as controlled for him as opioids had become.

He was slightly intoxicated, oscillating mentally in the alcohol induced version of that wonderful, temporary status between wakefulness and sleep, out on the precipice from which it was equally agreeable to tumble in either direction.

The bourbon before this beer had been too strong, with an odd taste. It was the worst mint julep he'd had in, hell, it was his first in decades, from before his incarceration. He'd never liked them he realized. "Had that one tasted as odd as the ones from 30 years previously," he asked his intoxicated self. The barmaid had teased him that nobody drinks a julep post Derby. Alcohol, another addiction.

What a crime that had been, the addicting of fellow citizens, but a crime so profitable that no one would be punished, except those dead from the narcotic. Perhaps a few of them lay dead nearby right now in this downscale neighborhood of the deceasing. There would be no penalty suffered by anyone else. Too much money. At the end of the proverbial day, the attorneys would have extracted their commission on misery.

Templeton was a bigot. He insulted the poor for laziness and the rich for being snobbish. Himself he found passable, but living adjacent to the fairway of a golf course had come to be a constant mockery of his own declining skills in that or any activity that required health.

Templeton thought of his last conversation with Ronnie, his old friend's words "Your mother confused me with my father, her testimony would not bear any level of scrutiny. So you walk again. She passed me the gun that you now hold in your hand."

Nearby, a patron laughed in such an isolated and private manner that Templeton shivered. People got shot by crazies all the time. He might even be a friend of Ronnie. Templeton stood carefully and left, having dropped a large tip on the bar as an exit fee. Outside, he laughed at his fear until he coughed, but forced himself to pursue the laugh, to the point of choking, gasping for air, dry heaving in an involuntary attempt to empty his stomach in order to make more room for his lungs.

"Screw them", he said aloud when he regained his breath, his faced turned toward the large window of the bar. "Screw them all. They are all either idiots or fools." He inhaled deeply but said his next words only to himself.

"The doctors should have been in prison for malpractice, and this detective Castorina Ertras, she is out of her depth."

He glanced back to the bar.

"It takes a thief to catch a thief, and it will take a murderer to catch this murderer," he informed the actor selling a cure for erectile disfunction on the screen visible through the plate glass window.

Jackson decided to visit a so-called gentlemen's club in order to think. Post Derby, traffic was nearly nonexistent, and prices had declined to overpriced. He was recognized immediately as law enforcement, but in this brief interlude between Derby and late May, both the staff and the customers were only going through the rehearsals of titillation. Jackson was here to think, to spend some of the city's overfunded vice budget. Jackson was frugal and kept tips to a minimum except if he received information in return. "That was more and more rare," he sighed. Here, he could ponder, and plan.

Jackson imagined the conversation in Frankfort, or maybe the governor was still in Louisville, hidden but close to the investigation.

"I should have never released him" the governor said in Jackson's script.

A political flunky offered, "There are holes in every timeline, we can do our part to make them bigger". The flunky paused and then corrected himself, "By our part, I mean my part".

The governor glanced at him, silent.

"The right timeline would show Templeton innocent".

The governor simply nodded and frowned, which the flunky took as approval. As did Jackson. They all have their monologue, talking to yourself is a method if you do it silently. It's called reflection. Aloud it is deemed madness. At least earbuds provide a disguise.

Cas had her method, it was crazy in his opinion. Strolling around a lake, it was only a pond to be truthful, a glorified ditch, and that was a secondhand technique of the late, Great Perch.

"Great, my ass," he muttered quietly, the dance music obscuring his voice from the few other patrons.

"He died like some convicted drug dealer in China, bound and executed. Why was he even on this case?" he wondered.

When his train of thought was interrupted by the 30'ish dancer who had approached his table, his mind pondered the amount of his current per diem.

Jackson wondered about cameras here. Who had the time or passion to concern themselves with the dead, he thought without noticing the irony.

Not far away from Cas's residence, Melissa was pensive. "The official unofficial story is that Templeton was the murderer with either her or another accomplice. Had she misjudged Grove? Shery Pregel had been dead for so long that the memory of her existence was not even a distant memory.

Like Ertras, Melissa considered herself afflicted by a private curse. Hers was having supernatural hearing. She heard much, much too much, and all that she heard was worrisome. Worse, she was conscientious, unable to either blot out or to ignore the need. And for that, she needed gods.

"If this god won't answer me, what good is he? I will find another; there has to be one or more for each of us, like curses. Stars are infinite in quantity, why not gods?"

Since her childhood, Melisa had pictured Death as a female, "Deathette", dressed in the requisite black, but with just a dash of color to give the soon to be dead a final illusion of hope. But now, now that she'd seen death up close, she told herself that she had been blind, and silly. The brutality was the behavior of a man. With death, there was no joyful sprig of bright color, there was nothing at all

Melissa wanted to remain local, despite her complaints to Joyce. She had done nothing wrong. She had suspected that Castorina and Ronnie were, or had been lovers. He had ridiculed the idea, and then, seeing that Melissa was serious, had sworn that his words were true. Melissa had forced herself to believe him. Now doubt had returned. Men had always disappointed her. That was their role. She recognized it as undeniable truth. Ronnie was no longer there to calm her, to provide the comfort and assurance. He had bristled at the gift she had given him at Christmas. He had called it a drone for a drone. And now Ronnie was a dead drone, shriveled in Cave Hill. He was another man who had abandoned her unexpectedly. Not, that wasn't quite true. She had expected it, it was her fate. She knew that time would pass, and that she would meet another man, other men, and they too would in turn disappoint her. She would need to move on, from a hole as deep as the one which now held Ronnie, from a position less than zero. She had done it before, she could do it again.

With men, it was so often about sex, they talked about power, but they understood the term only at a basic level. They were cute in their own way, but they were transients, drones who flitted around her for a while, and then disappeared. They were essential, but ultimately useless. She laughed, for sadness is unbecoming for a solitary woman, and drank from the crystal wine glass in her hand, then stopped to listen to the buzz of flying insects. "Here is to the next drone," she toasted.

CHAPTER SIXTEEN

Perch had auditioned for a local theater group. Despite his lifelong presence in Louisville, he was relatively unknown. Few of those not directly impacted know the names of those who are paid to protect them.

"Or avenge them," the director said in response to Ertras' opening question that Thursday morning after the murder.

"Was that his role?" Ertras asked.

"An avenger, yes I think that was his core."

"Playing the role of the villain was more the nature, the core, as you put it, of Templeton."

"Who?" asked the director

"Never mind," replied Ertras, "no one of consequence."

"Retirees are always searching."

"For what?"

"I'm not sure that they know the answer themselves."

"That sounds very sad. Terry, I may call you Terry, I hope?"

"Sure, I'm used to answering to any name, or insult."

"The life of theater?" Ertras asked politely.

Terry only smiled and nodded in response.

"Mr. Percheron, it was strange to hear him referred to by that salutation, didn't strike me as sad."

"No," asked Jackson, "but you said"

"Retirees are always searching, the lucky ones that it. The unlucky give up, they surrender."

"They surrender to what?"

"I can't explain it exactly, they just abandon the search. They turn around wherever they are and return home. Sometimes in a very literal manner."

"The search for what," Jackson persisted. "I don't understand."

"Theater has taught me a line that I like to misunderstand myself," the director said, trying to explain her theory." In Shakespeare the line is the Play's the thing, meaning that the performance of the play is itself the action that will bring a reaction in real life. All inside of the actual play, of course."

It was clear that she was not clearing any waters for either detective.

"The play's the thing," repeated Ertras in a questioning voice

"Yes, it just encapsulates existence."

Jackson glanced at Ertras with a bewildered look, one that she returned.

These actors love their time on stage was the thought in both their minds.

Ertras winked at her associate while waiting the next words of the director

"Beyond a certain point, we love to play. Think about it, cavemen painted dance scenes. They lived in caves and chased down their meals, but they still had time not only for play, but time to preserve the idea of play on cave walls. Life is tough, but there is time enough for play."

"And time enough for love?" asked Ertras before she could prevent herself from speaking.

"One can wish so, Detective," Terry replied before adding, "that says it all as far as I am concerned. Sorry, I got carried away."

"What did he do for you?"

"He volunteered here for several months. I didn't know him all that well. From what you've indicated just now, that was my loss. He assisted with our props, and wardrobe, items like that. He auditioned once I think, but he wasn't right for the role."

"Which role was it?"

"I'm not sure, I wasn't casting that piece. I can find out, if you like. Is it important?"

"Who knows?" Ertras sighed. "Let me know if you can, it might be relevant. Or not."

"He was still searching, it was perhaps his detective nature, or maybe just his nature. He liked the fact that our theatre stages mysteries, too many theatres just want to do artsy stuff," he said once.

"I didn't take it as an insult because I knew what he meant. We don't have the luxury of too much experimentation, but we do some. I'm optimistic that we can balance the artsy and whatever the opposite of artsy is."

"So he liked mysteries," Jackson prompted, anxious to leave this stage where neither he nor Cas had a part to play.

"Yes, I imagine that it must come with his job. It seems to me that he has left you a difficult mystery to solve, a regular mid spring dilemma."

The allusion passed by, unrecognized.

"Mr. Percheron was not ready to give up."

"Nor was he ready to act, in your opinion," Ertras stated, ready to terminate the interview.

"No, sorry."

The director asked about Jessica, "Did she really find the body"?

"Yes", Ertras answered, "she did".

"Jessica came to the theatre,", the directory began.

"When she was a kid?" Jackson asked politely, but ready to finish with this particular witness. Crestwood was nice enough, but it held no interest for him. They did theater to escape farm chores, he speculated, understanding immediately that it was not true.

The director was still speaking, "Yes, often. She was always talented. But I meant before and after."

"Before and after what?" Jackson asked, confused.

"Why the murder of that poor detective, Detective", she answered, frowning at the poor dialogue that she had created for herself. "Officer", she added, only compounding the awkwardness of the phrase.

"She visited here on Thursday and again on Sunday evening. I wasn't here on Sunday, and I heard that she only stayed a few minutes. Maybe she was looking for me and left."

"Are you saying that Jessica Villier was here twice, once on Thursday before Oaks, and again the Sunday after Derby", Jackson asked excitedly, pushing the thought of farm chores from his mind.

"What did she want?" he continued, as the witness nodded yes. Terry inhaled, making a conscious effort to avoid another botched line of her own making. She overcompensated and her words sounded theatrical, even to her own ear. "She did indeed, Detective, she did indeed". Modulating her delivery, she pushed on, this time at ease with the virgin line. "I was delighted to see her. I was honored knowing how numerous her local commitments must be. She was polite, gracious."

"But?" Ertras interrupted, following her own script.

The director paused expectantly.

"There is always a but in my line of business, Terry," Ertras said in explanation.

"There is in mine too. We are both in the business of drama, I think. For me it's entertainment, and you, I'm afraid, for necessity. But it's business all the same."

"You encourage drama and I try to eliminate it."

"We both attempt to channel it. That is how I see it." The director returned to the visit in question.

"I felt that Jessica had come to see me, particularly on Thursday, to do more than just say hello. I think that she was trying to gather information on your deceased colleague. He was alive at that time?"

Jackson nodded yes, and the director uttered "good".

"What did you tell her?

"About Mr. Percheron? The same as I told you. She wanted to know what he did, what he worked on here."

"Did that annoy you?"

"Annoy me? Not in the least. It did not surprise me either. What did surprise me however was her desire to see the prop room. You know, where we keep the sets, and costumes, gadgets, things like that. It's upstairs." Terry motioned overhead with her left hand, anticipating the question from Jackson.

"Overhead?" he asked.

"Yes, we are a small theatre."

"Why did such a request surprise you, aren't you two both interested in acting?"

"Jessica Villier has access to the most modern and comprehensive prop rooms in the country, if not in the world. Compared to those, we have nothing."

"May we see it?" Ertras asked with a smile. The director led them up the stairs located behind the stage and a minute later the three of them were standing in a musty room above the audience portion of the theatre. There, yesterday's extras awaited rebirth and another chance at a glamorous life. It reminded Ertras of Cave Hill for some reason. There was nothing relevant to be uncovered, the detectives quickly determined.

"Was there anything that Ms. Villier found of interest? You mentioned gadgets."

"Yes like fake cigarettes and blood packets, blanks, those sorts of things."

"Guns? Yes. They aren't real guns."

"Are the prop guns still here? Are they the same ones as before?" Jackson asked quickly.

They all understood what he meant by before. The prop guns were as they should be, it had been a short lived lead

Was there anything else she was searching for?

It was maybe a way to extend her time with me. Maybe she enjoyed visiting a simpler theatre, to have a chance to relive old times. She asked a bit after my cousin. Jessica is a polite girl."

"I see," Jackson said, his voice not hiding his disappointment.

"Did she ask any questions about Mr. Percheron?" Jackson hoped to resurface memories that were already fading from the mind of a woman who adopted false memories and imaginary back stories on a continuous basis.

"She was curious about an old murder. How could I have forgotten? It must be all the rehearsals. It's so easy to forget when one is trying to remember. I'd forgotten that Jessica was curious, not the murder of course. Jessica will probably put her in their new movie, or maybe they would have. It's probably canceled now.

"Who is your cousin, Terry?' Ertras asked, searching like the actress, to extend the conversation with this font on unexpected knowledge.

"She died a long time ago, she was the one murdered, Sherry Pregel.

As they were leaving, Jackson asked the title of the upcoming play.

"The Suicide Club: New Members Welcome."

"A comedy, then?"

"No, not really."

Ertras hid her disappointment. She'd been hoping for a comedy, one like *La Famille Bilingue*, a local production that she had seen a few years previously. No one had died in that play. "Only comedies in the future," Ertras promised herself.

CHAPTER SEVENTEEN

While he waited for petite Joyce, Templeton brooded and coughed. Death was nearly visible on the horizon, and he was anxious for the end. He just needed a few more days. Templeton was not pleased with having been born in the first place. It had been an annoying for him and nearly deadly for his mother. To be born once was more than enough. To do it again was unthinkable. It's a pity that you can't simply turn around and go back to oblivion, like reading the outside menu of a restaurant and deciding, no, that's not for me. No, the world was convinced of a second or a series of endless chances, repetitions of what was a bad idea to start with. He kept that multi-heretical proposition to himself. And if the world was correct, and he was wrong, well, apparently he'd be sentenced to spinoffs if not actual reruns of this tedious experience. His thoughts were cleared by Joyce's arrival.

Joyce Small was short and, if she'd been a man, one would have described her as wiry. Her blonde hair was cropped short, while her direct brown eyes and sharp nose gave her the appearance of an attentive hawk. The combination was a very sensual woman, to whom any man would respond immediately. Joyce was someone who could take down a wild horse or drive a docile man wild. Few men were that docile.

It was the Monday before Derby, and Joyce was seeing her least favorite patient. She took her role as a nurse seriously, but the world would be better off without Mosgrove Templeton.

She saw him twice a week but Joyce would be glad when his treatments were over, for that would mean that he would be dead. In the meantime, she would do her best to treat and cure him.

Joyce was blessed in having had a very misunderstanding spouse. The divorce was quick, and the marriage had been tolerable as it had been brief. She claimed to have green eyes. It was untrue but she was attractive enough that no man was foolish enough to correct her.

Templeton had noticed immediately noticed that Joyce, the nurse he'd like more with, wore an Assumption class ring, what they used to call a dinner ring, gold, with a long oval ruby color stone, in which was imbedded a long, more narrow oval of gold. He remembered that some of the mothers of Sherry's classmates at Assumption wore rings very similar. He had been absent from

Louisville for decades of his life, but it was still the same. The ring was another reminder of past lives and past connections. Louisville, big and small, international and parochial. Assumption, Bellarmine, Saint Agnes, and others and here was Templeton, a devil in the forest of Eden.

Templeton remembered the arrival of the new girl in the neighborhood all those years ago, as if it were last week. She had moved in with her family, whom he would later think of as her supporting cast, although at the time, he didn't think of them at all. Where they had moved from was irrelevant, and despite his learning that it was from a town only thirty miles distant, she was as exotic as if she'd come from a foreign country. It was meeting Ertras that had brought this old memory to the surface, her Spanish name and the blur events of the past few days were combining to blur the distinction between today and long ago. He was confusing himself.

"Damn his mother and her defective genes," he cursed silently.

The new girl was named Angela Pregel. The boys of the neighborhood learned that she was as adept an athlete as they were, faster actually. Her appearance coincided with the time in life when girls are the physical equal of boys. The period was brief, soon the boys would eclipse her in speed and power, and their thoughts would turn to topics other than sports. It was a magical time, special because of its brevity. Templeton remembered the day a few years later, the day he was a boy and a man, leaning against the girl's budding breast during a game, he abandoned all desire for sports, and knew instead that he wanted her, without clearing understanding what that meant. It was a drive to follow, a command to obey without question. But it came to nothing, time passed, and Angela went away to college. By that time, it was not Angela Pregel who was the object of his passion, but her much younger sister, Sherry.

Living on the outside was difficult, it entailed living in an uncertain future. In prison, the future was the same as the past and the present. This future was hard, it demanded so much effort and was full of so much randomness. He had opened one of his old books that had come to him from his mother's estate. It was his book, not hers. Inside he found a four leaf clover, a relic from happy days, pressed from the time that it was picked decades ago by Sherry. The leaf marked not only a page in the book he had never finished, but also the end of those halcyon days. Grove had convinced Sherry to give the charm to him, but the gift had brought both of them nothing but bad fortune. Would things have been different for her, and for him, if she had kept the treasure herself.

"You're staring at my ring again, Mr. Templeton," Joyce said. She refused to refer to him by anything other than Mr. Templeton, despite his repeated requests.

"Should I be staring elsewhere, Joyce?" he retorted lasciviously.

Joyce ignored the comment, male patients were all the same.

"Does it remind you of something?"

"The ring?" Templeton said more civilly, dropping his attempt at flirtation for the moment. "Yes, it reminds me of better days, younger days." He did not describe to the nurse what he meant by that. Instead he was thinking of Sherry, of Ronnie, and how he would like to answer this hot woman who acted so coldly to him with heat of his own.

He would answer her question with a bottle of cold, cheap Chardonnay to her head, neither the wine nor she would have time to breathe before she no longer had need to breathe. He was going to kill her, of that he had little doubt, but much anticipation. She continued to babble on, unaware of her upcoming demise, her rush of works leaving her breathless, in a preview of what was to come. She hesitated a moment, when she saw his smile, not knowing that he was congratulating himself on planning her final, surprise birthday party. She thought instead that he agreed with her, and continued speaking.

"Death would be a surprise to her, but not to him. But it would need to wait, until after Ronnie. It was better that way," he concluded, drinking from the glass of mediocre cabernet. Its bland taste did not distract him from savoring the expectation of Joyce's death.

CHAPTER EIGHTEEN

The prostitute resided in the apartment of the building where she conducted her business. That was evident from the wonderful odors of Eastern European cooking that floated silently in from an adjoining room. A block off Bardstown road, Jackson reflected was not a terrible location for a new restaurant. But no, the lack of parking made it an impossible dream. Maybe. Maybe this or maybe that. It was useless suggesting ideas to adults who were beyond a certain age. He had learned that lesson years ago, one relearned again more often than he could count. Advice was not a suitable gift for either the donor or the recipient.

Jackson was following up on a clue. He would pay her for her time like any other customer, he might be able to expense it if she had information. The police had been able to track a phone call from Percheron to the prostitute.

"Oh him," she said upon see the photograph of the dead detective that Jackson held in one hand.

The young prostitute was not yet resigned to her career. She tolerated it and brought to it all of her raw acting ability. She was still young enough to have other choices, what they were he had no idea. Jackson envisioned again a successful restaurant.

"How old was she?" he wondered. "Late twenties, but the doors were closing rapidly."

He surmised from her current situation that it been a series of poor choices, but had she been presented with any good ones?

"Yes, I remember him."

"What did he want?" Jackson asked, his voice neutral.

"The usual", she replied, letting the awkwardness build before adding, "for a detective. He wanted information. He paid as well. Your mothers raised you well. Not like mine."

"Uh huh", Jackson hummed noncommittally.

"Mine was a complete waste of motherhood. That's why I won't ever have a kid of my own."

Jackson nodded.

"Don't worry Sweetie, I'm not wasting your time, or your money, with my bitching about my childhood and my mother. I hadn't thought of her for a long time until he," tapping the photo with an index finger whose nail was in need of a polish touch up, "brought her up."

"Your mother?"

"Yeah, your detective, I forget his name, sweetie works for most men that I see, women too," she added with a wink and a fleeting smile, both of which had more sadness than mirth in them.

Jackson decided to stay silent, in this instance "Sweetie" was as good a name as any. This woman before him, she too could go by the same name, and he began to think of her as Sweetie.

"He wanted information, contact information really, on my mother," the newly christened Sweetie was saying.

"He was open about it, something to do with an old murder case from years and years ago. You know, we don't talk much in this business, to cops or to other clients, it doesn't do anyone any good, but with him it was different."

"How so? Was he special?"

Sweetie laughed, the humor genuine this time.

"No one is special, Sweetie. But with him, I saw a chance to treat my mother as bad as she had treated me. I was disappointed that he wasn't looking for her as the murderer. All I knew was that she was living with some guy or another in Ohio, but that was ten years ago, maybe longer. She could be dead now, or living upstairs. It doesn't matter to me, as long as I don't have to see her. I can see that you don't care about this."

"Did the detective mention any details about the case?"

"More than I remember. It was about some young girl murdered when my mother was a teenager. Once I realized that she was not going to suffer from it, I lost interest. And, yeah, one more thing, he mentioned some guy's name, Moses, or something like that."

During their brief conversation, Jackson had seen three or four messages appear on the witness's phone. Their own encounter was over, they both had other work to do. As Jackson stood to leave, the woman approached, gave him a peck on the cheek and said,

"Thanks Sweetie."

Jackson walked backed to Bardstown road, and stepped into a pub to review his notes.

He ordered a coke from the bartender.

Youthful drinkers arrived and departed like bees, threading their way to the bar and back to their seats, laden with a less viscous form of honey. There was a pause in the male dominated conversation.

That meant one of two things, either a fight was on the verge of erupting, or the arrival of an attractive woman. Good, it was the latter.

Jackson regarded each of these unknown faces, seeking to determine which if any were his designated replacement on the planet. But he would not be replaced today, not voluntarily. Jackson didn't drink, it did nothing for the talented but transform them into a melancholic, workaholic, alcoholics. Life was too long to settle for any of those buckets.

Despite these young adults rushing into middle age, Jackson believed that children grew up too slowly in the West, their parents do them no favor in trying to be kind. Jackson thought again of Sweetie. She was the exception that proved the rule. She had not been ruined by kindness

CHAPTER NINETEEN

The Monday evening before Derby was free of football. Templeton thanked the God that he'd never believed in for this small mercy. Templeton had seen some of this football virtual reality. He had seen grown men not in the least embarrassed to play this fantasy football in bars like overgrown six year olds. On their deathbed, they'll see someone else's life flash before them. It won't be a series of selfies, and it will add a final pathetic period to their pseudo existence.

He recognized purveyors of addiction when he saw one. They reminded him of the people who ran the prison libraries, no, not the trustees, but the do-gooders on the outside. They too offered a form of virtual reality. They called it education, culture, but it was all fantasy. The real world was not something you could absorb at your own pace. That was a fiction. It arrived as a flood. Taken at the flood, he remembered that for some unknown reason. Life was not controllable. "Where was he? He should take notes, he told himself for the umpteenth time. Notes for what? For nothing."

He found it more and more difficult to make decisions, however minor. He reflected on a pulp novel that he had read as a teenager, *Such Men Are Dangerous* , by Louis Block. When in doubt, do nothing, had been the motto of the protagonist, one that the, character struggled to uphold. Templeton had liked the concept, but had found the advice impossible to follow. Not even now, when was so tired. He had seen a copy of it on a shelf in Ronnie's home, when he had peered through the windows. What other books had he seen? It didn't matter. Where was this leading to? He had been thinking about his mother. Was the craziness of teenage years the first occurrence of dementia? Did it hibernate for decades and then erupt again later, like Shingles

At these times, he felt thankful for the cancer. His body and his mind were in a race to die first. Templeton had placed his bet on the lung cancer, it was more painful than his dying brain, but it could run like the wind that he no longer had. Templeton was not remorseful. He hated reliving history, his own included. If forgiveness was needed, he would grant it to himself. He needed no intermediary's, neither a human nor a deity. "He might be evil, but he wasn't bad," Templeton told himself.

"Virtual reality, another bad idea. Give him real life anytime, or at least for a little more time."

CHAPTER TWENTY

The man next to Cassie at the Heine Brothers' coffee shop on Gardiner lane was lonely for conversation.

"A third death likely a suicide, it looks like another opioid overdose. The police chalk those up as suicides without more than a glance. They blame the deceased, never considering the possibility that they were a victim."

Ertras smiled politely and began, "Statistics," but the less polite stranger cut her off.

"I know all about statistics."

Ertras doubted that, but she listened as he went on unhurriedly.

"I know about black swans and outliers, and standard deviation. I understand how organizations, the police included, work. They excel at mediocrity."

"Hmmm," Ertras responded, noncommittal.

"They treat most cases as the ones before."

"It's called method and procedure," Ertras said, instantly regretting extending this conversation.

"I call it laziness." The stranger looked directly at Ertras, "You may be right this time, maybe it was a self-inflicted overdose. But the big case, this Percheron one."

"I've heard about it."

"It's interesting, there is some much fake news about true stories, it is strangely refreshing to see the opposite."

"What do you mean?"

"They write about what supposedly happened at Cave Hill as if they had the facts."

"I think that the facts are clear, the police seem to have provided many details."

"Except the most important fact. I doubt that they are even aware of it. Black swans, young lady, black swans."

"I didn't see, I didn't read about any swans, black or white, being seen at Cave Hill."

She had heard that there had been swans there once, but that they had died due to some poisonous snail or clam in the cemetery's ponds.

"Black swans," he repeated. "There was no murder, it was all faked."

"Another crazy," she thought. "Or maybe just broken in some way. It was time to leave. They were everywhere, what had happened to normalcy."

CHAPTER TWENTY ONE

It was the Friday morning after Derby, and Detectives Ertras and Jackson were in her office, each reading a copy of Perch's report on the Pregel murder. They had found nothing new in it, and were discussing the section on Percheron's trip to Rose Hill, Pennsylvania. This portion of the report was more in the form of a short story, instead of the dry formal style that comprised most of the file.

"This is the most unusual police report that I have ever read," Jackson exclaimed, and across her desk, Ertras nodded in agreement. They stared at the words on their respective copies.

"There was no benefit to this trip," Perch had begun. "Rose Hill was full of people who placed all trust in a black swan event, the second coming, winning the lottery. Between these and the disbelievers, we expect wholeheartedly and simultaneously deny the existence of these life changing events. In this case, I returned empty handed. There was no black swan for me in Rose Hill."

"Where had she heard that term before?" Ertras wondered.

"I got to hear music from Moliere in a country farmhouse, it was well played. That was the least strange part of the trip.

Voodoo never caught on in Louisville, but since there was a relationship between a timber company in Pennsylvania and a wood product company in town, we came up with an idea.

Out of desperation, we ran a story in the Courier, actually I let it slip accidentally on purpose over a beer at R Place that we had done a remote reading with a psychic in a small village in rural Pennsylvania. The story garnered some good, short term publicity, and dozens of calls. These calls generated several leads, but none that led anywhere, neither from the callers nor from the psychic.

One of the callers even suggested that we needed to see the medium in person and we thought sure, that would be optimal but we didn't have any budget category for crystal ball consultation.

Without hesitation the caller, I'm not disclosing her name here, says that she will pay all expenses, she doesn't want anything in return, not a mention or a photo in the paper, no credit, nothing. But there is one condition, we must do this before Halloween. It was weird.

The sponsor of this expedition was a French expat who is convinced that Halloween is the time of best reception in the spirit world. I think that she just needed to make arrangements as the two best psychics in the town, Rose Hill, had both died in mysterious circumstances a few months previously.

It was strange enough that I was optimistic that it would lead somewhere.

I don't believe in the occult, but I was convinced that the bizarreness of the story would push a reluctant witness or even the perpetrator to come forward. The media spotlight can overwhelm people's reticence."

"Perch certainly knew people", Jackson commented.

"Rose Hill was very picturesque, sitting on the bank of a lake in central Pennsylvania. It had the feel of an upscale, camping village or retirement community. The small, cute, colorful cottages reminded me of the attorneys' offices in Pikeville.

The village was recovering from the death of several local residents who had died in bizarre circumstances. Two of the dead, a middle aged man and his twenty some daughter had been French nationals."

"That's odd," Ertras exclaimed.

"According to several psychics that I had spoken with, I had arrived in Rose Hill at the worst possible time. It would be impossible to assist him due to what was referred to as "mystic turbulence.""

"Figures," Jackson snorted.

"They stuck to what might have been the truth. A freak accident had killed two inhabitants of the Pennsylvania village, followed by the suicide of the girlfriend of the male victim. Apparently all of that had caused such a disturbance that the local psychics were unable to aid me with my investigation of the Kentucky killing. It was odd that both the FBI and Interpol had arrived in the village a few days before the deaths and had left almost immediately afterwards. There was talk of various romances among the victims and other inhabitants, but there is always talk like that after the fact. None of it was of my concern, and none of it furthered my search for answers in the killing of Sherry Pregel."

"It sounds like an interesting place," Jackson said.

"Seriously?" Ertras asked.

"Sure. Who knows?" her colleague replied.

They returned to the past.

"I remained a few more days, hoping that this spiritual storm would pass. In the interim, I discussed the Pregel case with local law enforcement, the sheriff of Rose Hill, who showed only a polite interest in the murder in Louisville. Nothing came of those discussions. To pass time, I attempted to engage the sheriff in what had happened locally, to no avail. Despite his admission that he spoke French and knew all of the victims, he declined to reveal any information on the deaths in Rose Hill other than what was in the official report.

He said that although we were both law enforcement, I was a stranger who would soon be gone, and as such, I didn't merit the effort of a freshly baked lie. I dropped that topic so as to not antagonize him.

The sheriff's son took me on a tour of the local attractions, which mostly consisted of a great number of large trees, and information on local tree spirits, of which Buck was a devotee if not some sort of high priest.

Apparently, these creatures were not affected by the events in town.

I even suggested that I had seen a wood spirit in a campfire one evening in an attempt to get info from Buck, but he was as reserved as his father.

Upon my return to Louisville, I stated that the trip had been useful and that we were pursuing several significant tips. But I had nothing. I kept that to myself."

"It's interesting to see his frustration, it makes mine more manageable," Jackson said seriously.

"The story ran in the local media, it even made some noise on the national scene," Perch's words continued.

"This was years before the Internet, amazing," Jackson said.

"Again we received many calls and leads, all of them adding up to zero."

Ertras smiled humorously and thought of an evening long ago.

"Police work is not for the timid," Perch had claimed one Wednesday evening after she had attempted karaoke at Check's. The next contestant had sideburns that ascended to where gravity

161

took over, and his head remained bare above his ears, the delineation as clear as an alpine tree-line.

"Why do men do that?" she asked. "Don't they ever see photos of themselves? I remember an old game, old even for my friends' parents. It was a board game with a bald man and magnetic hair."

"What are you talking about?"

"I don't have a clue," she answered.

Percheron filled in the gap in her memory, "Wooly Willy. That was the game. My mind is reduced to worthless trivial pursuit."

"Trivial pursuit is tomorrow."

"With the technology, policing is just not as much fun as it used to be"

"Is that how you envisioned police work, as sport? How did you ever last?"

"You have it backwards. If I didn't envision it as sport, I would not have lasted as long as I did, Castor."

"Perch really cared."

The voice of Jackson brought Ertras back to the present.

"Cas, sometimes I try to convince myself that I gave up caring about the typical victim years ago. It's like a doctor stitching up a drunk, it's just a job, a task that the patient could have avoided by behaving responsibly. If the jury knew the victim, there is a good chance that they would acquit the killer. They really need to filter out these, these modern duels, from the system. You know, the Kentucky oath of office requires that the office holder agree not to participate in any duel. In my opinion that means that it's legal for everyone else."

"We should bring back duels?"

"They never went away, they just went underground. They'd certainly make for less wastes of police and court time. It would also be better television than this constant sports garbage that we are fed."

Their debate was interrupted by a knock on the door jamb of the open office.

"There is someone here to see you, Detective Ertras. His name is Roger Walsh, and he claims to be a longtime neighbor of Detective Percheron."

"I had another friend die last month," Roger Walsh began.

"It was a freak accident, unusual enough that murder was considered, but your team quickly eliminated that as a possibility. And now after what happened to Perch, well, you know."

He was an elderly man, likely ancient in the eyes of Jackson, who was taking French lessons at the AFL with his granddaughter.

"I believed that we could do something that was equally challenging for the both of us. Boy, was I wrong. The lessons are so much easier for her. I should have suggested skydiving," eliciting a raised eyebrow from Ertras, but he was not serious.

"Gravity is the same for the young and the old," he joked, "but her parents would not have approved.

I see from your expression that you listened to what I had to say. I'm often discounted, neither seen nor heard. Thank you for not millenialling me. That's French for being elsewhere when I'm speaking to you. Anyway, we enjoy it, Perch suggested it to me, and"

Ertras said nothing, she sat patiently and waited. It would come.

"And now, I just don't know. You spend your life helping others, and once you are dead they bundle all the concern that you've shown others, well, they bundle it all in an oblong box and bury it in the ground, out of sight, like toxic waste."

Ertras saw that Walsh could have been referring to a future him, and not just Perch.

"He was one of the good ones," he said vehemently, leaving no room for disagreement.

Ertras regarded the elderly man again, but this time as if he had just entered the room. He was in the old man uniform, which to him was normal attire. Ball cap, a striped, short-sleeve collared shirt, imperfectly pressed. Walsh no longer had clothes laundered. He wore high waisted, relaxed fit jeans, these latter held in place by a brown basket weave belt once fashionable, but now considered out of date. The entire effect was ruined by the smart phone projecting from one of his pants' rear pockets. His granddaughter must have showed him that method. It was a look adopted by every American female under thirty years of age. "It didn't work," Ertras thought, "I'm surprised that Perch didn't tell him that it looked ridiculous. Maybe the phone was new, acquired since the murder."

Life goes on. That was the gist of this old man's anger. It wasn't anger, it was closer to sadness, with a dash of bitterness.

"Were you his closest friend, Mr. Walsh?"

"His closest friend? As in his best friend?"

"However you want to think of it".

"No, I don't think so". He thought a few seconds longer, then added in a regretful voice, "But he was mine." After another moment of reflection, the man who had lost his friend continued.

"I'm not really sure that Perch had friends, it seems that friendship went from him to others, and didn't make a return trip. That sounds idiotic, I suppose. You know, maybe he just didn't need any friends."

Ertras reflected on her own memories of Perch and admitted that the old man was more correct than he imagined.

"Perch had his work, and his friends, so to speak, for when murder was in the doldrums."

"Life was a diversion from death," Ertras stated, expecting no answer.

"You could say that," the man said nevertheless. "It sounds cold, however you put it."

"Tell me more about your conversations."

"That week?'

"Yes, that one. Yes. But any other conversations that you think might be relevant."

"Recently?"

"Recent or not recent. Again, I'm interested in whatever you remember that you think might be relevant. It doesn't have to be important, only relevant."

"With both of us being retired, we could keep some strange hours, but not being young and stupid, we didn't. I should say that I didn't, maybe Perch did, but I don't think so."

"And your wife?" Ertras asked, noticing the ornate wedding band on Walsh's left hand.

"I'm a widower, but I still wear my ring. I'm old fashioned that way, too. It's been a few days more than a year now, she died right after Derby, last year.. It's probably time to stop wearing this now."

He made a motion to remove it, and then changed his mind, probably thinking that it was an action to take in private.

"I'm sorry to hear that," she said. "Was your wife a local girl?"

"Yes, born and raised. I went to the cemetery the Monday after Derby, this Derby, it was back to normal, aside from some of the police tape. It was quiet".

"Your wife is buried at Cave Hill?" Ertras asked, keeping her voice calm. This might be a lead, or just another coincidence in a case that overflowed with them.

"Yes, along with other members of her family. I moved here after college, that was when I met the woman who became my wife."

"I see."

"I met Perch several times over the years, but I didn't really know him, we were both working until recently, it was only after he retired that we started spending any time together. It had been a bit awkward when my wife was alive."

"Oh? Why as that?"

"She knew Ronnie slightly from when they were kids. Well you see, my wife's maiden name was Templeton," the old man said hesitantly, searching Ertras' face for a negative reaction, but found there only mild surprise. Ertras had learned years before that life occurred in a small fish bowl for many people, at their essence they remained villagers. It was as true for Perch as it was for this man, and for herself, Ertras realized.

"Was your late wife related to Mosgrove Templeton?" Ertras asked, not wanting to assume more than what had been only implied. But she was not surprised when he confirmed her suspicion.

"Yes she was his cousin, second cousin, or third. I'm not sure exactly."

So now she had this man, the self-described not the best friend of the victim, before her. A man who was aware of the comings and goings and the schedule of Percheron, and who was

165

the widower of the prime suspect's cousin. First, second, or third, that made no difference.

"It's a small world, Ms. Ertras", the old man added. He had been retired long enough to drop formalities and the use of titles. "But she was nothing like him."

There was no need to mention the name of him aloud, the name that was at the forefront in both of their minds. Roger Walsh had arrived unannounced, like an unexpected royalty check. Ertras had welcomed him as someone who could be a key witness, but who had in the space of a few sentences, transformed himself into a possible suspect. The balance between witnesses and suspects was tipping more and more to the wrong side. Louisville was sometimes just too small, it was a village, a nightmare for a policeman. She had never felt more of an outsider than she did right now. Family and school ties were the language and currency of this place, this foreign land, and while she might speak the local dialect, it was with the mental accent of an immigrant.

"Perch was focused, dedicated," he said in praise.

"Intense?", Ertras proposed.

"Absolutely", the witness replied. "It could be, oh I don't know, wearisome. This", he paused, searching for the appropriate word, and failing, fell back on "intense. As you said. It was great, exciting, but only in small amounts. When he wasn't on."

"On what?" Jackson interjected. The old man had forgotten the presence of the second detective and was startled at the new voice.

"On himself. I mean when he was able to relax and become someone other than a detective."

"When he could escape?" Ertras asked, without thinking.

Walsh agreed instantly and emphatically "Yes that is it exactly, when he could escape."

"Can you tell us about your last conversation with Perch?" Jackson requested.

"We were talking in my yard, Perch would walk the neighborhood and stop to chat. I noticed that he was hoarse.

Walsh described the conversation in detail.

""Allergies", Perch responded.

"Allergies? Since when?"

"I'm seeing a doctor in a few days for a colonoscopy."

"That is the wrong end, Perch", I said.

"Yeah, maybe. But listen, I am done bitching."

"That's a first, Perch."

"In fact, I'm moving."

"You've moving? Where? I noticed the for sale sign, but didn't want to pry."

Perch ignored those questions as he had my joke of a moment ago.

"I've already told the girlfriend.'

"You'd better move soon, before she retaliates."''

Back with them in Ertras' office, Walsh asked them, "Do you think that she did? Retaliate that is?"

Jackson had ignored the question, like Perch had done a week ago, and instead posed it back to Walsh.

"Do you?"

"No" followed by a confused "maybe" was his response.

"What did you mean earlier when you suggested that Perch liked to complain, to bitch as you put it?"

It took a moment for Walsh to process the query, his mind was busy reviewing his entire history with Perch and his now aroused suspicions about the girlfriend.

"I was suggesting that he could find something new and exciting to replace his former career. I don't know, I hoped that maybe we could even find something together. He had found something by himself. I'm old enough to complain myself," Walsh said with a bitter chuckle.

"I'm disappointed."

"In Percheron?"

"No! Perch was a man of action. That sounds corny, I suppose," but Ertras would have described him using the same clichéd phrase. Jackson didn't understand Perch, Ertras realized. Maybe no one other than she did, and she might be overestimating her own knowledge of the man.

"I'm not a man of action", Walsh was saying. "I'm the one who bitches," He paused for such a long time that Ertras was on the verge of concluding the interview when he said,

"Disappointed with Perch? No, not at all. I'm disappointed and angry with myself, not him."

CHAPTER TWENTY TWO

Ertras woke as slowly as she could. Today would be a day for second tier and repeat witnesses. Cas had low expectations from either category. She had run these sorts of errands often enough to know from experience that it would be a long day. On the other hand, Jackson would enjoy seeing Jessica again.

The sunlight reflected from the thousands of leaves of fresh grass appeared as green diamonds extending across cemetery. Nearby, the intermittent hum of bees was a parallel to the thankfully absent sound of vehicle traffic. She had not hear the insects during her first visit to Cave Hill. Had they been resting that Sunday, or had they been frightened away by the presence of live humans?

The staff at Cave Hill was kind, yes that was the perfect word. Kindness was becoming passé, even here in Louisville, where politeness was natural as air. Like the rest of the country though, virtues were becoming vices to be avoided and kind was on the verge of switching to a metaphorical as well as a literal four letter word. Here in the cemetery the stone structures and tall surrounding walls delayed the invasion of modern sensibilities. The staff were funeral attendants without reprieve, faithful behind their ramparts and among them, kindness still reigned. For her, this too was a moment of rest among the eternally resting.
"We all need a moment in heaven, either here or there."
"Of heaven," her colleague corrected.
"I'll take my slice of heaven here and now, they may run out later."
Ertras stopped herself from nodding in silent agreement. "Sympathy was not available for her to dispense to just anyone, not to anyone at all," she admitted ruefully. She thought again of her life, and of her work, and attempted without success to think of one without the other. They weren't one and the same, no really they weren't. She had years, decades remaining and the luxury of money, now was the time. It was more than a waste, she was being given the opportunity to escape. It would be so easy, there was no outside force delaying her departure. She had seen all the parts of policing that were worth seeing.

"Why on Earth was she waiting? Whose permission did she need, Perch's?"

The answer was obvious now that she had posed herself the question. Perch had given his permission when he died.

"The cemetery closes as 4:30, 4:45. We sometimes stay open late around Derby, for private patrons. That day, we closed at the regular time, and just stayed to watch the race."

"What if someone was locked in?"

"We'd have left them out. But there wasn't anyone."

"And then you locked the gate?"

"Not exactly. We considered it closed, that was good enough. And we opened a bottle. We were going to get an hour or so of overtime, and we'd be paid to have a few drinks at the same time. It was our own private millionaires' row."

"So someone could have left, or entered and left, and you might not have noticed."

"I don't think so, but it is possible. You can see for yourself that we spot everything and everyone that comes and go."

"If you are watching.

"It's not as if we are TSA. The passengers here are dead."

"I'm glad that we did this second interview, Jackson. Some witnesses need time to ferment, to remember something that they had overlooked, or to decide to divulge information that they had withheld for some reason. Their testimony needs to age before I can swallow it."

"Like drinking at work?"

"Yes."

"At least that can't kill anybody on the job," he said unthinkingly.

"You know what I mean, Cas."

"Sure. I expected more of the local wannabes. They want to be famous, they should be coming to us by the truckload. These are the same people who are opposed to everything that we do, and doubly opposed to everything that we neglect to do. Sometimes we just need to wait, but I'm worried. It is too high profile, and after Derby is a slow news time. And the victim was a police officer."

"Between guilt and rewards, we will find the truth."

"I hope so. People have to confess and to feed their addictions. The old carrot and stick."

"I heard that our union and Cave Hill have both offered rewards."

"We know that Templeton was here on Derby, he admitted it. The guards noted his probable arrival."

"The guards noticed a big, old, fancy Cadillac arrive and leave about the same times that correspond to the times that Templeton claims for his coming and going."

"It appears that you were correct about him driving a Caddy," Ertras said in an attempt at levity. This case was depressing.

"We need to find that car," she continued, stating the obvious.

"We'll find it. But we will be damned if it belongs to Templeton and damned if it doesn't. Either it way it gives him an alibi."

"The guards don't recall seeing anyone else in the car. They can't even be sure if it was Templeton at the wheel. If he did this, his actions were incredibly bold, even careless."

"What was really heard by guard and others after Templeton passed through the gate? Was he driving fast enough to call it fleeing?"

"Not at all, he waved as he almost crawled by. If it was truly Templeton. We may be chasing some innocent octogenarian who stopped by to visit family graves and who is now on our most wanted list. Hell, his car might be in a garage until next year. He might even be dead. We need to find that car."

"There is no car registered to Templeton."

"Check every 1970s Cadillac registered in Kentucky in the past ten years, concentrate on Jefferson and Oldham, and Bullitt counties"

Jackson made a note.

"Whoever was driving had to have stopped at Baxter Avenue."

"And?"

"I don't know Jackson. Maybe someone in one of the bars nearby noticed the car. I know, it's a long shot."

"Cas, what was not heard before the Cadillac left the cemetery grounds? It is easy enough to muffle a gunshot, they probably discuss topics like that every Wednesday in prison classes."

"Maybe. But Templeton no longer cares. He is dying. You've heard him speak. He claims that it was suicide made to look like murder. He bragged in prison about doing that very thing, murder made to appear to be suicide. He knows better than to tell the truth to anyone, let alone to fellow convicts. Is it murder, made to look like suicide, made to look like murder? He is smart, you've seen his file."

"Once we arrest him, Templeton won't make bail, he has no money, no support outside of the internet kooks."

"If he were to be bailed, he will go after the governor."

"He already has."

"What? I hadn't heard that. When?"

"When Perch was executed."

"I don't follow you."

"If Templeton pleads guilty, that destroys the Governor's reelection."

"If Templeton claims innocence, and there is a lengthy trial, it's just about at bad for the Governor, maybe even worse."

"I don't understand all of the intricacies and political ramifications that might happen."

"The best thing for your boss"

"The governor is not by boss."

"Close enough. The best thing for him is for us to either find the other, the true killer, or declare it some elaborate suicide by Perch."

"That's crazy."

"I agree. But that is the politics of it."

"So the man who freed Templeton now needs Templeton to be innocent of the very murder that he, Templeton, bragged he was going to commit. The governor looks more and more like an accomplice before and after the fact."

"I sure as heck won't be voting for him."

"You never vote. You told me that you aren't even registered."

"I may register just to not to vote for him."

"Templeton can claim suicide, self-defense, little green men in flying saucers, but none of that fits the evidence. The bullets that killed Perch came from a gun in Templeton's possession and he tested positive for gunshot residue within forty-eight hours of the murder."

"You make it sound cut and dried."

"It is."

They never are, you know that. How many murders don't have some unexplainable inconsistencies, things that don't fit?"

"I know. Zero. But this case"

"Has plenty of holes. Such as, we don't have the gun, we can't even show that it was in Templeton's possession. The gunshot residue test could have been triggered by a number of things, some of which are in Templeton's residence. The evidence needs to be perfect."

"As you just said, holes are normal. Enough to not indict, or to not convict?"

"Maybe both."

"Let's go through what we think that we know."

They reviewed the evidence again, again without conclusion.

"Templeton wasn't good at the beginning, he was just lucky with his first murder. The weather was bad, witnesses were drunk. He was caught and convicted of other crimes. He was never good at his chosen profession. And now that he is old, sick, and dying, he has become a master criminal? I don't believe it. He made a mistake somewhere."

"His entire life has been a mistake."

The Cave Hill docent dressed the part of story guide, with his worn, broad brimmed hat, and his walking stick which was at once both spiraled and straight and topped with an unnumbered yellow billiard ball. The ball and staff served as both grip and defense against whatever dangers the celebrated cemetery might contain. The docent reminded Ertras of Father Time, who if not still in his prime was near enough to it to be interesting.

He had been with Jessica Villier when she discovered the body. As a teenager, she had appeared in amateur French plays at both the Alliance Française and the theater in Oldham County.

"More and more coincidences. I hate them," Cas complained to herself. They are like confident but dead witnesses for the defense, hard to discount, and impossible to completely refute.

"Given the recent murder, this staff provides protection against what up to now were only illusory threats, Detective. The residents who slumber in one of the few 19th century mausoleums, or who lay ensconced six feet below are no longer concerned about their safety. I'm sorry to hear that your friend is now among them."

"Yes, so am I.". Ertras hesitated, then confessed, "You seem to be from another era."

The docent smiled and laughed easily.

"Perhaps I am. I conduct many of the tours here, and seeing the end makes me appreciate the middle."

"Which sorts of tours?"

"Oh, famous people, artists, poets. Keat's brother lived here, he is still here," he said without hidden meaning. "And Madison Cawein, he is credited with *Wasteland*."

Ertras nodded her head, in the way that the docent had come to recognize as complete ignorance of the Louisville native.

"Tourists visit their graves. Few people today visit the tombs of their own ancestors. It was satisfying to see that Jessica Villier is an exception."

"I imagine so."

"Nowadays the dead are best quickly forgotten, the Great War expression, 'Lest we forget', overtaken by the more practical, lest we remember."

"When did that change take place?" Ertras asked, saddened by the turn this conversation had taken.

Instead of answering, the docent directed the discussion back to the matter at hand. He suggested that Ertras talk again to the staff, "they are here much more than I am."

"My hairdresser has heard it all", said the female guard, "at least twice. People come and go here, Detective Ertras. We don't have infrared, we are not looking for people breaking in. We have periodic issues with kids, but they are unstoppable."

"Let me ask you about the shots that you heard after the Cadillac left. How often do you hear sounds like that, could you really have heard them from here?"

"Yes the sounds were after the Cadillac left, at least fifteen minutes. They sounded like gunshots to me. That is really all I can say."

Ertras took her statement at face value. If the sounds she heard were shots, then Templeton was innocent. If not, if the guard heard, or missed, other sounds, earlier sounds that were gunshots as well, then it all fit. All they needed was the Cadillac and the gun.

"Did you hear any other sounds like those gunshots earlier, say within 30 minutes of the Cadillac leaving?"

"No, absolutely not."

That was absolutely not what Ertras wanted to hear.

"Tell me more about Cave Hill" Ertras requested, hoping for something, anything.

"Like what?"

"About your job, the visitors, the graves, whatever you like."

"Well, I don't have any strange stories, and that can be disappointing. We have a docent to do tours and such. Most visitors, and I mean tourists, want to hear of ghosts and visions, not to be frightened, but comforted."

"Comforted?"

"Yes they want to believe in the supernatural. But with our lack of sightings, they expect that we are here so often, that we would be in the know. Where was I?"

"The lack of ghostly sightings."

"Oh yes, us not seeing phantoms frightens them more than if we had. Most people are afraid of nothing than they are of something, even hell. If you ask me."

"I am."

"I've been tempted to make up a few believable hauntings but that would compete with our tours."

"Tours?"

"The ghost tours that we offer here. They aren't very good, but the public demands it. I should not have said that the tours aren't very good. Please don't put that in your notes, I'm just being honest," she requested meekly.

Ertras smiled and made a show of scratching out a line in her notebook.

"We do have hoaxes from time to time, a few occultists who are immature kids, regardless of their actual age. Most of what I see here is private grief, solitary sorrow. Is that what Percheron was doing here? No, that's stupid of me. According to what I heard, you think that he was brought here Derby afternoon, alive, and then murdered?"

"Yes. Do you think otherwise? You were working here at the time."

"Yes, I was working. Watching the races, to be honest about it. We don't have regular rounds, well we do of course, but it's not every hour, especially during"

"During Derby?"

"During the day. Visitors are generally well behaved during the day."

"Not this time," Ertras interrupted. Don't interrupt she commanded herself silently.

"No, I guess not."

"Still, it could be good thing."

"In what possible way could my friend being shot to death in your cemetery be good?"

Ertras again cursed herself. Her outburst was not helping.

"Sorry. I didn't know that he was your friend."

Ertras gazed around the small office until her flare of anger cooled.

"No, there is no reason that you would know that. What did you mean about it being a good thing? Don't worry, I asked you the question and I would like to know your thoughts."

The guard was hesitant, she was not used to be questioned by police, especially not by angry ones.

"No, not really good, but"

"But what?"

"Well, if he was actually killed here, a former homicide investigator, 'the' homicide investigator according to Facebook. Anyway it could help the tourists get what they want. I could come up with a sighting now and again. It would keep his memory alive, and if you don't catch his killer," the guard's voice trailed off.

"What makes you say that? Of course we will catch whoever did this."

"Well the way that Facebooks says that he was 'the' homicide investigator, I naturally figured that you would have a problem solving the case." She paused, not sure if she should continue. Ertras returned the guards gaze.

"Please, continue," she said encouragingly.

"With him not around to solve it for you. If you see what I mean."

"Go on."

"So if you don't solve it, but you will, just like you promised, well, just like you said, it could attract publicity and visitors, and the sightings of his ghost could provide comfort to people, people in general. He might even," again the guard paused, attentive to either anger or encouragement.

'He might even what?' Ertras requested, her voice adjusted to pleasant.

"He, his ghost"

"The ghost that you are going to see soon?"

"Might even give you some clues, help direct you, your efforts. He might even solve it for you. If you see what I mean."

CHAPTER TWENTY THREE

Melissa and Joyce met to talk. It was the Tuesday before Derby.

"It's over with Ronnie."

"You and Perch are through?"

"I'm afraid so. He broke it off, he said it was the honorable thing to tell me in person."

"Honor? Don't be an idiot. Honor is the male version of romantic love, survivors outgrow it. And now you're thinking of leaving Louisville? Do you want to abandon all of the connections that you have here?"

"Maybe. I don't know what I want."

"A change. The big change. I've heard that before. Let me tell you, Melissa, the big change is a big letdown. It isn't like in the movies, if it were, they wouldn't make movies about it. The big change doesn't exist."

"Ronnie was so Ronnie. He was so calm, while I sat there repressing my urge to move and smack something. I told him that men complain about women and our emotions, don't even mention menopause. I told him that men are that way for decades in their own version of crazy. I've come to understand that it is their strength and their weakness, Joyce. I told Ronnie that he was just too damned too emotional, never satisfied, constantly searching. And that it made him look foolish."

"What did he say?"

"He wanted something different."

"Different," Joyce echoed.

""Dye your hair," I suggested. He thought that I was kidding, that I was being, oh what word did he use?"

"Flippant?" Joyce offered.

"Yes, flippant. See how men think alike, Melissa said, "They know the big words, but don't understand English".

"Not even Perch?" Joyce asked, genuinely curious.

"Ronnie is better than most. If I had advised him to buy a motorcycle and drive around the entire country, that would have struck him as more reasonable than spending fifty bucks at a salon. Well maybe not Ronnie, but what I've just said would apply to most men that I've known."

Joyce had survived but not yet prospered, 'yet' being the lottery ticket on which she wagered constantly. Her current relationship was too normal. It was doomed to successful unhappiness. Both she and Melissa and Joyce had dated police officers who had made detective, they were supposedly more cerebral. Joyce had kept the most recent one a secret.

"But they still think as men do, not at all," they said simultaneously, giggling from the strong Australian wine.

Joyce was not fond of the sound of Joyce Jackson, she would become a JJ, but it was not only the prospective nickname that made her noncommittal in the relationship. She also perceived that Jackson was losing interest by the week. It was time for her to move on. If not, he would.

Their respective careers of nurse and cop made them a cliché. She had been attracted immediately to him. He was a nice, handsome, ambitious man. She saw the ambition growing in her short term but soon to be ex-boyfriend. The ambition had outpaced their couple-hood. She wished him well, and in doing so accepted they she was saying goodbye. It was probably due to Derby, it gave Louisville an exaggerated sense of its own importance, and that had worn off on Jackson. Who knew where it would end? Post Derby there was a sense of fatigue and disappointment once the celebrities and the spotlight that accompanied them departed as quickly as they had arrived. And what about Jackson? Oh, he would still be in the local spotlight but it was not as brilliant as those that had shone when the national press was in town. Life had become a derivative of itself. Sports had replaced sports activity and now they are being replaced by fantasy sports. At least Jackson wasn't into that.

"Why do grown men jump up and down when they see someone throw a ball, and another one catches it? My grandmother can do that.

What was that old phrase my granddad liked to use, 'once they've seen Paris it's hard to go back to the farm.'"

Once Paris and Dubai and Hollywood landed in Louisville, surrounded by the intoxicating fragrance of money, power, and sophistication, it changed the locals who had direct exposure to it. Jackson had the luck and the misfortune to be one of those infected. He was too easily tempted, she understood that minutes into there was first date. Jackson was not Perch, whom she had met several times at Melissa's. No, that one had been immune from temptation.

"For the most part," she told herself, "everyone wants a bite of the apple at some point."

Returning to her analysis of Jackson, "what did she think of him? More importantly, why was she still thinking about him?"

He was too normal, even for Louisville where the unofficial motto of 'keep Louisville weird', only served to highlight its normalcy. Joyce valued normalcy, excitement brought its own share of scars and hangovers. The few weeks of Derby were enough weirdness for her, it was like an extended Halloween or a pleasant staycation where you were able to sample tastes and activities that were usually overlooked.

Joyce wanted more than perfection. Perch had been perfect for Melissa, but that had come to nothing, and now it looked like it never would. Jackson might very well be more than perfect, yet she knew intuitively that Jackson did not share that opinion about her. It was over, she would pass on the traditional breakup dinner, it was a waste of courtesy.

Melissa had had hers. Hearing about it secondhand had been enough anguish for a while. She and Jackson had been together long enough for it to be appropriate. It hadn't worked for Melissa, from what she surmised it had been unpleasant. Perfect to the last is too much to bear. The breakup scene is overrated as much in movies and is real life. She'd text Jackson tomorrow.

CHAPTER TWENTY FOUR

Mrs. Villier claimed that Jessica had left for California. Upon learning that she and Jackson were with the police, the mother apologized

"Oh, please come in. I thought that you two were more reporters. I'll go ask Jessica to come down."

While awaiting the actress's entrance, Ertras reviewed the mass of photographs on the wall and on the mantle. It was the typical selection of multi-generational images found in millions of homes. A few of the photos included Perch. The same trace of dust on the frames left by their housekeeper indicated that those photographs had not been placed there recently, simply for Ertras' benefit.

"Jessica didn't know that you were stopping by," she told herself mentally in an attempt to ratchet down her out of control suspicions.

The wall devoted to Jessica contained only professionally taken images, and these frames were free of dust. "That was the mother's shrine," Ertras concluded.

"Did Ertras' own image merit such an honored place in her parent's home? Probably not," she decided, swiveling to face the actress who had just entered the room.

"What can I do for you, detectives?"

"We spoke to Terry at the Oldham County theatre. I was surprised that you went there, given your busy schedule," Ertras began.

"I make time for what is important to me."

"Why was it important?"

"I performed there a few times, it brought back pleasant memories."

"We were told that you asked about Perch, and old cases, and that you were interested in the prop room."

"Yes, that's all correct. Why do you ask?"

"That's my question, why did you ask? Its curious, given what has happened."

"Yes, it is. It was a coincidence."

"There was that hated word again," Ertras and Jackson both thought.

"I wanted to do more research, in case Perch decided to bail out on the project. It was too good of story not to go forward, with or without him."

"And now?" questioned Jackson.

"I don't know. It is still a story, more than a story. I'm part of it now."

"In what way?"

The actress chose to not answer the question.

"Visiting family graves has become a tradition for me. You probably weren't aware of that. I try to keep a few parts of my life private. I went back to before the beginning."

"Before what beginning?"

"It was something that Perch had suggested years ago. Thanks to him I discovered a grave in Portland Cemetery. A woman of the 19th century, a direct ancestor who was also a complete stranger. What would we have in common? Anything? Our world views would be completely different.

Anyway, few of the graves were visited, the most recent burial being that of a young girl decades earlier."

"It was funny in a not so funny way," Ertras thought. "There was so much extraneous death surrounding this murder. It had an excess of coincidences, close, almost incestuous relationships, and death before, during, and after. Should she expand the investigation to find the truth, or wrap it up as rapidly as possible, and ignore how ugly the finished package would be?"

"Stopping at that grave and others graves has become a tradition, you might say a good luck charm. I asked Perch if he wanted to join me there."

"Did he?"

"No. If the dead were not as unfamiliar to me as I once thought, the west end had become a foreign land to him. Only twenty miles distant, it was the other side of county, not the other side of the country. It was too far to drive, he said. Here he was planning a move to France and he was uncomfortable contemplating thirty minutes behind the wheel."

"France was only a secret to Melissa. Why was that?" Jackson wondered.

"Do you believe in charms and omens?" Jessica asked them earnestly, but this elicited no response. The actress was not used to her interlocutors forgetting their lines and less used to being ignored.

"Jackson," she said in her exquisite voice, bringing her captivating gaze to rest on the assistant detective.

"I'll take that as a no, unless you are too embarrassed to confess to an unpopular belief."

She moved slightly, and Jackson exhaled.

"Here I am, asking the police to confess."

She continued with her monologue.

"Many people trust in omens. And in spirits, too."

Ertras recalled Perch and his uncooperative spirits.

"I don't," Jessica continued.

The detectives were lost, trying to make sense of those words, when Jessica added, "Confessions. I don't believe in them, myself. I don't expect you to confess," she admitted, trying to bring humor to the odd conversation.

"Now Perch, he might well have had some faith in omens," Jessica said, her words shocking Ertras back to listening attentively to the words of the beautiful actress. Ertras needed to focus, but Jackson was not experiencing the same drift. From all indications, he was fixated on her, but it could have been her face that was the target of his concentration and not her words. It was claimed that the most beautiful women east of the Mississippi were in Kentucky. Jackson had embraced that particular dogma.

Jessica was still delivering her dialogue in a soft, measured tone.

"My parents told me that he had even visited a psychic or two somewhere up north. My parents would know where exactly."

"Really?" Ertras asked, bringing a nod to the head of the actress and raised eyebrows from her subordinate. Ertras had surprised herself. She wasn't sure why she hadn't just agreed and moved the conversation on. The fact that Jessica was aware of the Rose Hill visit was more impactful.

Aloud, Ertras commented, "That is interesting, it may be useful." Even to herself her words sounded nonsensical. Jessica was sticking with her own delivery.

"Anyway, ever since, I've paid my respects at several of the Louisville cemeteries, you know about Cave Hill," the mention of the place bringing sorrow to her expression. "But also Portland cemetery, as I've said. Who knows if it is a result of that, I'm not certain myself, but I was lucky enough to appear in several movies."

"But you are a big star, you're a huge success for Louisville," corrected Jackson

"Several good films, thanks," agreed Jessica.

"It may sound silly but I don't want to lose it. I like to try different ideas, new, maybe even controversial themes, but I do it the same way."

"Like a bakery," said Ertras, thinking of her parents' business. She noticed Jackson's curious expression.

"In a bakery, you may make a new cake or a new bread, but you follow the same process."

"Yes," Jessica confirmed. "I don't really care how or why it works," her voice accepting no disagreement, "but so far it has brought me good luck so I continue to follow it. It's my one ritual."

"I see." Jackson said.

"I visit the graves, this isn't being recorded, correct?" That had been one stipulation for the previous interview; Jessica controlled her image or there would be no meeting with the police, no in person questioning.

"What do you during these visits?" asked Jackson.

"We talk," and then added, "I talk. And I listen."

"What do you hear?"

"She hears what she wants to hear," Ertras answered Jackson's question silently. "What else would she hear? Jessica was no less human than the two of them."

"Feelings mostly. I hear, feel support or hesitation. Some of them have never seen a film."

"Some of who?" Ertras asked, knowing full well who Jessica meant. The interview was off track. Soon it would be the killer ghost of Cave Hill. With a sequel no doubt.

"My ancestors of course. It's not ghosts, detective, they have been dead for many years. It is," Jessica trailed off, unable to read the words of a nonexistent script.

"It's just a feeling."

Jackson spoke up suddenly, his voice too loud and high pitched to conceal his excitement.

"Do you think that we could combine the two?"

"There might not be an expense problem, you know how they scrutinize the budget. With Jessica's, I mean Ms. Villier's assistance, you know with travel and permission, and of course," adding ingredients to this unknown recipe as they popped into his head, "We would do this undercover."

Pausing to take only half a breath, he then pushed on.

"It would be a documentary, Jessica," he said, again ignoring formality. "Then if it works, or it doesn't, it could make a great scene. You know what I mean, Jessica, Ms. Villier," Jackson concluded as he surfaced for air.

"Jessica is fine, Jackson. I like that name, it is so trustworthy."

The actress was accustomed to stream of consciousness creativity, it was the native patois of Hollywood. She saw already the possibilities present in Jackson's inspiration.

"This was another omen, she must heed it," she told herself. It was as if the room lighting had switched from a steady yellow to a flashing crimson. It was a wonderful and welcome sign, delivered by police escort no less. "What could have been the worst of times," she told herself, a drop of guilt landing and evaporating in the interval of a single heartbeat.

"We can fly there in the next day or so, you can get approval later."

"Forgiveness," Jackson said, correcting Jessica's terminology.

"Yes," laughed Jessica, flirting with this newly discovered talent. "I can help with either or both."

Ertras had not followed this suddenly private dialogue. The actress and Ertras' energized assistant were reading from the pages of a script held only by them. Ertras hands fidgeted, as if attempting to materialize a copy of her own from the heat generated by her palms as she rubbed them to and fro. No revisions appeared in her grasp.

"What the hell are you talking about?" she finally demanded

Jessica rotated slowly to face the question and explained as if to a child, "Jackson suggests that we fly to this village up north, I think somewhere in Pennsylvania or upstate New York."

He and Jessica quickly explained their plan, each taking turns to describe it in detail.

"We go there, the three of us, maybe with a small film crew."

"The Lear can transport all of us."

'And we see if the psychics there can help us to solve Perch's murder. They might fill in some of our gaps. We might use some of the same psychics that Perch consulted years ago."

"That would be fantastic," exclaimed Jessica in a raised voice, before muttering dejectedly, "Yeah, but those psychics failed him."

"How do you know that?" Ertras interjected.

"It's obvious. Oh well," she continued, once again perky, "that would still be ok, the older psychic fails, she is losing her powers, but another younger one succeeds."

"Or they both fail, but you discover your own gift. It only required that you visit the village once and you solve the case."

"No one has solved anything," Ertras fumed.

"This guy was talented," Jessica thought.

"With the aid of your own deceased relatives," Jackson finished his sentence.

"You are wasted here—Jackson," Jessica cooed, pausing to recall the name of her new discovery.

"Either way it works," she squealed in delight while Ertras saw the death of a friend transition to whatever plot would attract more credulous movie patrons.

"You two are nuts," spoken by Ertras brought the hallucinations to an abrupt end. The two fantasists offered Ertras their best look of contrition and Jessica gave a wonderful interpretation of sincere regret, but Ertras resigned herself to the inevitable: this case would soon be out of control, if it wasn't there already.

"During these visits to the cemeteries, Ms. Villier, what do you say to the dead?"

"I tell them what I want to hear. They are dark mirrors that reflect only my image and my thoughts. They can do nothing but confirm my decisions. The dead have made us and in turn, we remake them. We make of the dead whatever we want, the irony is that the dead are not fixed in time, we can dress them in any sensibility that we like."

"What the hell is a sensibility?"

"A prejudice or opinion. We can transform an ogre into a saint or a saint into an ogre just by assigning them beliefs that they held or didn't hold during their life."

"More pity them," Ertras thought, disgusted with the direction of the discussion.

"You really are vampires, sucking the blood of others, and worse, injecting blood into the dead, forcing them to lead lives not their own, all for your benefit. You create an imaginary world and profit from it. It's clear now why you are so attracted to the supernatural angle."

She paused for breath.

"You don't care about solving a real murder, or even that a kind man that you knew as well as anyone in town is now dead. You disgust me," she said passionately, not caring herself that she was making an enemy of a powerful woman.

"Yes," confessed Jessica. No, it wasn't a confession. It struck Ertras that, far from shame, the actress' yes had been an acknowledgement of fact. Jessica was proud of her status as a vampire, and while she would have employed another word, something less ghoulish, she enjoyed her work and saw no need to apologize for her contributions.

Living vampires who prey on the dead, it's a reversal of roles. They construct their own reality and then sell the believable lies that they fabricated around it to a public who bought them.

"What did Perch do? When?" Cas wondered.

He acted similarly. Evidence was used to build an image of the murder scene. It was a set arranged for the climactic actions of one of the actors. He enjoyed it. He had more in common with Jessica, they both inhabited a world that was equal parts imagination, illusion and reality. Instead of planning a move east to Paris, he should have considered California where he could have played the same murder game on film. It necessitated only a change in the ratio between the real and the unreal. Jackson wanted to seize the opportunity that lay before him. It was tempting to toss all this work away for something more profitable and less emotionally draining.

"You should have headed west, Perch. Or east. It didn't matter now. You should have just left sooner. We'd have gone together," the thought arriving unbidden, but not totally unwelcome. He was a convenient escape, he didn't offer that to her now. It would not have worked in any case, there was no sustainable passion between them. Perch would have offered her a familiar face in an unfamiliar place, nothing more. That would have been enough, for a while.

The dead can no longer move, neither to the illusion across the Atlantic nor to the one bordering the Pacific. "But can the dead think? Do they have regrets?"

"This woman in the room across from her, this actress, perfectly coifed, with perfect diction and poise, she was dangerous. Her objective was delivering beautiful lies to as many uninformed people as possible, while hers was what exactly?" Ertras asked herself.

"Beautiful truth? That didn't exist." Ertras would settle for tolerable truth, pure truth was rare. "Truth without makeup is a poor contestant against gorgeous myths," Ertras acknowledged. She felt another premonition of defeat whip through her mind.

"Jessica was a witness and an improbable suspect but moreover she was a threat. Was this defeat? The investigation into the death of a good man churned into a circus?"

On her drive home, Ertras noticed the flag. She had grown accustomed to seeing flags flying at half-staff, but rarely was she aware of the latest horror responsible. The country was constantly at war against something. More and more often this something seemed to be itself. Was it this way during the real wars? She had no idea, she'd need to ask some friends whose family were longer term Americans. Today's war had no discernible victories. There was no visible, uniformed enemy, just demolished trucks, usually Toyota's for some odd reason, in a country of little importance. The wars had become play wars, except for the dead soldiers on both sides who shared the same fate of being as hidden away after death as they had been in life. She felt herself in their company.

CHAPTER TWENTY FIVE

The excitement of Derby was increasing on that beautiful spring day, three sunrises before the biggest sporting event in the state of Kentucky.

Certainly, they would help each other.

It was the old time village attitude they both understood implicitly, one with ties nearly as close as familial bonds. Community sense was relocating online, where it became wider, but not deeper, it spread like water across a frying pan, to evaporate at the first sign of high heat.

"This campaign to keep Louisville weird, what is wrong with just keeping it friendly. Friendly is more important than weird. It won't sell. To whom, weirdos? We have more than enough of those already, we don't need to import any more. We shouldn't even fertilize the ones that we have."

"You are one to talk, Grove," Melissa quipped.

"Let me give you some advice Grove," Melissa said.

"Does your advice involve compromise and settling?"

"It involves change and choices."

"All those words are synonyms for prison. I've learned to not take advice. As far as change, that can be for the better or for the worse. Why chance it?"

"Why was she expending this effort on Grove, did she really care about him?" wondered Melissa. She was simply trying to save a life. She happened to be the first one on the scene.

"You can revert to being clever and cynical tomorrow," Melissa said. "Today is reserved for kindness and courtesy."

"Kindness and courtesy are likely lying in shallow, adjoining graves."

"And hope?"

"She's been missing for a few years, from what I gather."

"You would know, Grove."

"Kindness is overrated because it is free."

"Everything in life is overrated, it comes with the territory."

"And here I thought that I had the monopoly on pouting."

"Everyone has regrets."

"You're wrong there, Melissa. My backpack of regrets is empty. I sewed the flap shut decades ago so that none could climb aboard and crawl in. You should do the same now, but first you need to empty yours, it is overflowing."

"Don't do anything that you will regret, not now, not at this late stage. As you said, my sack is full. So is my bag of injuries. I don't need another.

I had low expectations with Ronnie. They sank even further the longer that we dated. It's crushing to find out that your lover would rather do anything than make a life with you."

"He wanted to spare your feelings."

"He only made them pain more."

"Truth is worse than useless. Give me fantasy any day."

Melissa said nothing, it would have been a waste of breath to state the obvious, men and their fantasies, the fantasy of honest being one of the worst.

"Ronnie is too thoughtful."

"Too human?"

"That is the perfect description."

"People should be careful about being too human. It's bad for their health."

"Meaning what?"

"Don't be melodramatic, there is no hidden meaning."

"I didn't invite you here to be melancholy. How is the treatment going?"

"Finally, you picked a more pleasant subject. Pour me some more wine and I will regale you with my health."

The conversation shifted like a rivulet of sudden rainwater, running off to easier and less resistant topics, this one forgotten for a while.

"He had taken up birdwatching," volunteered Melissa a few minutes later.

"Had he?" asked Templeton, neither surprised nor unsurprised.

"He gave that up, like me. I guess that I wasn't special enough."

Melissa sometimes felt like an ivory billed woodpecker, alone in a deep wood, extinct to all the world but herself, crying for a response but hearing nothing in return, not even an echo.

She drank more wine. Bars, even home bars, are like confessionals with the occasional penance of a hangover.

"Your mother forgot that she hated Ronnie. She lived in her own twisted version of *Ground Hog Day*, bouncing somewhere in a fifty year span, landing on randomly colored days of her own internal roulette wheel. But the cycle didn't stop when she found happiness. Every day was different in its sadness. He was kind to her, Grove."

Templeton remembered a conversation that Ronnie had forced on him after the death of Sherry Pregel.

"Years ago, Melissa, Ronnie came back from some crazy trip to a psychic village, and tried to bluff me into a confession, using so-called information he had received from the 'other side'. I should have demanded that we talk at the police station and videotape everything. I could have made a bundle on that and put an end to both his career and his persecution of me. He talked about some lumberjack who spoke to tree spirits. Here in Kentucky, I told Ronnie, our best spirits come not from a tree, but from a grass, good old corn. Maybe the lumberjack was enjoying too much of our spirits when he began hearing from his own. Yeah, that was a missed opportunity. But I was kind to him, Melissa."

"I see."

"You want to have both Eden and the apple. Broken promises are not my fault."

"If you say so Grove," Melissa responded, no need to add sarcasm to the recipe of words they both knew by heart.

CHAPTER TWENTY SIX

She was almost the next of kin, but she did not feel the loss as family would have. Their final breakup had eased the way. He had retired, not died was how she would remember him and the event.

It was only a few days ago that she and Joyce were commiserating over the men problems, now they were mourning.

"Are you here to gloat, or to banish Ronnie's ghost from your dreams?" Melissa asked Templeton bitterly as he stood on the front porch stairs, regarding herself and Joyce.

"Neither. You know me better than that. I simply came to offer my condolences."

"Well, you've done that now Mos," Melissa replied.

Her refusal to call him Grove at such a time as this was a dismissal. He would stop by again later.

"I want to be alone for a while, here with Joyce. I can't see you now, not for a while."

"You should have called the police, that man is crazy dangerous," Joyce said in an anxious whisper after Templeton had left.

"Not to me. He likes me"

"And what about the rumors of the girlfriend he supposedly killed years ago?"

"I am certain that he killed her," Melissa answered nonchalantly.

"What?" exclaimed Joyce.

Melissa repeated the answer, her clear voice eliminating any doubt that she had misunderstood Joyce's question.

"I am certain that Templeton killed Sherry Pregel."

"Call the police right this minute," Joyce commanded. "Tell them that he murdered that young girl."

"The police already know that, Joyce. Ronnie knew it. I'm not clear however, that Grove knows it."

"What?" Joyce asked, her voice low and her throat dry

Melissa continued her explanation.

"There was no proof and only scraps of evidence. If anyone could have delivered an indictable case to the city attorney, it would have been Ronnie. He had decades to do so, and still, he failed. He even went so far as to visit a psychic village somewhere in Pennsylvania".

"Rose Hill?" Joyce suggested, intrigued by this bit of information.

"Yes, that sounds correct."

"I've heard of it", Joyce said. "So Ronnie really consulted psychics, that doesn't strike me as something he would do."

"He was desperate."

"It was a long time ago, thirty years more or less. From what I remember hearing, he could not have chosen a worse time to expect help from those people at Rose Hill They had their own unexplained deaths, and apparently the FBI and Interpol was somehow involved. Nothing came of Ronnie's trip, nothing at all. Me, I suspect some sort of cover-up. They let Grove skate."

"Let's talk about the here and now, Melissa. That is what concerns me. If this Templeton character"

"We are all characters to one or extent or another, Joyce. Grove, you, me. Grove likes me."

"You just informed me that he is a murderer."

"Yes, he is."

"And that does not bother you?"

"No."

"Please don't answer with just yes, and no. I am really worried."

"Grove likes me," Melissa repeated like a young school girl repeating an irrefutable truth that she had just learned.

"I bet that he liked Sherry Pregel just as well, and he killed her."

"Grove loved Sherry."

"There you go," Joyce exclaimed, leaning back victoriously, her argument having prevailed.

"Grove likes me," Melissa repeated. She said it in such a way that Joyce could only stare at her friend, perplexed. Joyce remained relaxed, her back resting against the plush wheat colored couch. She said nothing, looking expectantly at Melissa.

"Grove likes me, he loved Sherry. He likes me too much to murder me and he loved her too much not to kill her. Some men are just like that."

There was an awkward pause, during which Joyce attempted to make sense of what she had just heard. She'd known Melissa long enough to recognize when her friend was teasing. This was not one of those times. Melissa spoke at a pace appropriate to the rate that Joyce was able to absorb it.

"Sherry rejected Grove, all of him, and in return, Grove acted."

"Logically?" suggested Joyce, instantly regretting the bitterness that was in that one word. She should let Melissa finish. Melissa ignored the bite of her friend's response.

"Logically? No, not to me," she said, smiling. "Don't worry about me Joyce, I'm not going all weirdo on you. I must sound that way," she added, and saw the confirmation in Joyce's eyes. She smiled again. "His reaction wasn't logical to you me, but it was predictable. I think that is the essence of friendship."

Joyce forced herself to count to ten, and then extended it to twenty, and then beyond, as the silence in the brightly lit room continued for a full minute. This visit had become much more than spending time with a dear friend who was in mourning, drinking wine and watching movies they'd selected to make themselves cry. It had gone from sorrow, to fearsome, and then crossed over into creepiness. Finally, Joyce could resist no longer, and asked quietly, like a shy student of a tenured professor, "The essence of friendship?"

"Yes," replied Melissa. "You know your friends better than they know themselves, and they know you better than you know yourself."

Based on what she'd heard Melissa state only a few minutes before, Joyce thought that Melissa was proof of just the opposite.

"In a strange way, they help you to live your life by leading it for you. I think that is a great accomplishment, Joyce. Grove likes me," Melissa repeated for a third time.

It dawned on Joyce what Melissa was saying with those three words. Grove liked Ronnie too. So, for Melissa, there was no need to fear Templeton.

"How had she and Melissa ever become friends?" she wondered suddenly. What Melissa had said in the past few minutes had been so unlike any conversation that Joyce had with anyone, ever. Melissa had preached to her that we know our friends better than we know ourselves. Joyce was inclined to disbelieve everyone, especially preachers, frocked or not. Joyce

197

thought more of Melissa's words. If Melissa was correct, then we don't know our enemies at all.

It was time for her to leave.

CHAPTER TWENTY SEVEN

Even those who had little or no interest in horse racing attended pre Derby parties. For Jessica Villier, Thursday evening before Derby at an estate in Anchorage would define her image for the remainder of her life. This was two days after Melissa and Templeton commiserated in a way that defined the rest of their less glamorous lives.

Scientists in California had invented a new shade of black, THE BLACK it was termed, blacker by ten thousand times than any previous black, and the young actress, petite et menue, had wrapped herself in what came to be called the dress black. What the dress black covered seemed to vanish from view, leaving behind not a silhouette but the theory of one, a disembodied but compelling face. Her image hovered among the other guests at the cocktail party like an oracle in an avant-garde London play.

In the next few years, the photo of Jessica taken that evening would become iconic, to the point that today this same photo hangs in New York's museum of modern art.

.

CHAPTER TWENTY EIGHT

Jackson was moderately happy one week after the Kentucky Derby.

"Cas, we have a confession, just not the one we want. Here are the highlights. Two brothers came in and confessed to the theft of Perch's car from the hospital parking lot. They claim to have noticed the car Friday evening when the parking lot was nearly empty. The car had a for sale sign on it, and when they got out to look, they saw keys underneath the driver's side front door. They claim to have found his wallet in the glove compartment and used the credit cards inside to buy gasoline. That is their version of events."

"So maybe they kidnapped Perch as well and then took him to Cave Hill and shot him there. But why would they do that? It doesn't fit."

"It does if they were Templeton's accomplices. They are young and strong enough to control an older man."

"An older man," Ertras had never considered Perch old. "To Jackson he was old. Did her assistant see her as oldish as well?"

"Maybe all three were there, these two help Templeton to abduct Percheron, they take the car and its content as payment and go on their merry way. Twenty-four hours later, they help Templeton commit the murder, either driving Percheron's nondescript sedan that the guards at Cave Hill don't notice, or they are hidden in the back seat, with the victim, sorry Cas, Percheron locked in the trunk.

Days later, when they discover that the owner of the car that they stole has been murdered and was a retired policeman, they decide to confess to stealing a car from the hospital parking lot, claiming to have found the keys lying beside the driver's door. They have already been seen driving it, they used his credit card, if they confess to the theft, they might escape a murder charge. If the pressure is too much, they modify their story and can drop Templeton as being the leader. He probably was."

"You may be right. They sound like common thieves, I'm not familiar with their previous crimes but if they are just stealing cars that have the keys available, I can't see them organizing this complicated of a crime. Can you?"

"Maybe."

"Plus, there was no sign of a struggle in the parking lot. If it was a crime of opportunity it has too many coincidences. No, I think that the brothers just might be telling the truth, they stole the car Derby eve".

"I disagree. There had to have been at least one accomplice, we know that."

"We think that."

"It's a logical assumption."

"If the brothers aren't involved, then we have two separate crimes within say twelve hours at the same location."

"It wouldn't be unique."

"I just wish the hospital had better video retention. I know, I know, lawyers."

As Ertras sat and pondered this new development, Jackson reflected on the details of his questioning of the thieves.

It was clear that the thieves felt more secure in jail than they would have felt outside, driving the stolen car of a murdered policeman.

Their adrenaline needed an outlet, and their mouths served that purpose.

"Justice is carved in stone on the outside of courthouses because you won't find it inside. It is like the so-called gentleman clubs advertising the prettiest girls. You won't find those either on the inside."

"It's an innate sense of justice," Jackson explained.

"What does that mean?"

"Innate? It means invisible," piped up the second thief.

"Innate means something that we are born with."

"With what?"

"A sense of justice."

"That's the word I asked about. What does justice mean?"

Jackson frowned, frustrated at these inane games that some suspects insisted on playing. They weren't very good at it as a general rule and it only delayed what was inevitable.

The second thief took advantage of Jackson's hesitation to offer his worldview.

"Justice is a game like polo, made up by rich people so they can get people like us to behave as they want us to."

"Like shoveling crap?" asked his brother.

"Yeah, shoveling crap."

Jackson decided to remain silent and let them finish their routine. Who knows, they might have some clever lines.

"You know how women make things up to get what they want?"

"What else is new"?

"Why do you think we boosted the car? Hey, there is no sense in lying about it," he added in response to his brother's angry glance.

"Well, women like to get their way, you don't believe that men don't just as much. It's all lies. They say, "I'm sorry men, but you are going to jail, that's justice." I've never seen this Justice and I've never seen Santa Claus. Now this big man, Justice, wants to send us away forever, for something we didn't do."

"It's forever for Detective Percheron. If you are innocent of the murder, then for the car theft, it's only, oh, a year or two. A year or two is not forever," Jackson said wearily.

"One or two years this time. It will be forever, in two year doses, life in prison on the installment plan."

"And these policemen here," the older brother continued, as if bringing up to date an unseen stranger in the interview room, "they are working for Justice. They tried to frame Coz,"

"Templeton," Jackson translated silently, "but old Coz outsmarted them."

"We aren't that smart," the younger brother remarked. "I don't like where this is going."

"Let me tell you, Jackson, what's happening here. You're a detective, and that might impress some people, maybe some kids at Whitney Young"

"Whitney Young?"

"It's an elementary school. The kids there are good, their parents are clued in, the teachers get results. But they are just kids."

"They believe in Santa Claus," the other brother summarized for the detective.

"And while your off the rack suit and shiny badge might amaze these children, you are just a runner," the first said, "You don't know the big story."

"It's called strategy," the sibling said concisely.

"And you two, high end automotive movers, out there boosting luxury Impalas, you are current with this strategy?

I'll eventually get to the truth. It will be with your help or without it. It all pays the same. It doesn't matter to me, it's a job. Only criminals understand freedom. Someone told me that recently. I have to admit it, I agree. You know, I admire you two, in a way."

"And we like you too, Jackson," one of the brothers said, straight faced. The three of them appreciated the farce that this interview had become.

Jackson considered the criminal mindset. Thieves, gang uniform, where was their plainclothes unit? The grunts had their tattoos as their self-awarded medals and combat ribbons. As far as their detectives, there they were sorely lacking for they had none. Or was he wrong? Were the modern criminals clueless or so good that he was unaware of its existence?

He wondered if the old man, the bereaved grandfather of the Portland murderer, was aware of the thief brothers. He had begun to think of them as an act, one that could be booked for family events, depending on how one defined family.

"Your boys couldn't convict Coz for some killing years ago. We are in the clear on that one, dear brother," he quipped to his sibling, "we weren't born then. Right, detective?"

Jackson said nothing in response to the accusation phrased as a question.

"Soooo, since you couldn't pin that murder on him, you'd press him on this one. Payback is a bitch."

"Press?" queried Jackson.

It was the other brother's turn to speak.

"Squeeze, pin, frame. You need to spend more time with the public you serve."

"That there is justice."

"I see," Jackson said, pausing before appending, "I'm disappointed."

It was the older brother's turn to be caught off guard, but he said nothing, waiting.

"I expected a more original story."

The older brother leaned back in his chair and smirked. In an assured voice, he said, "There's more."

"I'm listening."

"Follow the timeline."

The younger brother's face shouted either genuine surprise, or an act worthy of applause. Jackson guessed the former as more likely, these two boosters could not be that good. The storyteller went on.

"Coz is released after a long time behind bars. He hasn't repented. And now here he is back in town, living here like a man from Mars."

"What did that mean?" Jackson wondered, but said nothing.

"A few weeks later, boom, or should I say bang, bang, your boy is dead. You don't find the gun in a land full of guns, you don't find Coz's car in a land full of cars. And lookie here, what else don't' you have. No witnesses, no footprints, no forensics, no finger prints from what my police informant tells me. Oh, don't look so shocked, Jackson, information flows both ways. It's an information highway, not a river. Get it? But let's talk timeline. The witnesses, your witnesses, our witnesses." he said with a beatific smile.

Jackson returned the smile. This was the fun part. The late Percheron may loved the puzzle, but he, Jackson, savored the drama. He so loved the game. These two street criminals were correct in that regard, justice was crap, no more than a game. How it was scored was arbitrary, but so what. All games are made up, as were their scoring systems. All that counted was whether or not they were fun, and whether or no he could win. Up to now he had done well, but he was growing weary of the game, especially in this minor league town. A voice broke into thoughts and returned him to live action play.

"And so, what to conclude?"

"I don't know, you tell me. You seem to have all the answers and the better snitches".

"I've been trying to tell you that for the past thirty minutes, Detective Jackson", the thief said.

"Here it is. Someone that Percheron busted wanted revenge and framed Coz. It is all a coincidence of timing". He paused, then said quietly, "Or."

"Or what?"

"Or y'all did this yourselves." Seeing the look on Jackson's face, the suspect mocked him.

"Don't look so shocked Jackson, it makes you look gay". The brothers laughed, secure under the protection of Sony cameras.

"I ask myself, who and why? You must be familiar with these words. There are a few more, but I see that you are already struggling. I'll give you the spoiler. Cherchez la femme". There was a pause, during which the players regarded each other for signs of credulity and deceit. "It's French, you know. Find the woman".

Jackson was indeed struggling.

This interrogation, screw interview, was out of control. The brothers were polite, calm as hell. They were in control and he was the one panicking, he needed some air. He could walk out, it wouldn't be a retreat if he left slowly. He stood and turned to leave.

"Cherchez la femme, detective Jackson," the thief repeated.

"She's probably in the station, her name is Ertras."

Jackson wasted no time He walked quickly to her office.

"Cas, we need to talk."

"I'm busy," she replied, but she looked anything but busy.

"So am I," Jackson said matter of factly, "but this is important. The rumor is that you are involved in this case."

"Of course I'm involved."

"Involved as in being a suspect."

"What?"

"I'm just the messenger."

"Should I shoot you?"

"That isn't funny, Cas," the male detective replied, then quickly added, "Maybe tomorrow. Shoot me tomorrow. I have plans for this evening."

It was then that he mentioned the thieves' confession.

After considering their statements, Ertras conceded to Jackson, "They present a plausible theory, one that a journalist might find compelling."

Criminals were lazy with plenty of free time, in general that reminded Jackson of his aunt's cats. They weren't super intelligent, but provided with sufficient time, they eventually came up with a solution.

"This was all theater," he realized suddenly, all the players in this drama had their own unique script from which would spring some cobbled together version of a resolution, if not the truth. He might need his own plausible solution. Sure it was the murder of a legendary colleague, but one little more than a stranger to him. This was just a case, one on which he was not the lead investigator. There would be others.

"It was Percheron's death, let him be honest with himself, this Perch was dead and buried. But he, Jackson, was very much alive. So was Cas, but yeah, for her, it was personal. Maybe it was too personal."

Was it just another coincidence that one of the car thieves had brought Whitney Young into the conversation? He had read an online article a few minutes ago about it being a bilingual public school, with French as the language of choice. How the school administration had been able to achieve this was another example of local passion. Schools were usually better than the usual and chronic complaints indicated. If these off the path criminals recognized the school's value, well someone was doing something correct. On a more practical level however, the brother's reference was an additional French connection in this case. It was odd, was the brother clever enough to have offered that as some sort of obscure clue?

"Had the two thieves spun a true tale? Screw it. This was just a case, not his case. He would have others." He returned to the interview room.

"We stole the car, but we did not murder anyone. We have alibis."

"What is your alibi?"

"We were on a road trip. The credit card was good, and it was never reported stolen. So, we stayed within a gas tank distance of Louisville. We had to leave town."

"Why is that?"

"Try getting a hotel room during Derby. The prices are criminal," the other chimed in.

"Why not use the card for a hotel?"

"They ask for ID."

"We drove to Saint Louis where we have family. We stayed with them. You know detective, what we did was really just mischief. And when we heard about the murder, we came here and turned ourselves in. We even had the car detailed. I suggest that we call it even."

CHAPTER TWENTY NINE

It was a beautiful Derby morning, but as usual there was a forecast of late afternoon showers. Jackson parked in the nearly empty Kroger parking lot and started towards the grocery store. A young woman walked ahead of him, the hypnotic sway of her jean covered hips captured and held his admiring gaze. Kentucky had the prettiest women, he told himself again.

Inside the store, the rose garland for the upcoming Derby winner was on display, hundreds of red roses stitched into a magnificent blanket for a champion. Jackson liked to see it early, privately each first Saturday in May. In a few hours, it would be placed into a Kroger van, and escorted by blacked out county sheriff's Suburbans, driven to Churchill Downs for eventual delivery to as of yet unnamed recipient.

It looked to be a wonderful day, despite the chance of precipitation. He expected a quiet weekend, one that would not test his law enforcement skills. He was uncomfortable that police work has gone from being a job, before he joined, to a profession, and now to an art, like acting. Success was precarious at the best of times, and was predicated on image and illusion. "It's not surprising", he had told several of his friends, "We hang out with each other because no one else is safe. And I'm not certain about a couple of you".

The public demanded of him unrealistic behavior and fashionable attitudes, like an actor who, once having donned a particular costume, was destined to play forever that character, even offstage. The public's credulity was essential for him, but today it knew no bounds. People were open to any rumor or conspiracy. Truth was relative. Half the community were convinced of that police were sinners, the other half saw them as saints. Both were wrong.

An unwillingness to believe a common truth mocked and destroyed the best attempts at honesty. "Oh well," he shrugged. "He had his friends, odd, even criminal gangs craved their own companionship, they too called it a posse."

Jackson was tall, and took private instruction to counteract the political correct remedial training that he feared would get him killed if he were to follow it blindly. He'd enrolled in classes conducted by an aged Memphis cop, long retired, who had convinced Jackson that an elderly man or a 105 pound woman could kill a person just as dead as any criminal in peak condition.

Jackson had the Louisville accent, not Southern, but unique in its own right. It was difficult to describe but readily recognizable.

He shaved in the evening because he was lazy enough not to want to worry about it in the morning. His lethargic nature in this one area had the ironic effect of making him appear dedicated and hardworking. His early five o'clock shadow was evidence to his superiors of his diligence. His bosses were easily impressed, which in its own appearance of irony, made them not worthy of being impressed.

It was a religious warrior mindset that the private training exuded. That used to be normal.

Truth will set you free, but lies will make you happy. Lies is just a vulgar term for inspiration. Our strength comes from being able to hold two conflicting ideas in our heads at one time. We are creatures that succeed by deploying tools.

God is like one of those solid police flashlights that we used to carry. It worked when on to illuminate the scene, and it worked when off to bash whoever needed bashing.

Belief works like that, you turn it on and off as needed for the task at hand. There is no paradox.

Jackson was a young policeman who risked and injured his health not in some grandiose good war, but in the never-ending fight against one facet or another of tawdry crime. Drugs were the perennial favorite, more reminiscent of sports, where there was neither enduring victory nor loss, only next year's season of promise and dash hopes.

There were losses and casualties on both sides, it was war and peace at the same time, in the same neighborhoods.

CHAPTER THIRTY

One of them had been removed from the case, and her partner was clearly in the process of stepping back from the coming train wreck that would annihilate both of their careers. They said their goodbyes, it was a cordial but not an intimate parting. What Jackson thought could have been, if Cas had been receptive, had been never been more than a dream.

Jackson reflected on what had just happened.

"You've been on the case since the beginning," the chief had begun.

"From the beginning, that makes it ten days," Jackson counted silently.

"How do you feel about taking over this investigation? You have the drive and the experience to see this thing through. Of course you have the support of everyone on the force, including me. We need a quick resolution, Jackson."

As he replayed the short conversation in his head, Jackson forgot the precise terminology used by the chief, but the message was clear, "You are now primary. Good luck you poor schmuck."

However it turned out, Jackson reasoned, he was not going to make any new friends . If he found evidence to convict Templeton he would have made a personal enemy in the form of a sitting governor who was famous for his temper. If he couldn't get a conviction of Templeton or someone else, his future employment in Louisville or anywhere in Kentucky would be brief.

The problem was that there was no other promising suspect other than Templeton. The good news was that he was dying. If he died before any conviction they would have to vacate the indictment and the population would be satisfied and probably the governor as well. "If Templeton would just die before being indicted that would solve everyone's problems, except for Templeton," Jackson concluded silently , and then chuckled aloud. "Better than a confession," he thought. The best outcome was that with Templeton dead, the whole investigation would freeze and sink from view. Jackson said a quick prayer for the future departed Mosgrove Templeton.

The couple adjacent to Templeton were dropping the F word as if they were cold reading a scene from a pornographic script, one written for the modern lack of sensibilities. The formerly offensive word was used as an all purpose adjective, said with neither emphasis, emotion, nor ultimately without meaning. The couple was oblivious to their own crudeness, or maybe he was just too sensitive to enjoy the modern era. For them, this was their water, he saw it as polluted. The worst was that the woman could not be quiet. Quantity for quality was not a beneficial exchange when it comes to dialogue. She was modern enough to be criticized. Her partner was an idiot.

Templeton turned his attention to one of the many large television screens projecting some sporting event. The female commentator was saying something but the volume was turned off and he was not interested enough to put on his glasses to read the closed captioning. For some reason the woman had apparently modeled her appearance on the queen insect from "Aliens", with tubular hair arranging her head into an elongated pod shape, while her fingernails reminded him of an Indian recluse who had passed his days in worthless meditation. Even the freaks were finding it more and more difficult to distinguish themselves from what passed for normal representatives of contemporary humans.

He glanced again at the female half of the vocabulary challenged couple. She used the F word in a way that spoke of needing to meet a quota.

Jackson reflected on Cas, the former head of the Percheron investigation.

Ertras' career had followed a trail of happenstance. It was a job that had changed who she was. Maybe there was a reverse quantum effect, observing changes the observer's outcome. Or maybe jobs are catalysts, changing the worker, but not the job. Jackson had noticed a change in Cas even before Perch's murder, and it had only accelerated since then.

Along the way the demands of the job and the people that she encountered, saints and sinners, he recalled the phrase from that first morning at Cave Hill, had changed who she was. How had Templeton put it, needs versus wants? If she was going to consider that man as some life coach, she was beyond hope.

Jackson was no Castorina, nor was he another Percheron. But he was no fool either. This was not his case, it had not been his from the beginning. Depending on how things went, he could either be a hero, or use his get out of jail free card and claim that the investigation had been damaged beyond repair from the beginning by the actions of lead detective Ertras. He had tried to salvage it but Ertras had botched it, whether this was due to her closer than known at the time relationship with the victim was not for him to say. She was gone, the case was growing murkier by the day, and it was every man for himself. Every woman as well. Hell, Cas herself had bailed out. She knew something, or had seen something that he and others had missed. He didn't think it possible, but maybe Cas had been somehow involved.

Well he knew a few things as well. He could not prove them all, but they were true nevertheless. One, Cas had not been totally open during her debriefing. It was evident to him that she had withheld information. Had it been out of spite of having been pulled from the case, or for another reason? Second, Cas understood Percheron better than anyone else on the force, but that meant little, and third, he was not going to permit his career to be derailed by this one murder. Whichever career that he now had or would have going forward. He thought again of the famous actress, once an unknown local girl.

Jackson was still bothered. If the Percheron murder were to make the leap from crime to entertainment, then he would need to balance himself. Crime is brutal and callous, true crime entertainment even more so. He would need to be on good terms with Cas. It was strange to find himself in a relationship with Cas, as a friend and close colleague , similar to the one between her and Percheron.

On the other hand, from a purely police career perspective, he needed to be as distant as possible, throwing Ertras under the proverbial bus if necessary. It was a tightrope on which Jackson needed to balance. This damned case, it was both a gift and a curse. What was he missing? Enough for tonight, he would sleep on it.

It was a game of rock, paper, scissors, which to wager? As he began to drift, he thought of paper wrapping rock. This case was a rock, obscured by evidence that was precise but inaccurate, irrefutable but misleading, true but false. The evidence led invariably to a paradox. If he considered the evidence as only a portion of the puzzle, then the resolution was child's play, but games of children were dismissed out of hand. The answer was too simple, and while more than plausibly true, it would not pass the adult demands for process instead of facts and insight. We understand numbers and rule but we fail to comprehend people.

Percheron had always been in command until one day when he wasn't. The same for Cas. The abrupt change recalled to him a song by Coldplay. He thought then of the term depersonalize, a word used often in a long ago modern police course. "Don't depersonalize either the victim or the suspect had been the theme of the too long seminar."

At the time Jackson had found the message ludicrous, in his world victims were without exception depersonalized, an action usually accomplished with the aid of a 9mm handgun, and if the majority of the commonwealth's citizens had their way, the perpetrator would be equally depersonalized. Jackson saw for the first time what the term meant outside of murder. For Percheron, retirement was depersonalization. And so?

Jackson projected himself into this murky future and wondered if this would be his fate also. Probably, he answered himself, and moved on contentedly to other, less important questions.

Percheron had been a hero, a veritable icon to some, he still was to many of the old timers. The respect was testimony to his character, but was Jackson obliged to consider it as evidence?

His mind was racing, but he was going nowhere. What was relevant to him was not necessarily admissible. His was the first court of appeal. No one admitted that reality, but people were not good with reality at the best of times. Murder did not qualify for the best of times.

This damned case was collapsing from the weight and weakness of the evidence. And from the strength of these personalities, there were no amateurs on this stage. He just wanted to sleep on it, to make Perch leave him alone temporarily, like death averted. A few hours' sleep, a pause of a few hundred minutes would suffice.

CHAPTER THIRTY ONE

The axiom that sports is a metaphor for life had now made the transition to where life had come to be the metaphor for sports. Or so Castorina concluded in seeing the headline *Ertras, Ergo, Her Gone*, written by someone hoping to be promoted from serious news to series sports.

It was a novel experience to be talked about in the third person. It was like gossiping about one's alter ego, or attending one's own funeral. She saw her image on TV and on LOU247.

When Ertras had ended the phone call late yesterday, one week post derby, she could not believe the conversation. Even now, twenty-fours hours later, replaying in her head the words of Perch's attorney, she was still in shock. She was one of two primary beneficiaries of Perch's will. Perch had left her his home in Lake Forest. Why? That would certainly cause ripples, as large as any she could imagine. But she didn't have to imagine. The attorney had also informed her that the second recipient of Perch's generosity was Melissa. The press was going to love this.

It was inevitable. Her assignment had raised both eyebrows and expectations, when Percheron's protégée had been designated to lead the investigation. In this horse town, she might have even been seen as his well trained, professional offspring.

Once the fact that she was also the beneficiary of the sale of his house, her position was untenable. The life insurance payment was destined for the ex-girlfriend.

Two women, each with a now clear interest in Percheron's death, one the lead detective, the other a suspect, made the case national news.

Some were already referring to it as the case of the dead bachelor; it was on the verge of complete chaos. She knew that her replacement would need to restart from zero, even her notes and previous work would be considered as suspect.

She'd taken the photograph from Perch's home purely for sentimental reasons. As far as she knew, no one other than she was aware of its existence or disappearance.

If that "theft" became public knowledge, the photo would acquire an importance that it didn't merit. It would be hidden evidence, proof of some incomprehensible conspiracy and subsequent cover-up. Better then, to say nothing.

There were two schools of thought on the sale of the house. One contingent expected that the notoriety of the murder would cause the home price to skyrocket, while the other half expected the price to plummet, for the very same reason. In fact, both were wrong. The house would subsequently sell in the normal time at a normal price. In death, Percheron had the same limited impact on events as he had despaired of in life.

"Was everything tied to Perch's first case? If so, why that one, and especially why now? No one cared about the case today, the old dead are ignored as are the old living.

Oh, sure there are a few friends and family still left, but they were neither numerous nor important. Or was this all part of a complex ruse?"

Cas dismissed that idea completely. Perch was clever, but this was too much, even for him. Jessica Villier had raised the idea of a hoax, but death, not here and not in the psychic village of Rose Hill, had no sense of humor.

No accomplices were seen in Templeton's car, they would find it soon, she believed. Neither was Percheron seen, either in a car or on foot. Templeton's was a bold move, or possibly an action emboldened by drugs.

The counter argument was that Templeton was sufficiently strong to act alone, he lacked only stamina.

The dying convict did everything but confess to the killing. He enjoyed the celebrity spotlight, and then he would claim poor memory. With the police, and in his own mind, he bounced between guilt and innocence.

Ertras felt untethered. In normal times, this case would have grounded her in what she did best. She could hide behind her police shield with all of the procedures and regulations that it provided. She thought of herself sometimes as a skilled surgeon called to set things right. Tonight, here in the darkness, she was a failure, here career ended. This was not her unique loss, she was only one of Perch's student, not the master himself.

It was too simple, a clear case with gaping holes. It was too simple, so simple that a jury would hang on a verdict and Templeton would escape. Only Templeton had ever beaten Perch, once, decades ago. Was he going to do it again?

Essentially, the evidence would prove nothing to the jurors and they would discount it.

Ertras supposed that human interaction was always reciprocal, no one was really a catalyst, immune from the impact of these continual collisions. It was like the sunshine that struck her that morning at Cave Hill, the bright light on that beautiful blue spring days helped to illuminate the awful sight, while the cumulative damage of those same gorgeous solar waves would be learned only at some later date.

She had become what she needed to be to succeed in her job slash career slash profession, but had she sacrificed her own wants? Templeton had as much as said that to her face.

She laughed at the thought and at herself. She inhaled a breath as if her lungs were tasked with forming the next words instead of her mind.

"I've retained my sense of humor," she said, beginning an internal dialogue.

"Yes, because I had to. But is a humor without joy, it was a need as necessary as a spare magazine for her service pistol."

She had to take another breath, as the wrong words had been exhaled. This time the lungs pushed out the correct phrase.

"I'm less fun," she thought ruefully. "It was an acquired regret," an older officer had once told her. She had never understood what he'd meant until now.

She would find her own life in Paris, it might not be any better, but it would be hers. It would be a life unplugged, disconnected in all of its meanings. She could withdraw into a place where solitude was treated as a reasonable choice, and not as a disorder.

The relationship between Perch and Ertras was worse than taboo, it was ultimately unachievable. Love has its own peculiar limits, and they had discovered them. Love limits friendship as much as friendship constrains love. It was as simple and impossible as that. They were friends. More would have been a fantastic cruise, a beautiful, temporary world that would inevitably collapse. And in the interim, they were...

"Content?" she had asked him once, years ago.

217

He had laughed quietly. "Contentment is not for mere mortals Castor, a lucky few are able to steal a small cup of it from the gods."

"So this is hell?"

He laughed again, incongruously, given the seriousness of the question.

"No, this is not hell. You're here, I'm here. We are here together. Hell would be"

"Hell would be what?" she had asked quietly."

"Not this."

She had no family within 3000 miles, how many kilometers was that? She was acquainted with no one except the dead and their entourage of bizarre characters. There were no personal ties that required her to stay, no family, no meaningful lover, not even a tomb among her own ancestors that awaited her. Perch was gone, and even alive he had been an older brother. That had not been not enough.

Castorina sat alone in the dark of her bedroom, talking silently to her naked reflection.

She possessed a rose golden parachute in the form of a European passport. It would permit her to emigrate from a place that she had begun to think of as the Old World. Her return, as her parents considered it, was what they desired, and that which Ertras had resisted. Perch's death had disrupted both his plans as well as hers. She saw this as an omen, one of those signs that Templeton had ridiculed.

"But," she thought, "Templeton was a chronic liar, even when he spoke what she knew to be true, it came with a sour taste. Had he spoken more truth than she had realized? Sweet or sour, it was no longer for her to judge." Decisions had been made for her. She had been pushed by her current boss. She paused then told herself, "And pushed by her former boss." She did not enjoy being pushed. She preferred to push. That had been one of the attractions of policing, pushing those who needed to be pushed. She was done with that now, she was too fatigued to push anymore. All the effort had not resulted in the birth of a child, but she had delivered herself. She would deploy her European parachute and land safely thousands of miles from Louisville.

Somewhere in France, perhaps Normandy. Perch would like that. She would not stay there forever but it would be perfect for a while, until. Until when? Until was until. She felt a part of her American-self begin to slip. A shiver of fear and anticipation sped through her naked body. She could be useful again, this time to herself.

The sky was darkening, a few recalcitrant clouds hovered low overhead like helium filled blimps that were reluctant to leave after the Derby festivities, but this was not a joyous occasion. The day seemed anxious to close, as did Ertras, who was struggling to keep her eyes open. "Let this day be over for me as well," she thought.

Louisville remained small enough to be livable and relatively understandable. It was debatable if Louisville qualified as a city or had the misfortune to have grown into one, like a reverse version of the ugly duckling. But it would soon belong only to her past.

Ertras' mother had told her once, "You expect too much. Women expect less than men, we are more practical. But you, you act like a silly man, you still demand too much." Cas had agreed with her mother, but what was wrong with expecting so much. "Hadn't they come to America for that very freedom?"

Cas was a hybrid, she had been sufficiently Americanized. Was that why her parents had returned to Spain? Had they seen their daughter's transformation, one invisible to Castorina herself, and they feared the same effect on themselves? Her mother had failed to convince their daughter to return with them. In hindsight she saw their efforts as desultory. They would flee not only the US, but also their daughter, a failed Frankenstein experiment for which they took little responsibility.

Cas had only returned once to Europe as an adult, a college age adult, too young to appreciate what Europe offered other than easy transportation, readily available alcohol and inexpensive lodging. She saw it in comparison to home, she thought of Kentucky as home, and Europe came up short. She remembered one castle in Luxembourg, it combined in one well maintained ruin the summits and despairs of human existence.

From the isolation of a chained man in a windowless, low ceiling cell, to the grand hall with paintings, hearths, and the faint, imagined sound of wind instruments.

But she was no longer a college age adult, but a complete adult. She would feel at home there now. Or so she hoped.

Cas reflected on the events on this Sunday, a week after beginning the investigation of the murder. This Sunday, the day that she now considered her last complete day in Kentucky.

She had gone to the house early arranging to meet Perch's agent around 11 in the morning.

Cleaning out the house was maid like, it was clearing the detritus of a stranger, half used tubes of toothpaste, and unemptied trash in the kitchen. Once off the case, she was off the case, and now, or soon, she would be off the force. The department had finished their search of the house, if there were any remaining secrets or any skeletons, she did not want to discover them.

She recalled from her visit, was it only days ago, that the house was uncluttered, the refrigerator was spotless inside, the bed in the master bedroom had been stripped. At the time she had chalked it up to a possible accident before his scheduled colonoscopy.

On checking the dryer, she had found the bed linens, cool enough that she had first thought them damp. Everything was organized, tidy, evidence of his upcoming departure, one planned and by all appearances, well in motion.

A realtor's business card sat on the kitchen island, while the calendar on the door of the stainless steel refrigerator had the previous Thursday circled and '10:00 realtor' printed in blue ink. That missed appointment would occur today with her, the beneficiary in Perch's stead.

The realtor had little to say, she had planned on meeting with Perch to review any the current state of affairs as Perch was moving overseas, Paris she remembered, and would not be there for any closing.

It would be this same realtor who would later sell the house or Ertras' behalf. Ertras herself had only been inside the house once or twice after Perch had retired. It was easier to consider

Perch retired, rather than dead, ensconced in a Parisian apartment, their paths unlikely to cross again but still possible. His would have been the best of her many friendships that faded from view and then from existence. Ertras signed the contract that the realtor had brought, handed over the keys, and left the residence forever.

Life offered only one rotation on the carousel. It was time to hop aboard. Cas would find a solution, a refuge, somewhere less manageable. Handing over the key was her last managerial decision. She would only make decisions in case of emergency. Doing nothing would be her default inaction, like that character in the Leonard novel that she had found at Perch's. He had mentioned it a few times, but had never followed the protagonist's motto of "when in doubt, do nothing". It might be harder to do than it seemed. She could, she affirmed to herself. This one time, she could succeed where her mentor had failed. She would probably read the book herself, but that could wait, she could do nothing for now, she had its essence.

She would follow Perch's lead once again. He had made it as easy as it was inevitable. Her superiors had in their own way, ordered it. So be it. As far as Ertras knew, she herself had no enemies of sufficient intensity to be of serious concern. But then, she would have said the same about Perch, up until the moment when she saw him lying dead with two bullet holes in his back. She would have discounted Templeton's prison bravado. Even today, she was unable to grasp the level of hatred that Templeton must have had for his former friend. What did she know, really, of strong emotions? She was neither a psychologist nor a psychiatrist, not even a psychic like the one Perch had consulted decades ago.

Friends. Had it always been this way with Perch, did he have a blind spot for his old friend? It all comes back to the neighborhood, their neighborhood. It struck her as some generations old feud from the hollers of Pike County. Ertras had only been in the eastern Kentucky County once, in Pikeville itself, where the attorneys' offices were as cute and colorful as the pink and green jaws of a Venus fly trap. She jumped suddenly to images from the Rose Hill village that Perch had included in the Sherry Pregel file. The psychic's cottages were just as picturesque and approachable. Both they and the attorneys would tell the client whatever they wanted to hear, making up the rules as they went along.

Ertras was out of sorts, tired of thinking but powerless to not continue. She was a newcomer in a country much younger than the one of her birth. She felt cheated of having her own long history, one that merited enough passion to commit murder across generations.

It came down to generations. A moment ago, she was positive that the neighborhood was central. Maybe they were one and the same.

Ertras sometimes wished that she could create her own characters and direct the mystery rather than just lead the investigation. She envied the theater director that she'd spoken with the other day, Terry. As a director, Ertras would have the power to cast her own suspects, rather than manage with the real ones that she was forced to accept. They were so often pitiable in their banality, undistinguished in the malevolence. Her whole life, had consisted of following rules and guidelines that others had created for her. She was a good girl, she followed the instructions laid down by her new country, her new teachers, her employers, her new friends. And now, even as a soon to be former senior detective, she followed the rules, including, she thought bitterly, even those of the low life criminals associated with the case. She felt that her life was for rent. Jessica Villier had uttered those words too, recently. In trying so hard to fit in, Ertras only felt more and more alone. House for sale, now house sold, life for rent, indeed.

CHAPTER THIRTY TWO

Jackson sat in the interview room with Mosgrove Templeton and his attorney, in a meeting that felt incomplete without the presence of Castorina Ertras. It was Monday morning, a new week, a new beginning. Mosgrove Templeton was under arrest.

"Ronnie was not perfect," Templeton said, smiling. "Punctuality was one of his flaws. It saves me. I have your witnesses. They save me. I have, or rather you have, the gun. That saves me. Congratulations."

"Your witnesses, our witnesses," Jackson smiled in return.

"Maybe. But maybe what they heard were not gunshots, or they were some other gunshots. Reasonable doubt works for us as well."

"Us? You mean the police? Or just us as in you and Ertras?"

Jackson ignored the question.

"We found the car, the caddy," Jackson, crowed, wishing that he could stand and high five his former, absent, partner.

"We found the gun, it is a match."

The car was last registered in Templeton's mother's name and he kept it parked in a neighbor's garage.

"You thought that you were clever, hiding in your neighbor's garage. You were so arrogant that you left the gun in the trunk."

"Clever, arrogant, good looking and a celebrity. I should do well on Tinder. Especially for women who aren't looking for a long term commitment."

"They can see you on visitors' day."

"Anything else?" asked the attorney.

"Gunshot residue and DNA evidence in the vehicles."

"Vehicles, as in more than one?"

"I'll get to that in a minute."

"The Cadillac was kept at my neighbor's for two reasons, Jackson," Templeton began.

"I'm renting the house where I'm staying, and the garage is half full of the owner's junk. It was a tight fit for the car. My neighbor had room in his garage, he's divorced. He likes to tinker on old cars. He has all types of fluids in the garage that would trigger as gunshot residue. Really, the garage stinks with all those chemicals. Its probably why his wife left him."

"That makes sense, detective," the attorney said.

"I wasn't hiding anything."

"There are other suspects," the attorney said, as way of introduction to Templeton's theory.

"Ronnie made it look like murder or more likely Melissa or even that Castorina Ertras did it to collect on insurance because you can't collect on suicide. Melissa had access to the gun, she was the real estate agent for my mother's home sale, she knew Ronnie's schedule, and they had broken up. It all fits."

"No, it doesn't."

"As far as detective Ertras, she has probably framed other innocent people. Ballistics and DNA testing, who is charge of that?"

"She was. We checked on the life insurance policy, it was written more than two years ago, it's valid. Even in the case of suicide.

Detective Ertras and I have both reached the same conclusion in our roles as lead investigator. The kidnapping was perpetrated by the two car thieves, not by your client directly. There was no DNA evidence in the Percheron car other than that of Percheron himself, the two thieves, and Melissa."

Jackson did not disclose that no one could place Templeton at the scene of Percheron's disappearance, and neither the thieves nor Melissa admitted to the crime or to even knowing Templeton in the case of the two brothers.

They claimed that it was all a coincidence, they happened to steal the car of a man who disappeared at the same time, and was later found murdered. No one believed in coincidence when it came to this case, probably not even the car thieves.

"DNA evidence from Percheron was found in the trunk of your client's Cadillac, as was the murder weapon."

"Planted," Templeton said simply.

"DNA?" the attorney asked innocently.

"Counselor, I can see that you are young and that you are new to this business, but you must have heard of DNA."

"Of course, detective. My client just suggested that any DNA found in his mother's car was planted by the police, a claim that large segments of the public would find plausible. DNA has been around for a long time now and, maybe because I'm young, DNA is no longer magic. In some cases it is weakened by its very certitude. It is irrefutable and true that DNA is often assumed to be false because it can so easily be placed at the scene."

"Is that your response too, counselor, that it was planted?"

"No, not necessarily. The car belonged to my client's mother, and from what other witnesses have told me, Detective Percheron had a habit of checking in on the late Mrs. Templeton. Its reasonable that he had occasion to perform certain activities that would result in his DNA being deposited in the trunk. Bringing in groceries or changing a tire are two of the numerous activities that come readily to mind.

Do you see my point on how DNA evidence can be discounted, particularly when there was no other supporting evidence."

"Forensics proves that the bullets that killed the victim came from your gun," Jackson said, then added, "So, your possession of the murder weapon proves that you are innocent? You were too self-confident or too drugged up to not retain it."

"You will need to prove that the gun that he gave me is the same one that shot him."

"We have proved it."

"No, you haven't. The gun that you found may very be the murder weapon. But someone planted it in my car."

"Who would do that, and why?"

Templeton indicated outside of the interview room with a wave of his right hand, thumb extended as if he were hitchhiking.

"Anyone on your team. Even players who were recently cut."

"Where is the gun that you state detective Percheron gave to you?" Jackson asked calmly.

"I don't know. Maybe you swapped it out, maybe someone else did, maybe I dumped it on my way back from Cave Hill. Dumping it is likely as your framing me. I'm sick and forgetful, you know. I need to write things down. If I'd killed Ronnie, I would not have kept the revolver."

"That is for a judge and jury to decide, Mr. Templeton. We are done here."

One man, with or without assistance, kills another, and then dies before trial. The case is resolved, if not officially closed.

MosgroveTempleton died a few months later in prison, awaiting both a fair trial and medical treatment. He remained adamant that Percheron was alive when he left the cemetery.

Ertras left for Spain, or perhaps that was just her point of arrival in Europe and she may be this moment living her life in Paris.

Melissa remained in Louisville and later married a retired doctor.

The betting ticket found in Perch's pocket remains in evidence, as the case itself remains dormant. This winning ticket for Inutile, French for useless, is now without any value as Kentucky racing commission regulations mandate that winning tickets expire after sixty days.

There is a rumor that the ticket will be awarded to whoever can prove to a court's satisfaction who killed Henry Percheron. This small piece of paper has taken on a mythic quality, and the term Perch's wager has come to mean, among Louisville police, something unobtainable.

The son of Inutile is projected to follow in his father's hoof prints at Churchill Downs this coming May.

Henry Percheron rests in peace at Cave Hill Cemetery. The marble headstone on his grave has slate attached to its reverse side as per his last wishes. Those who knew him, and those who did not, are able to write on its surface anything that is not favorable. It is impossible to prevent both kind words and obscenities from appearing on its surface, but the rains of Derby and other times erase the scribblings.

The powers that be refuse to accept my conclusion as to what happened at Cave Hill during the Kentucky Derby. My theory fits all of the facts but lacks the definitive proof.

It's been claimed that everyone lies in criminal investigations. I suspect that I will not be invited to any upcoming Derby parties, when this, my contribution to the mounting volume of conspiracy papers and books is published.

I believe that all witnesses told the truth when it mattered. This is what I believe happened, from the morning of Oaks Day until shortly after the horses bolted from the starting gates of Kentucky Derby the following afternoon.

It was a fair trade, death for life, and life for justice.

It seems inconceivable that someone who devoted their life to combatting murder would, in effect, murder himself. It is said that desperate times call for desperate measures. I don't know about that. But desperate people do desperate things. And Henry Percheron was desperate, despite so much evidence to the contrary.

Retired detective Henry Percheron walked to his parked Chevrolet Impala after his successful colonoscopy. He regretted that his last meal had been yellow jello. He opened the car door and retrieved his secondary cell phone from the glove compartment, along with a small bag that he slipped into one of the large front pants pocket. Into his jacket pocket he placed a similar bag. He then donned a ball cap and dark glasses.

Percheron locked the car and placed the keys on the ground, half hidden by the left front tire of his vehicle. He turned and walked towards the McDonalds across Breckenridge avenue. Not entering the fast food restaurant, he adroitly applied a false beard and mustache, silently thanking Terry for the opportunity to practice in the theatre prop rooms. Next, he opened the Uber app on his phone and requested a ride to the Starbuck's on Baxter Avenue. The phone was tied to a false identity, one that had served its purpose.

Once at Starbucks, he waited a few minutes, removed his jacket, slung it over his left arm, and walked the half mile or so to Cave Hill Cemetery, entering on foot by the main gate.

He walked unhurriedly to the Smith Mausoleum. He had nothing but time now, more than twenty-four hours to wait. He would be hungry and thirsty, but he would be clean and he would leave no evidence. He would not be too cold in the chilly tomb. He entered the burial chamber unseen, opening and then reclosing the lock that he had broken months beforehand. He spread the reflective blanket and covered it with the section of black material that he had been able to obtain thanks to Jessica.

He would now wait, but waiting came naturally, even on this, the last stakeout of his career. Percheron passed the night alone with his thoughts, there was no light to read by, but at this stage there was no purpose in reading anything. Once morning came, he treated himself to one or two packets of sugar that he had picked up at Starbuck's.

As the hour approached, he called Templeton to remind him of the meeting.

A few minutes before the designated hour, he walked to the rendezvous location. At this point, he had to rely on luck, on the weather, and on a lack of visitors.

Templeton arrived on time, their short meeting went as Templeton later claimed. Percheron was perhaps surprised that Templeton did not kill him, but he was prepared for that disappointment.

After Templeton left, Percheron stooped down and, obscured from passers-by, pulled out his secondary smartphone and dialed a number. A few miles away, a drone hummed to life in his backyard. It would arrive soon.

Percheron disliked technology, disliked technology so much that he would use it against itself. He had one final match to play, like a John Henry with a badge and a gun. But he no longer possessed either. If the best police technology could solve his murder, then it deserved to win. If not, then people like him still had a place in the world. He would be his own black swan. Maybe Castor would solve this, but he had taken steps to remove her from the board. Grove would be a good pawn. Besides he did need to suffer for what he had done to Sherry Pregel all those years ago. He would understand. But no one would believe him. Anyway, they were both terminally ill, one of cancer, he of boredom.

The drone arrived and he guided it to the surface of nearby headstone. He had been worried about rain, but his luck held.

He admired his handiwork. He'd been able to learn enough, using the internet from a library in Nelson County to construct his own miniature predator. It was fitted with two tubes that would fire nearly simultaneously, sending into his body two already fired slugs from the revolver that Grove now had in his possession.

He so wished that he could shred the past half century of technological innovation, as he'd shredded his own unwanted computers and incriminating paperwork.

He looked around at the dead all around and thought, not for the first time, "Life is always more attractive from the other side of the grave."

After he had taken the next step, which would start a thirty second countdown, he placed his hands behind his back, attached zip-ties, and tightened them the best he could. A minute later, its fatal message delivered, the drone departed, taking with it the bag of evidence that Perch had loaded unto it.

It had been the easy choice for this new millennia, the one click checkout. It had been simple. Press one for Paris and whatever diversion it held there, or press two, and remain here forever, his life if not complete, completed. His left forefinger had hovered over the digits and then pushed two softly. He felt a strange sense of power as he passed the final command to his personal angel of death.

"Did the drone settle on the surface of the Ohio, near where Sherry Pregel had entered the water so many years previously?", Castorina wondered from time to time in Paris, her mind picturing again the flock of geese landing on Lake Pointe. Unlike the birds, the drone would not have floated tranquilly on the surface, but immediately and forever submerged, joining Percheron in whatever oblivion awaits us all.

FIN